DEAD RINGER

BY

KEN DOUGLAS

A BOOTLEG BOOK

A BOOTLEG BOOK
Published by
Bootleg Press
2431A NE Halsey
Portland, Oregon 97232

This is a work of fiction. Names, characters, places, and incidents either are the product of the author's imagination or are used fictitiously. Any resemblance to actual persons, living or dead, events, or locales is entirely coincidental.

Dead Ringer. Copyright © 2003 by Ken Douglas

All rights reserved for this book. No part of this work may be used or reproduced in any manner whatsoever without written permission except in the case of brief quotations embodied in critical articles and reviews. For information address Bootleg Press at 2431A NE Halsey, Portland, Oregon 97232 or visit wwwbootlegpress.com.

Bootleg Books may be purchased for educational, business, or sales promotional use. For information please e-mail Kelly Irish at kellyirish@bootlegpress.com.

Bootleg Press is a registered trademark.

ISBN: 0974524638

Cover by Compass Graphics

Printed in the United States of America

November 2003

For three Angels

Jack Douglas
Richard McPartland
&
Whitney Barr

Father, Friend and Lost Child

Heaven, I'm sure, is a better place,
Because of their company.

DEAD RINGER

Chapter One

Horace Nighthyde stood at the bus stop on Atlantic in front of Sammy's Bagels, a black bakery in Downtown Long Beach. He checked his Timex. Five to twelve. Five minutes before he was supposed to kill a man. He heard the drone of a small plane, looked up. A Cessna was on a straight out over the harbor. He sighed. He had his own Cessna. Flying soothed him, Mozart on the CD player, the ocean below, like he was God looking down on his creation.

The sky had just cleared. It had been raining earlier, the kind of hot rain that's common in the south, but rare in California. He heard the hiss of Striker's tires against the steamy pavement before he saw his black BMW. He took a last, quick look upward, saw the clearing rain as a sign, a good one. He stepped off the curb, got in the car.

"Ready?" Striker slid over a pump shotgun. He was a big man, dark hair cropped close, white walls, like he was back in the Army or still on the force. He looked like a fight waiting to happen, but he was the kind of man who stayed in the background, a planner, a fixer.

"Yeah, I'm ready." Horace fingered the shotgun, playing calm, but his nerves were on fire. He wished he was anywhere else, but Ma was sick and she had no insurance, so here he was. It was out of his control

"There's a small convenience store up the street," Striker said, getting right to it. He had a deep voice, like one of those game show hosts on TV. "The Jap goes in every Monday at twelve-ten, gets a bag of dope from his connection and buys lottery tickets."

"Junk or coke?" Horace said.

"Smack, but he's not a junky, he smokes it," Striker said.

"Like that makes a difference."

"He's a snappy dresser, you can't miss him."

"What's the name of this place?"

"The convenience store?" Striker pulled away from the curb. "Quick Shop."

"Quick Rob is more like it," Horace said. He called convenience stores "stop-and-robs." You stop and they rob you with their high prices. "So what's the drill?"

"You walk in, blow the fuck away. After, walk to the back of the store. Next to the freezer section you'll see a door. Go through it into the back room and out the rear exit. There'll be a four door Chevy waiting, engine running. By the time anyone figures out what happened, you'll be gone." Striker gave him a quick look from behind the wheel. Horace saw a hint of amusement in his eyes. The bastard was enjoying himself.

"Jesus, I'm gonna be seen."

"No one's gonna notice you, and after that gun goes off, they're gonna be grabbing floor."

"Shit."

"We're here." Striker pulled up to the curb in front of the store, tires throwing water.

"Hey!" It was a pretty blonde. She had to jump out of the way to keep from getting sprayed.

"Sorry," Horace said from his open window.

"Sure." She went into the store.

Horace couldn't help taking a quick appraisal of her figure and shoulder length hair. He was a sucker for women, even though he wasn't too lucky with them. She had blue eyes. He loved blue eyes. And she was dressed in designer clothes, beige silk blouse, scarf that matched her eyes, classy skirt. She belonged in Beverly Hills, not downtown Long Beach. Maybe she worked for one of the attorneys down by the courthouse. Maybe she was an attorney herself. Maybe she was slumming. Who could tell?

"Okay, go!" Striker slapped him on the thigh.

Horace got out of the car, holding the shotgun down by his side. He looked both ways as he crossed the sidewalk. Nobody noticed. He stepped into the stop-and-rob, saw the Jap right off. He had a bottle of Johnny Walker Black in his hand. Two people were in front of him as he waited at the cash register. Horace took a quick look around. The store was full of customers, a man and a kid at the magazine rack, others in the aisles.

He almost called it off, but then he met eyes with the Jap. The Jap saw the shotgun, recognition flooded his eyes. He knew who the gun was for. Horace stepped forward, stuck the gun into the Jap's chest, braced himself for the kick, pulled the trigger.

The Jap flew backwards as if he'd been kicked by a tornado. His body slammed into a counter of canned goods, sending beef stew and baked beans rolling among the screaming assholes seeking cover. Striker had been right, nobody was looking at him.

Horace turned toward the rear of the store, found himself face to face with that blonde from out front. She'd seen his face then, she saw it now. Her blue eyes blazed. He brought the shotgun up to her face. She didn't shrink like the others.

Finger on the trigger.

She stared right into his eyes, as if daring him.

The seconds screamed to a stop. Everything seemed slowed down, like he was that comic book character, the Flash. She was a witness, a problem. Squeeze on the trigger and the problem would go away.

He pushed her aside. He couldn't kill a woman. He chanced a quick look around, almost screamed when he saw another Jap in a suit. He tried to get the gun around, but the bastard was running for the door. He was out and safe before Horace could fire.

Horace grabbed another look at the blonde, then rushed to the back of the store. The door was unlocked. A dingy back room, dust. Horace despised dust. And the place sold food. The back was unlocked, out in the grey day it had started to rain again.

The Chevy was waiting as promised. The engine running as promised. Horace jumped in, pulled it out of park, smashed his foot to the floor. The Chevy fishtailed on the wet pavement, but Horace knew how to drive, loved to drive. He got quick control of the car, made a right at the first street out of the alley, another right, another and he was on Long Beach

Boulevard. A couple minutes later he took the on ramp to the San Diego Freeway south. He got off on Bellflower, near the university. He turned toward Lakewood and home.

His head was spinning. He laughed. He couldn't believe it. He was high, like he used to get when he was a punk in school. Who woulda thought you could get off on killing a man?

But did he get the right one? That fucking Striker. Maybe he'd been a tough soldier and a hero cop, but he sure as shit couldn't plan a job. Two Japs. Christ.

Fifteen minutes later he pulled behind a liquor store on Candlewood, near the Lakewood Center Mall. He wiped the shotgun down, then heaved it into a dumpster. With that taken care of, he drove to the mall and left the Chevy unlocked with the keys in the ignition by the south entrance. He entered the mall, adrenaline pumping. He bought hot chocolate chip cookies and cold milk, greedily wolfed them down.

He left the mall, passed the stop where he'd caught the bus to Long Beach. The sun was out now, burning off the rain clouds. Crisp air, and clean. A good time to fly, but he had to get home and check on Ma.

A couple of young blondes, still in school probably, got out of the car parked next to his van. Seeing them made Horace think about the blonde in the stop-and-rob. She'd gotten a righteous look at him, like it or not, he was going to have to tell Striker, but about the other Jap, he'd keep that to himself. If Horace brought it up, Striker might hold out on the money.

He climbed into his van. What the fuck, he'd done the job, he deserved to be paid. He put that other Jap out of his mind.

He thought of the blonde again and white knuckled the wheel. What if Striker wanted him to do her?

Chapter Two

ABORTION, A HORRIBLE WORD. Unthinkable for a woman who wanted children, never mind a Catholic who held life sacred. Maggie let go of the shopping cart, rubbed a hand across her stomach. Life, and she was going to kill it. She fought tears. What else could she do? Three years she'd been faithful to a fault. Except once. One time and it had happened.

How could she have been so stupid? A party, a few too many drinks, but not too many that she didn't know what she was doing. No, she couldn't blame it on the drink. She couldn't blame it on Conner's persistent advances either. He was, after all, only twenty-one, ten years her junior. He was just doing what all men his age did, trying to get laid. She was the one who was supposed to know better.

But she'd been flattered by his attention. And when he asked if she'd like to leave the party for someplace more private, she surprised herself by saying yes. He took her to the Marriot out by the Long Beach Airport, not some cheap motel, and that impressed her. He'd been a slow and considerate lover and that impressed her even more, and he didn't complain afterwards when she told him she had to get back to her car so she could be waiting for her husband when he got home from work.

When Nick got home a little before one in the morning, she was in bed where she belonged. He'd wanted to make love and she responded with a passion she hadn't shown him since before they were married. She loved her husband and, curiously enough, she didn't feel guilty about what she'd done with Conner.

That night had been wonderful, wonderful with Conner, wonderful with Nick, but now she was paying for it with an ache that tore at her heart. She couldn't keep the child, not and have Nick, too. He had two sons from his first marriage, wanted no more, and to ensure it, he'd had a vasectomy before the wedding.

After she quit racing they settled into what Nick called the perfect life. He had his job, she had her work at the magazine. He was happy. She told herself she was, too. Now she was shit. She wondered if she'd blame Nick for the abortion later on. It wouldn't be right, not really. After all, he didn't even know.

She picked up a pot roast, turned it over in her hand, studied it with a remote detachment.

"Got you!" a voice boomed at her.

"What?" Maggie dropped the roast into her cart. Goosebumps peppered her arms. It was high noon and hot outside, but it was Alaska in the frozen foods section.

The man blocking the aisle was huge, with hammy hands, a flat face, flat nose and black eyes, almost crossed. He wore new jeans and a white T-shirt that almost looked starched, with a pack of cigarettes rolled up in his left sleeve, like Marlon Brando or somebody from one of those old black-and-white biker movies. His hair was going to grey and he had a five o'clock shadow. He seemed slow.

"You're in my way." She started to back away, but he grabbed her cart. "Let me by," she said. But the man didn't let go.

"Saw you in the newspaper."

"What are you talking about?" She tugged on the cart, but it was no use.

"Leave the woman alone, Virgil," a squeaky voice coming up behind the big man said.

"It's the one you showed me, Horace. The one in the paper."

"Shut up." Horace slapped the big man on the arm with an airplane magazine. His sportcoat was hanging loose. It parted and Maggie saw the shoulder holster underneath. A policeman. A plain clothes detective.

He turned to look at her. He was short, wiry with a face like a ferret. Close, squinty eyes. Long, thin nose. Scrawny mustache. Hair slicked back, covering his ears. He wore a silk shirt under the sportcoat tucked into baggy pants that just touched spit shined loafers. His thin lipped smile was false and his eyes went wide when he saw Maggie. He looked like a '50s movie killer. There was danger there, policeman or not.

"It is, it's her!" Virgil was still holding onto her cart.

"It's not. Let her go!" Horace grabbed one of Virgil's wrists and squeezed. Virgil winced and let go of the cart. Horace was stronger then he looked.

"Thanks." Maggie started to back away.

"Has he been bothering you, ma'am? He can't help it." Horace's stare was as cold as the meat she'd just dropped in the cart.

"No, it's okay."

"Pretty women remind him of his mother."

"I see."

"He's harmless." He shoved Virgil aside so she could pass.

Maggie pushed her cart on by, turning at the end of the aisle. She passed a Pepsi display, stopped the cart and walked away from it. The big man had unnerved her and that Horace character had sent cold worms curling up her spine. She didn't want to cook dinner anyway. They could eat out.

For a second she toyed with the idea of telling Nick about the baby over pizza at Armando's, then rejected it. No matter how much she hoped Nick would say he forgave her, that they'd raise the child together, it wasn't going to happen. He'd feel betrayed. He'd want a divorce.

She stepped through the electronic door out into the noonday heat. The temperature was in the nineties, without a hint of breeze, rare for the beach. Normally she'd jump in her air-conditioned Mustang and be on her way, but Nick's ancient Mercedes was in the shop and he'd never dream of walking. Besides, he'd said, she was the fitness nut.

She started to walk home, stopped. She was supposed to meet Nick in a couple of hours at the

Menopause Lounge. If ever she needed a drink, now was the time. She headed east toward Second Street.

Shouldn't drink, she thought. Bad for the baby. Oh what the hell. It'll be dead in two days time.

A bus stopped in front of the Safeway, Nick's smiling face plastered on its side, an advertising banner for the Eleven O'clock News.

She put on her Sun Clouds, Horace and his friend Virgil gone from her mind as she turned on Second Street, walking slowly on the shady side. She loved the Belmont Shore section of Long Beach—the college kids, the beach, the ritzy bars, the trendy restaurants, the holiday atmosphere. But not even the Saturday buzz could take her mind away from the baby she carried.

"Hey, Maggie." It was Stacy, waving from behind the counter at Yoghurt Heaven. Maggie gave a half-hearted wave back. She knew people here, had friends. What would they think if they knew about the baby? If she kept it, she'd have to move away. She couldn't imagine ever leaving.

She caught her reflection in a book store window, frowned at the reflected lettering on the UCLA book bag she used as a purse. She hated missing work and she was going to be out for a week. Her T-shirt, peach colored and large, would have made a good maternity smock. Would have. It was wrong, but what could she do? Keep the baby and lose her husband? She watched herself start to cry.

If only she hadn't done it. How stupid. She covered her stomach with her hands, as if she could protect the life inside. She couldn't. She thought of Conner, tried to picture him behind her in the window mirror. Would the baby have his brilliant green eyes? His jet black hair?

She pushed the sunglasses onto her forehead, wiped her eyes with her fingers. Time for that drink. She turned away from the dismal reflection and pulled her sunglasses back on to hide her puffy eyes. A few minutes later she took them off and dropped them into her shoulder bag as she entered the dimly lit restaurant.

She saw Nick right away, but what was he doing here so early? Three o'clock every Saturday. Three to whenever. Nick was never early. Golf was his religion, Saturday his Sabbath.

He was siting at the end of the bar. Where else? It was where he greeted his fans. Nick was the local celeb, the Menopause Lounge his hangout, that barstool his throne. He was talking to a redhead young enough to be his daughter, his hands moving as fast as his lips.

Maggie checked out the redhead as she approached. Early twenties, tanned, years younger than her. Cascades of orange hair down her back. Breasts like cannons. Nick liked long hair and tits. But Maggie didn't mind, because he never touched, only looked.

She sighed.

"Maggie," Nick said, "this is Stephanie." She looked like a Stephanie, Maggie thought.

"Hi," the redhead said.

"I'm starved," Maggie said.

"I've gotta go. See you." Stephanie jumped from the barstool, wiggling her ass for Nick when her feet hit the floor.

"Kinda young," Maggie said as the redhead flowed out the door.

"Journalism student at Cal State." Nick gave her his sloppy smile, ran a hand through his shocking white hair.

"Pretty," Maggie said.

"She has the fire."

"What do you mean?"

"It's like she's totally focused, energy all flowing in one direction, and Heaven help anything that gets in her way."

"And where's all this energy flowing to?"

"A network anchor desk someday. I'd bet on it. But right now it's flowing toward a group of high school kids that are selling big time drugs over at Wilson High School. She's gone undercover to make a drug buy. We're doing the story this afternoon. Gonna film the bust live."

"How come you didn't tell me?"

"I didn't want to worry you. I was gonna tell you later, after it was over."

"You were gonna stand me up?" She looked into his eyes.

"Gordon's coming in at 3:00. He was going to keep you company till I got back. I'm sorry you came in early, I wanted to surprise you with the story on the idiot box up there." He pointed to the television mounted above the giant mirror behind the bar.

"Surprise?"

His cellphone rang and he pulled it out of his pocket. "Nesbitt." He listened for a few seconds, then, "I'll be right there." He slid off the barstool.

"You're leaving?"

"Gotta go. I'll be back to watch the Six O'clock with you. Don't dance Gordon's legs off." Then he was out the door.

"You two not fighting, are you?" It was Richard McPartland, AKA Skinny Dick, the bartender. He was a wisp of a man, thin but wiry, strong the way ex-cons are. He was bald, with saucers for eyes and a smile that opened up under a thick white mustache.

He was sliding into sixty and had spent most of his adult life behind bars for this or that, he'd say, but he'd been going straight for the last five years and was the best bartender on the Coast. Ask him, he'd tell you.

"No, we never fight." Maggie climbed up on the barstool Nick had vacated.

"The usual." He set a rum and Coke in front of her. That's what made him so good. He remembered you, remembered your drink. You didn't have to order here, Richard knew what you wanted before you did and he had it down on the bar before you could raise your hand for his attention. He knew your limit, too. No drunks allowed in the Menopause Lounge.

"You read my mind." Maggie picked up her drink.

"I got a good shoulder if you need it," he said.

"I'm okay. I'm just gonna nurse this and wile away the time till Gordon gets here."

"All right, but you wanna talk, gimme a shout."

"Thanks, Richard, I'll remember that." She sipped at the drink and Dick went to wait on a guy in a three piece suit that had just come in and sat at the opposite end of the bar.

She set the drink down and went to the phones in back by the restrooms. She fished a quarter out of her bag, dropped it in the phone and punched the numbers.

"International Off Road Magazine," Ron Cook, her boss answered on the first ring.

"Somehow I knew I'd catch you there."

"Maggie, you never call in on Saturday. What's up?"

"I need some time off. A week, maybe two, starting now."

"Kevin and Mike are both still on vacation, that's gonna make it kind of rough around here." Ron had a whine in his voice. He never said no, he just whimpered and acted hurt till he got his way. He didn't want to give her the time, not now, and Maggie understood.

"I'll do the Sara Hackett piece when I get back."

"Enjoy your vacation." All of a sudden he was Mr. Nice Guy. He'd been after her for over a year to do a story on Sara, till now she'd resisted. She hadn't been ready, she still wasn't, but she couldn't hide from her fear, from Sara, forever.

"Thanks, Ron." Maggie hung up.

She felt faint. She went into the restroom, splashed some water on her face, then faced herself in the mirror. She closed her eyes and all of a sudden she was back in Borneo, the green jungle grabbing at her as she drove, foot on the floor with Sara shouting, telling her the road went left. Maggie cranked the wheel and saw the boy. She jerked the car to the right, lost control and the car slid into the child, killing him instantly. And she'd come apart. That was her last race. She walked away from the sport and now Sara, her navigator, was famous, one of the top drivers in a worldwide sport dominated by men, while Maggie worked at a magazine that wrote about it.

Nick, who at first loved the idea of being married to a race car driver, was glad she'd quit. He confessed to her that toward the end he'd been worried sick every time she shipped her car off to some exotic location. Well, he didn't have to worry on that score anymore. Since that day, she hadn't even driven above the speed limit and she probably never would again.

She told Ron that racing was wrecking her marriage and he hired her immediately. Her writing was good and she got along well with everybody at the magazine. They were a family, but at times she envied Sara. She'd been putting off doing the interview, not wanting to admit to herself that Sara was the star now, but those feelings didn't seem to matter anymore, not with the baby coming.

Back at the bar she saw Richard drop a couple of Buds in front of a young couple that looked like they'd just come in off the tennis court. They were sitting close, touchy feely the way young lovers are. It had been a long time since she'd sat like that with Nick in a public place.

Nick, what was he up to? He was an anchorman, not an investigative reporter. Maggie pictured the redhead. Nick said she had the fire. What did he mean by that? Maggie sipped at the drink. Bacardi Select, like butterscotch floating in Coke. Then she looked up, saw her reflection in the long mirror behind the bar. God, she looked awful. She fought tears. What in the world was she thinking of? How could she ever doubt Nick? She was the one who'd had the affair. The one who got pregnant. The one who was going to kill her baby.

* * *

Horace Nighthyde saw the sign above the door. Millie's Coffee Shop. "Come on." He squeezed Virgil's elbow, pointed him to the door. "We can't stand out here forever." The woman had just gone into the restaurant type bar across the street. They could sit and watch from a window table. Horace needed time to think, time to deal with Virgil, time to get himself together.

Inside the coffee shop he took a quick look around. The place had an early American decor. The kind of restaurant that served biscuits and gravy for breakfast, more at home in New Orleans than Long

Beach, but here it was, complete with waitresses in red gingham dresses. He saw a vacant booth by the window and went to it. Virgil slid in opposite him.

"Can I help you?" The waitress dropped menus on the table. Her silver hair was tinted with a blue rinse.

"Coffee," Horace said.

"Yeah, Coffee." Virgil always ordered what Horace did, decisions made his head hurt.

"And two of these." Horace pointed to a picture of a burger and fries on the laminated menu.

"What are you looking at?" Horace said as the waitress made her way to the lunch counter.

"Nothing." Virgil took his eyes away from the waitress's ass. Horace wondered if he'd ever had sex. Most likely not. For a second he wanted to ask, but he was afraid it would confuse Virgil and that was the last thing Horace wanted to do right now.

He looked out the window. He had a clear view of the entrance to the Menopause Lounge on the other side of the street. The thought of doing her made him want to puke. He couldn't get those haunting blue eyes out of his mind. He had to do it eventually. He knew that. But it made him feel cheap, like less of a man.

If only she'd left it alone.

But she had to tell the cops what she saw. Striker said she'd been over to the police station looking at photos. They had a shit load of books down there, with thousands of pictures. Sooner or later she was gonna come across his. He was a lot younger when he'd been arrested, had short hair and no mustache, but the way they'd locked eyes in that stop-and-rob, Horace felt sure she'd recognize him.

Still he hadn't been able to kill her. Stalk her, yes. Kill her, no.

Horace shivered, blamed it on the air-conditioning. He felt good after he'd blown away the Jap, better when he found out who it was. Frankie Fujimori, a low life the planet could rotate very well without.

But when Striker told him he had to do the woman, he'd resisted, saying it wasn't right, but Striker had threatened to bring in one of those Yakuza types that his bosses at the construction company had hanging around all the time. Then Horace had to see it for what it was. A job, no more, no less. Besides, if he didn't do it, it wouldn't be no blonde those Yakuza fucks would be going after.

And when they came for him there wouldn't be a thing he could do about it. Striker had too many resources. He was untouchable. There was no going against him.

So he'd stalked her, building his resolve, convincing himself he could do it. But when he was finally ready, she pulled a disappearing act. Now all of a sudden she pops up in the Safeway in the Shore. If he hadn't seen her with his own eyes, he wouldn't have believed it.

"It's the woman you showed me in that newspaper, isn't it?" Virgil said, interrupting his thoughts. "I was right, wasn't I?"

"Yeah, Virge, you were right. You did good."

"I knew it." Virgil was glowing with pride.

The waitress brought their burgers and fries. They ate in silence as Horace pondered the problem of the woman across the street. There was no way out of it. He was going to have to go over and see what was what, maybe do her in the bar if he got a chance. Maybe she'd go to the can. He could follow her in, cut her throat and be gone before anyone had a clue.

"She's been over there long enough. I'm gonna go and serve the papers. I might be awhile, maybe a half hour." Ma and Virgil thought he was a process server. He'd told them he worked for the DA and that his job was to find and serve papers on difficult subjects, people who had the money and means to avoid a subpoena.

After all, he could hardly tell them what he really did for a living. He couldn't tell anyone. It had started right after he was arrested for a B and E all those years ago. Striker cut him a deal. Horace snitched on his friends and walked. But he was never free, Striker kept him on a short leash. When the man needed someone leaned on, he called Horace.

When a guy owed Striker money, a favor, information, anything, and didn't deliver, Horace paid a visit to his wife and scared the shit out of her. It always worked. Horace had to give Striker his due, it was way better then breaking arms or busting heads. It was amazing how you could get a guy to do what you wanted by fucking with someone he loved.

Only once had he ever had to hurt anyone. Striker sent Horace after this guy's kid brother, because the guy wasn't married. But the bastard wouldn't deliver, so Horace broke the brother's arm. Fucker was kissing Striker's ass the next day.

Horace sighed. Only once, till he'd blown away the dude in the stop-and-rob.

"I could help," Virgil said, shaking Horace back to the here and now.

"You did help, Virge. You spotted her in the store. That was good."

The big guy was all puffy, eyes wide with pride. Horace smiled at him. Virgil was five years older, but followed Horace around like a puppy dog, as if he were the younger brother, and in some ways he was.

Virgil had a memory like a trap, but he couldn't read. He was dyslexic and slow, no more than eight or twelve in some ways, an old man in others.

"So how come I have to stay while you finish the job?" Virgil squirmed in his seat. "You wouldn't have found her if it wasn't for me." His eyes were begging.

"Virgil, when I serve papers I'm an officer of the court. I'm deputized, like a policeman. We can't have civilians helping us. In fact, if my boss knew I was here with you while I was about to serve papers on the woman over there, I might lose my job. You wouldn't want that, would you?"

"No."

"So, although you helped, we gotta keep it secret or I could get fired. You gotta sit here and be good till I get back. It's important you stay in your seat and drink your coffee. Hey, I got an idea." Horace raised his hand, got the waitress's attention. She came over. She had her notebook out, pencil ready to write.

"You got hot cherry pie with ice cream?" Horace said.

"Yeah."

"Make it a double helping for my brother here."

"Really?" Virgil was drooling now.

"And if he wants anything else before I get back, bring it to him," Horace said.

"She sure is pretty," Virgil said, after the waitress left.

"She's older than Ma," Horace said.

"Not the waitress, Dummy. The woman across the street." Virgil's hands were shaking, Horace hoped it was nothing.

"I'm not supposed to notice things like that." Horace shook his head. So that was it, Virgil was smitten. Probably had been since he'd seen her picture in the paper. Horace had been surprised when he'd seen it. He'd told Ma one of his subjects was on the second page. Of course she couldn't see it, but he'd forgotten about Virgil.

"What'cha thinking about?" Virgil asked.

"About how low a man can sink," Horace said.

"Whatdaya mean?"

"Nothing," Horace said, but it was something. He'd always considered himself a man with standards, principles, and now he was about to go against everything he believed in. He was gonna kill a woman. It ate at him, but he didn't see any way out.

"Pass me your switchblade under the table," Horace said.

"Why?"

"In case I got to defend myself, why do you think?"

"Okay." Virgil reached into his pocket, handed the knife over. Horace slipped it into his own pocket, was about to get up when he saw the trembling in his brother's eyes. Like Ma, Virgil got the fits, but if you were lucky and caught them in advance, sometimes you could prevent them.

"Hey, Virge, I think I'll just hang here with you for a bit and have some pie, too."

"Really?"

"Yeah, I can serve the papers later." Horace raised his hand for the waitress again. He hated these fits Ma and Virgil got and was afraid someday he'd be afflicted, but so far it hadn't happened. He didn't understand them, what brought them on or what made them go away. They didn't hurt Ma so much anymore, she'd learn to roll with them and she recovered pretty quick, but once one got a hold of Virgil, he'd thrash like a mad dog, then, when it was over, he'd sleep for a day. The trick with Virge was to catch it before hand and calm him down, sometimes that kept them at bay.

The girl across the street just got a reprieve, but maybe not. She'd been in there awhile, maybe she'd be there awhile longer, maybe she'd still be there after Virge calmed down.

Chapter Three

Maggie took another look at herself in the mirror behind the bar. She made a comb of her fingers, brushed her hair back. Her lower lip quivered. She was about to cry again. She steeled herself against it.

"Maggie, I need some help." Dick put a margarita down in front of the woman sitting next to her. "That old woman." He nodded to a Japanese woman standing at the far side of the bar, next to the man in the suit. "She can't speak English."

"I'll see what she wants."

"And I'll love you forever."

"You say that to all the girls."

"And I mean it, each and every time."

Maggie smiled. Dick could always make her laugh. "Save my place." She slid off the stool.

"I'll have another drink waiting, on the house."

"Hey, maybe you really do love me."

She moved through the crowd toward the Japanese woman. The middle of the day and the bar was full. A testament not only to the bartender, but to the food. When Dick and his partner bought the place it had been called Taco Town. They changed the name and decor, but kept the staff and the Mexican food, because everybody said the cook, Juanita Juarez, did the best Mexican this side of the border.

"*Konnichi wa. Watakushi wa Maggie desu. Anata no onamae wa?*" Good afternoon. My name's Maggie. Yours?

"*Oshima Tomoko desu. Nihongo o hanasu n'desu ne. Sore wa ii desu ne.*" I'm Tomoko Oshima. You speak Japanese. That's good. And she continued on in her own language. "My husband was supposed to meet me here, but I don't see him."

They talked for a few more minutes, then Maggie turned to Dick, standing behind the bar.

"What?" He had his hands spread wide, palms upward.

"She says an American friend, who works for Visa in Tokyo, said this place has the best Mexican food in the world. Her husband was supposed to meet her here after a business appointment, but apparently he got hung up."

"Did you hear that?" Dick said to the couple in the tennis outfits. "Even in Tokyo they know about the Lounge." He was beaming. Then to Maggie, "Tell her I got a Japanese car. Wait, no don't, I'd sound like an idiot."

"You are an idiot," someone said.

Laughter.

"Show her to a table. Tell her lunch is on the house, drinks too."

"Hey, Dick, you never gave me a free drink," someone else said.

More laughter.

"You didn't come halfway around the world just to eat in my restaurant either," Dick said. "So get hosed."

Everybody was laughing now, Maggie too.

They took a table in the middle of the dance floor. The Lounge served a mean Mexican lunch, but when lunch was over the tables were cleared away, the Lounge became the classiest pickup place in the Shore.

"You speak Japanese, do you read as well?" Tomoko had her purse on the table in front of herself. She was fidgeting with the handle.

"Yes."

"Good, because I don't, not without my glasses." She took an envelope out of the purse and handed it to Maggie. "Can you read this? My husband left it at the hotel reception for me, but I lost my reading glasses somewhere in Disneyland yesterday."

"KCS," Maggie said.

"What?"

"Kanji Chicken Scratch. It means your husband has sloppy handwriting. It's what my mother called my Kanji when I was a little girl." She smiled, read the note. He says he had to reschedule the appointment. He wants to meet you here an hour later at 2:00."

"I feel so stupid."

"Don't. Actually it's a good thing, for me anyway. I'm meeting someone myself, but not till 3:00. We could have lunch together, if you don't mind. I really need somebody to talk to."

"I'd like that." Tomoko's fingers were calm now. She was smiling.

"Do you know Mexican food? Or would you like me to order for you?"

"I'll trust you," Tomoko said. "And I'd like to have one of those margaritas."

Gloria, Juanita's daughter, was working the section they were sitting in. Maggie signaled her.

"*Hola, mi amiga,*" Gloria said

"*Hola* yourself." Maggie laughed. Then ordered them each a taco combination plate. "*Y dos margaritas, tambien.*" And two margaritas also, she added.

"So you speak Spanish, too," Tomoko said. "Do you speak any others?"

"French, but Japanese was my first language. It's my favorite. I like to think in it. It gives my thoughts clarity."

"Your first language after English, you mean."

"No, my mother was Japanese. It was first. My father was American. English was second. A close second, but second, nevertheless."

"You don't look Japanese."

"I know, there's a story behind that." Maggie studied the woman, wondering how much to tell her. She'd probably never see her again and she desperately wanted to talk to someone. She'd start at the beginning, but she'd make sure she got to the end.

"In 1970 the Vietnam war was going strong. My dad was in the Marine Corps and he had an affair while he was stationed at Camp Pendleton. He told me he didn't love the girl, but he was going to war soon and, well, you know how it is. The girl got pregnant, but she didn't find out till after my dad met my mom, got married and shipped out.

"She wrote and told him, but by the time the letter caught up to him, he was in a VA hospital in Hawaii, I was already born and she was dead."

"Dead, your mother died?" Tomoko said.

"Yeah, her name was Belinda Moorehead. She was nineteen years old, estranged from her parents and living in this motel in San Diego. Two weeks after she got out of the hospital she flew off with some Marines in a small plane to see a Grateful Dead concert in Santa Barbara.

"They never made it. The plane went down over the ocean. The bodies were never recovered. I had a twin and till the day I die I'll never understand why Belinda took her and left me."

"Why would a woman leave a two-week-old baby behind?" Tomoko said.

"I don't know," Maggie said. "But that's what she did. The authorities took the surviving baby, me, to Belinda's parents. But they'd written their daughter off and didn't want anything to do with her child and since it wasn't possible to get a hold of my dad, they contacted his wife, my mom. She grabbed right on to me. She couldn't have kids of her own, so I was like an answer to her prayers. When my dad found out he took care of whatever had to be taken care of, and he and his wife raised me. So you see, I've had a Japanese mother ever since I was two weeks old."

"Your mother must have been pretty special, most women wouldn't accept a baby born like that, the product of a husband's affair, even if she couldn't have kids."

"They didn't even know each other when he had the affair, remember? But, yeah, she was special, my dad too. They met on a Monday and were married on Friday. It was really love at first sight."

The drinks came.

They picked them up, held them to toast. "*Kanpai*," they said, and sipped.

"They sound like exceptional people, your parents." Tomoko set her drink on the table.

"Oh they were. My dad was a geologist and worked in Libya and Saudi Arabia while I was growing up. His work schedule was usually three months on, three off, so we lived in Europe. Majorca when he worked in Libya and Paris when he was in Saudi. We came back to California because Dad wanted me to go to high school in America."

Tomoko sipped at her drink, looked at Maggie with liquid brown eyes. "I had three brothers, they all went to *Too Dai*, Tokyo University. For me they found a husband. One didn't waste money on girls back in those days."

"They married you off?"

"Yes. Oh how I hated them for that. I suspect my husband wasn't so fond of me either. He was the youngest son of four brothers. His siblings also went to *Too Dai*, but Kendo wasn't considered bright enough. However we learned to love each other, and together we worked, bought a small business and turned it into a giant electronics firm." She paused, took another sip of her margarita, licked some salt off the rim. "Now, tell me, did you go on to college? Did your father ever find oil? What happened to your mother?"

Maggie found herself laughing as she thought of her father. "Yeah, he found oil, lots of times, in Libya, but every time he did, some young Libyan right out of college took credit for it. It would make him so mad. He'd tell me and Mom about it and we'd think his head was going to burst, he'd get so red and puffed up." She ran a finger through the salt on the rim of her glass, but didn't drink.

"Mom and I had our first real fight when it came to college. I wanted to go to the Sorbonne in Paris and study art. She wanted me to go the University of Hawaii in Honolulu, because they had a program in Japanese Studies where you spent two years studying in Japan. She wanted me to know my heritage."

Maggie smiled at the memory. "Every day of my life I was my mother's child, as Japanese as she. If anybody ever said different, they met the full force of her wrath. You didn't mess with my mom, let me tell you. She was hell on wheels."

"So you went to Hawaii?" Tomoko said.

"We made a deal, get the degree from U of H, then, if I still wanted, they'd send me to France. So I got that degree, but I never went to Paris. By the time I graduated, I was pretty tired of school. Besides, I'd met this great guy from Nevada in my senior year. He'd come to Hawaii on a two week vacation and stayed till I finished school. He could drive like nothing you'd ever seen. He had oil instead of blood in his veins and he taught me how to race a car in the dirt. He was an off road racer."

"I don't know what that is," Tomoko said.

"He raced cars off road. You know like the Paris-Dakar race, or the Camel Trophy. He raced in jungles, deserts, the bush, you name it. Sometimes the races last less than a day, sometimes they're as long as a couple weeks—grueling conditions—mud, rain."

"You can make a living doing that?" Tomoko asked.

"If you're good, and Bobby was. We lived together for three years and I became his co-driver and navigator, till I caught him in bed with a couple racing groupies. I was supposed to be at a co-driver's meeting getting the route for a race, but I forgot my phone, so I went back to get it." She laughed at the memory. Bobby in their hotel room in Mexico two days before the Baja Five Hundred. Shocked as he was at being caught, he couldn't wipe the smile off his face. The girls were beautiful and couldn't have been older than eighteen. What was it about men?

"I went out on my own after that, got my own sponsors and my own car, a Mitsubishi Montero. I have an overactive imagination and I imagined myself famous, on television doing the talk shows, a woman at the top of a man's sport. And it was starting to happen. I was starting to get coverage, my sponsors we're paying more. I fell in love with and married the guy on the local news here. I was on top of the world." Then Maggie told her new friend about the accident and why she didn't race anymore.

"So I got a job at a magazine and started to live a normal life, till now."

"And now," Tomoko said, "we get to the reason why you're telling me all this. A stranger who can't speak English. Someone you can trust won't tell your friends, or worse, your husband. It's not his baby, is it?"

"No." Maggie didn't ask how the woman figured out she was pregnant, how she knew it wasn't Nick's. She just picked up her drink, held it up. "*Kanpai.*"

"*Kanpai.*" Tomoko said. They both drank.

"We've been married for three years," Maggie said. "He can't have kids. He had, you know," she made a scissors out of her fingers, "snip, snip."

"Ouch," Tomoko said.

"Usually men say that," Maggie said.

"I have an imagination too," Tomoko said.

"Anyway, I met this man, boy really, from Ireland. He was a young race driver I was interviewing for the magazine."

"This boy is the father?"

"Yes."

"So now you are in *itabasami*."

"Yes, I'm stuck between two walls, between a rock and a hard place. I lose no matter what I do."

"And you don't think your husband loves you as much as your mother loved your father? I'm not surprised, women love more deeply, suffer more pain."

"Of course Nick loves me. What are you talking about?"

"Your mother accepted you. Loved you before she knew you, because you were her husband's child. But you're not willing to give your husband the same chance with your baby. You assume he'll reject it."

"The situation's a little different. My father wasn't cheating, I was. My mother wanted kids, my husband doesn't."

"I still think you should tell him. Maybe you're underestimating him."

"He has this stupid pride."

"Pride," Tomoko said. "Maybe men should be gelded after their wives give birth. That would take care of their pride."

"Yeah." Maggie laughed despite how she felt.

"You should tell him."

"How can you say that?"

"Isn't that why you told me? So you could get an honest opinion about what you know you should do anyway."

"He'll divorce me."

"Not if he loves you."

"If he does, what would I do?" Maggie couldn't imagine living without Nick. He was the rock she counted on. He was always there for her.

"You'd do what a lot of other single mothers do. You'd raise your child."

The taco plates came and they ate in silence. Maggie thought about what Tomoko had said. She wanted to tell Nick. Wanted to keep the baby. But could a man with his pride live with another man's child? She didn't think so. As much as he loved her, he'd leave her. It was the way he was.

"Maggie," Dick said from behind the bar, "phone call for your friend." Maggie translated and Tomoko got up to get the phone. It was her husband telling her he wasn't going to make it after all and could she take a cab back to the hotel.

"*Meishi onegaishimasu,*" Tomoko said. Here's my card. Maggie took it. She didn't have a card of her own, so she scribbled her phone number and address on the back of her gynecologist's card, then gave it to her new friend. Tomoko promised to write. She wanted to know what Maggie decided to do about the baby. Maggie promised she'd let her know.

She took her place back at the bar after Tomoko left and ordered another rum and coke. Maybe she could get the baby drunk. Maybe then it wouldn't hurt so bad when they killed it.

The DJ had just finished setting up his stuff behind the dance floor when Maggie heard, "Hey, good looking."

"Gordon!" She turned toward a handsome man dressed in corduroys and a yellow Polo shirt. He was wiry, graying at the temples, had a dimple in his chin that set off his wicked handsome face, and a smile that could light up the Forum.

"Nick said he had to stand you up, something about a hot story he was working on." Gordon took the stool next to her. "It was too much for me, a lady waiting for a man, I had to come."

Maggie laughed. Gordon Takoda was Nick and Maggie's downstairs neighbor and landlord. Their duplex on Ocean was across the street from the beach.

"I've decided to let the pet store have the bird," Gordon said. "They promised to find him a good home. Besides, they say they can get me over a thousand bucks for him."

"Aw, Gordon, not Fred, you're gonna miss him."

"I miss Ricky, I won't miss his bird." Ricky, his partner, died of leukemia six months after she'd moved in upstairs with Nick. Gordon and Ricky were the first gay men she'd ever known and in no time at all they had become fast friends. And she'd grown closer to Gordon since Ricky's death. If asked, she'd have to say he was the best friend she'd ever had.

"I guess he must be a handful."

"Damn bird attacks me every time I feed him." Fred was a yellow-naped Amazon, twenty years old, a loquacious talker, and at times meaner than a Rottweiler with a hot poker stuck up its ass.

"Yeah, I can see why you'd wanna get rid of him."

"How long you been sitting here sipping those?" He nodded toward the drink.

"Too long."

Gordon turned to the DJ. "Hey, Brian, you got the Rolling Stones handy? A fast one, 'Start Me Up.' Something like that?"

"Got the one you want." Brian was a six-five homophobic weightlifter. When he wasn't doing the music, he was the bouncer. But as much as he claimed not to like gays, he got along well with Gordon. He put on the song Gordon requested.

"Come on." Gordon pulled her from the barstool to the dance floor and she started to work up a sweat.

Two hours later they were still dancing, only now to Elvis singing the slow one Maggie loved the best, 'Love Me Tender.'

* * *

Several hours and several cups of coffee later and the woman was still in the bar. What was she doing, drinking the place dry?

"You gonna be okay here, Virge, because I gotta go over there and do my job."

"I think so," Virgil said. He looked all right now and Horace felt a little better about leaving him.

"Just remember don't leave till I come back."

"I won't." Then, "Can I have some more pie?"

"Sure." Horace motioned for the waitress, then eased out of the booth.

The woman had been over there for ages. All of a sudden his ass puckered up. He hadn't thought about why she'd been shopping so far from home. Could the police have been following him? Could the meeting in the store have been a setup? All of a sudden he didn't want to go into that bar. But he wasn't a coward. Besides, it'd be dark. If there were cops there, he'd see them first and slide right on out, slicker than rat piss.

He jaywalked across the street, turned toward an afternoon breeze, a slipstream of cool air on this miserable hot day. Ma would say it was a good sign. Horace sighed, Ma was nuts.

He stepped into the bar and saw the woman right away, dancing with some guy. They were the only couple on the dance floor. She had her head on his shoulder. Her eyes were closed. It looked like she was at peace, in love. Striker was supposed to know everything about her, how come he didn't know she had a boyfriend?

He passed through the crowd and took a seat at the end of the bar, careful to keep the mingling people between himself and her in case she opened her eyes. He didn't think she'd recognized him in the Safeway, probably because she'd been concentrating on Virgil, but his brother wasn't with him now and he didn't want to take any chances.

"You come in here often?" A girl's voice.

"What?" Horace turned to the woman on the stool next to him. She looked like a hippy from the '60s. She had waist length hair, parted in the center, and she was wearing a kind of flower power skirt made out of that thin Indian tapestry material.

"I said, do you come in here often?" She had a voice like music.

"No, first time," Horace said.

"I'm Sadie." She had a boyish figure, small tits, but lips like a sexy model. Her mouth was all Os when she talked.

"Nice to meet you, Sadie, I'm Horace."

"That's your name, Horace? Really?" she said.

"Yeah."

"I like it. It rhymes with romance. You look romantic."

"It doesn't, you know, rhyme with romance," Horace said.

"It could if you wanted." She leaned into him, graced him with the most beautiful smile he'd ever seen, a cross between an O and a pout. She was the hottest thing that had ever come on to him in all his forty-four years.

"I've been romantic," he said.

"I bet you have. I saw you watching them dance. Do you?"

"What, dance?"

"Yeah."

"I do, but not now."

"Why not?"

"You wouldn't believe me if I told you."

"Try me."

"I'm working."

"At what?"

"I'm a private detective. I'm watching the couple on the dance floor. They're married, but not to each other."

"Oh." Then, "If you took me out there you could watch up close."

Horace thought about that for a second, leaned closer to her. "I'm wearing a shoulder holster. I wouldn't want it to frighten you."

"Why would it do that?"

"If we danced and you felt it against your, you know, your chest."

"Come on." She hopped off the barstool, took his hand and pulled him along as she wound her way through the crowd.

Horace sighed, felt a surge of relief when another couple followed. The woman was still slow dancing with the older guy, still had her eyes closed. Horace turned away from her as Sadie wrapped her arms around his neck. He put his hands around her waist.

"I feel it," she whispered into his ear, "your gun, up against my, ah, chest."

"Look," Horace whispered back, "I might have to leave quick like. You know, if they go. I gotta follow them."

"I know," she said.

"I wouldn't want you to think I was running out on you. I'm working, it's my job."

"You could call me when you finish. Sadie Sanders, I'm in the book."

"It might not be tonight, tomorrow okay?"

"When you can. It's okay." She rested her head on his shoulder.

The DJ played another slow song and another after that. Horace had trouble keeping an eye on the woman as more couples took to the dance floor. Soon most of the bar was dancing and he was tempted to forget her and concentrate on Sadie. But then he remembered Virgil across the street. He had to be getting plenty worried by now.

"Do you believe in fate, Horace?" Sadie whispered.

"Yeah," Horace said.

"I think there might be something for you and me. Maybe not right away, but I think we're destined for a relationship." She pulled him in close. He felt the heat of her and it caused him to shiver. "You don't have be afraid," she said.

"I'm not."

"You are."

"Maybe a little."

Nothing like this had ever happened to him before. Sure he'd had beautiful women in his time, but he'd always had to work at it, and in the end they'd always left. For a time he blamed it on his family. After all, who in their right mind would want anything to do with Ma? And then there was Virgil. But as he got older he had to admit the fault was within himself. He'd never been able to commit to anyone. It didn't take women long to figure that out.

But there was something about Sadie. Something different.

"It's kinda quick," she said. "But you know when it's right."

"Yeah," he said.

"They're going, the ones you're supposed to be watching."

"Damn, I forgot." He pulled away from her.

"Just a second." She still had her arms around his neck. She pulled him in. Kissed him hard. "Just so you don't forget to call."

"I won't."

"Go." She kissed him again, quick.

"See ya." Horace backed away.

Outside, he saw the couple turn the corner and head down toward the beach. He sprinted across the street. Inside the diner he dropped a fifty on the table. "Keep the change," he told the waitress. Then to Virgil, "Come on, we gotta go."

Chapter Four

JASMINE WOULDN'T STOP worrying until her mom was back and they were inside the condo with the doors locked. She peeked through the blinds. She had a good view of her condo from the clubhouse on the third floor.

"This is a stupid way to spend Saturday," Sonya said. She was Jasmine's best friend, they sat next to each other in school. She turned eight a week ago and she'd been lording it over Jasmine, the age difference, and she'd keep it up till the week after next when Jasmine's birthday came around.

"The Ghost is back." Jasmine pushed her blonde hair out of her eyes. They'd been up here since breakfast without the air-conditioning on. It was hot.

She was sweating. They had the window open a crack, but the little bit of sea breeze that slipped in wasn't enough.

"Let me see!" Sonya's brown eyes were open wide as she replaced Jasmine at the window. Tiny, honey brown fingers pulled the blinds apart. She was afraid of the Ghost. "He's so spooky."

"He's a policeman." Jasmine moved up next to her. The one that looked like a ghost had come before, with the police, so Jasmine guessed he was a detective, because he was wearing ordinary clothes, even if they looked like he'd slept in them. She was a little afraid of him, too, but if anyone could catch the killer, a ghost could.

The other man was wearing a dark suit with a vest, way too much for the beach on a hot day. He was the one who brought her mom home from the police station after what she'd seen in that mini market store in Long Beach. He'd been wearing jeans and a flower print shirt on that day, but Jasmine recognized him because of his long ponytail.

The Ghost knocked, then opened the door and they went into the condo. Darn, she should've locked the door. For a second she thought about going for the security guard. Danny could kick those guys out of there real quick, but she didn't want to leave her spot at the window.

She bit the inside of her cheek, felt blood with her tongue. She didn't mean to do it, she'd been concentrating too hard. She thought about how her mom had left on another of her religious retreats. A quick kiss on the cheek. A fast ruffle of her hair, then she was out the door with her suitcase. Gone for a week, praying up in Big Bear. Did she know the cops were gonna come around? Was that why she took off?

No. If she did, she'd have taken her with her. Her mom was a scatterbrain, but no way would she have left her behind, not if she knew the Ghost was in town. Jasmine could hardly wait till tomorrow. She was supposed to be back then. Tomorrow everything was gonna be okay.

She'd miss hanging out next door with Sonya. No prayers, that was probably a sin, but somehow at Sonya's house it didn't seem so bad. No restriction on television time. That was for sure a sin, her mom had said no more than an hour a night. No broccoli, no cauliflower, no string beans and no spinach—her mom would hate that. Jasmine smiled, what her mom didn't know wouldn't hurt her. But would it be a sin if she didn't tell?

She stuck her lower lip out and blew her hair back from her forehead. Still, as much fun as she was having at Sonya's, she wanted her mom back. Every second she was gone worried her more. What if the killer had gotten her?

Down below the Ghost looked out the door, almost as if he knew the two girls were watching. He seemed to be looking out over the ocean, but Jasmine wasn't fooled. Those spooky eyes saw everything. It was scary. He walked to the fence between the condos and the sea, bent down and picked up a handful of sand, then he stood and let it slip through his fingers, almost like she did when she played at the beach everyday. Why'd he do that? He turned, went back to the condo, but just before entering, he glanced up at the clubhouse and for a second, Jasmine imagined those ghosty eyes could see through the wall. She shivered, but he went into her house and she couldn't see him anymore.

* * *

Gay Sullivan was singing 'My Girl' along with Smokey Robinson as she turned off the Pacific Coast Highway and into the drive for the Huntington Beach Sand and Sea Condos. "Beach Front Homes on the Sand," the sign said. She braked at the security gate, turned off the CD player. The dashboard clock said 3:00, she checked her Rolex, 3:15. The dash clock was still slow, and they said they'd fixed it. She sighed. A classic XKE Jaguar was like a boat, you paid for the maintenance, then you paid to have it done again.

"How's it going, Mrs. Sullivan?" the guard at the gate said.

"Okay for me, Danny boy." She knew it pleased him, his name said that way.

Danny wore a frown. He was a fifty-eight year old black man with skin dark as Gay's, who claimed never to have had a bad day in his life. He was the eternal optimist. So the frown worried her.

"What's wrong?" Her first thought was of the girls.

"The police are back. First they want to see Mrs. Kenyon, now they think she's missing."

"She's not missing. Margo's off on one of her retreats. Jazz is staying with me."

"You know it and I know it, but the cops don't know it."

"You didn't tell 'em?"

"I don't talk to cops."

"Danny, I've got a feeling Margo's in trouble."

"Me too. You know what it's about?"

"Nobody told you? You're supposed to be the security here."

"I guess the real cops don't have any use for guys like me."

"Well, I sure do, so listen up. Margo was standing in line at the check out behind Frankie Fujimori, at a convenience store in Long Beach, when some guy walks in, pulls out a shotgun and blows Frankie away. Guy pointed the gun at her, apparently changed his mind, then took off. Nobody saw the shooter's face except Margo."

"I saw that on the news. Nobody told me Mrs. Kenyon was there."

"You're surprised? You know how she felt about Fujimori. She would've walked barefoot through hot coals if it would've helped put him back where he belonged."

"She's a tough one all right." Danny had that wistful look in his eyes. Gay thought she smelled marijuana. Ah well, God didn't put her on this earth to judge others. She had enough trouble keeping care of Sonya and her own self.

"Yeah, she's tough, but that shotgun in her face really shook her up. A cop had to drive her home, guess it was after you got off or you would've known. I had to drive her to the police parking lot in Long Beach the next day to get her car."

"She left that brand new Porsche in a parking lot all night long? In Long Beach?"

"Police parking, but yeah. That's how shook up she was."

"I should know this stuff." Danny narrowed his eyes. The faraway look was gone now. He was one hundred percent concentration.

"The cops want to keep it quiet. I think Margo does, too. So don't tell her I said anything. But it's stupid of them not to tell you. I mean, what if the killer found out? What if he tried to get by you? You know, to get to her."

"Nobody gets in here without a tenant clears him. But just the same, I'm gonna be twice as careful now that I know." He slapped his holstered pistol, a gunfighter ready for battle. "And don't you worry, I won't let on you told me."

"Good." Gay smiled at him. Stupid cops. Not telling Danny. How dumb.

"How's she handling it now?" Danny said.

"That's the weird thing. She was all shook up at first, but she got over it quick. God will protect her, you know how she is."

"Yeah." Danny smiled, went to the security bar, raised it.

Gay used her clicker to open the gate for tenant parking, found her spot and parked. At her condo, she saw the door next door was open. She clenched her fists, tensed. She didn't like the thought of police in Margo's home. She wasn't a criminal.

"Yo." Gay recognized Bruce Kenyon's voice. He must've come in right behind her and parked in the guest parking. She turned and waited. "So what's the deal?" he said. "The guy at the gate says there's cops here to see Margo."

"I don't know anything about it." Gay sighed, she didn't like Margo's ex. She didn't know anybody who did.

Bruce walked into Margo's apartment without knocking. Gay followed. They were in the living room, making themselves at home. The Hispanic one sitting in one of the rattan chairs had his hair pulled back into a ponytail, the other one, the albino, was sprawled out on the sofa. Gay could spot a cop in a crowd any day, but these two would've fooled her.

"Mr. Kenyon." The one in the chair got up, hand extended to Bruce, but it was the albino on the couch who didn't get up that caught Gay's attention. He seemed too relaxed, too at ease, as if he had every right to be where he was, as if he were sitting in his own home, in his own living room. She wondered if anything ever fazed him.

"How'd you get in?" Bruce took the offered hand, shook it. Gay saw the look on Bruce's face. Contempt.

"Alvarez, Jesse Alvarez. Homicide, Long Beach. That's my partner, Abel Norton on the divan."

"I asked how you got in," Bruce said again, voice tough, like he was brow beating a witness on the stand. Lawyers, Gay didn't like them, never had.

"Door wasn't locked." Norton made no move to get up. The albino had shoulder length white hair, whiter skin and pale grey eyes. A pair of hippy cops.

"You have a warrant?" Bruce said.

"We need one?" Norton shifted on the sofa, caught Gay's eyes, smiled. It was sincere.

"If you don't, you're gonna be looking for a new job." Bruce had a sneer in his voice now.

"Relax, counselor." Alvarez tapped his chest, indicating he had the warrant in his inside coat pocket. "We're covered. As we were when we came in the other day and looked around."

"You were here Monday," Gay cut in, "but you didn't go in her house."

"We came back Wednesday, about 2:00, 2:30, something like that," Alvarez said.

That figured, she thought, Danny's day off. He'd have told her, had he known. "We were at the movies, me and the girls. My daughter and Jasmine."

"Say again," Norton said from the sofa. He looked so relaxed in his rumpled cord sportcoat, brown over a plain yellow shirt and faded brown Dockers. The other one seemed uptight in a three piece suit.

"You got a hearing problem?" Bruce said, confrontational. He was a big man, probably a bully when he was in school, Gay thought.

"Sorry," Norton said. "We thought your wife and daughter had disappeared. Now I hear your daughter hasn't gone anywhere at all and I'm curious."

"Nobody's disappeared." Gay clenched her fists again. None of the men noticed. "It's Spring Break so Margo doesn't have any classes. She's spending the holiday up in Big Bear. Jazz is staying with me."

"Doing what?" Alvarez wanted to know.

"She's on a religious retreat."

"Boy, you guys are stupid!" Bruce Kenyon said. But Gay knew he didn't know where Margo was either. Otherwise, he wouldn't have shown up at her doorstep like he did every Saturday afternoon to annoy her by taking his daughter for whatever was left of the day. Had he known she wasn't home and Jazz was staying next door, he wouldn't have bothered.

"Don't fuck with us." Norton smiled when he said it. The effect was ghostly.

"Who the hell do you think you're talking to?" Bruce said.

"I think he's serious," Alvarez said to Bruce.

"Fujimori raped that little girl two weeks after you got him off," Norton said. "How'd you feel about that?"

"The DA didn't have a case."

"Yeah, well you lost on the second one."

"Can't win 'em all."

"He got paroled last month."

"And you guys let him get killed. Some police force."

"That's it." Norton was up quicker than Gay thought a man could move. He grabbed Kenyon by the arm, spun him around, cuffed him and slammed him face down on the sofa he'd just vacated. "Frisk him!"

"Pleasure." Alvarez ran his hands over Bruce, checking everywhere. He wasn't gentle. When he finished, he pulled him up by his shirt collar, turned him and set him down on the sofa, hands behind his back.

"You guys are off base here." Bruce didn't seem so arrogant anymore.

"Maybe. But we got a couple witnesses say you were in a car parked outside when Fujimori was shot. Everyone knows how crazy your wife was about him getting out," Norton said.

"I was following Margo. She went in the store after Frankie. I didn't have anything to do with him getting shot. Besides, she's the one that wants the bastard put away, not me. I'm his lawyer for Christ's sake."

"Your wife didn't take off before the police showed up. You did. You haven't been cooperating with us, she has," Alvarez said.

"Did she tell you I was there? Is she the one?"

"Get him out of here," Norton said.

"Get up!" Alvarez grabbed Bruce by the arm, jerked him off the sofa, dragged him toward the door.

"I didn't see anything out of the ordinary." He was whining. "I didn't have any reason to talk to the cops. I was just trying to catch Margo harassing Frankie, so I could get a restraining order against her."

"You make me sick." Norton turned as Alvarez led Kenyon away.

"He's a jerk," Gay said. "But he didn't kill anyone."

"I know," Norton said. "But he was there."

"How'd you ever get a judge to sign off on an arrest warrant?"

"He's a good lawyer, but he's a prick. Winning isn't good enough, he's gotta rub your nose in it. That's never a good strategy, because someday the attorney you creamed in court, than ridiculed in the press, might become a judge."

"You didn't read him his rights."

"What for? He'll be out by this afternoon. Still, I enjoyed it."

"So did I," Gay said. "Thank you for letting me be here."

"No problem. Thank you for clearing up the whereabouts of Mrs. Kenyon for us.

"Glad to be of service."

"Appreciate it." The albino smiled at her again, tapped his forehead in a two fingered salute. Then he left.

* * *

Jazz had seen her dad go into the condo with Gay. She was afraid he was telling the police her mom was unfit to be a mother. Yeah, that's what he was doing. They were gonna take her away and make her go and live with him. She hated that he'd tried to get her in court, because he didn't want her, not really. He only wanted to hurt her mom. He hated her mom. How could he be so cruel?

They were coming out. Her dad and one of the cops. Good, they were leaving. She sighed. Then her dad looked right up at her. She could feel his eyes, like he was looking deep into her. Any second he could come charging across the lawn, then up the steps after her. She had to get out. Now.

She took her fingers away from the blinds and ran to the door. She had it open in a flash.

"Jasmine!" her dad called out.

She was outside now, charging for the staircase. Holding onto the rail, she flew down the steps, skipping every other one.

"Jasmine!" her dad yelled out again.

Halfway down, she stopped, turned toward him and was shocked to see him between the two policemen. They were holding onto his arms. His hands were handcuffed behind his back. He wasn't going to come up and get her after all.

"It's my daughter," he said.

"It's okay!" The Ghost said as he let go of her father's arm, but Jazz didn't believe him.

She looked around. Mrs. Emerson from 1210 was putting her key card into the beach gate. Jazz didn't need an invitation. She waved, hoping to fool the policemen. She started down the steps, keeping her eyes on Mrs. Emerson as she pulled her card out of the slot.

"Hey, lady," the Ghost yelled out. He must have seen where she was looking.

"What?" Mrs. Emerson started to swing the gate open.

Jazz took the remaining steps as fast as she could, then hauled out at a dead run for the gate as Mrs. Emerson opened it ever wider.

"Close the gate!" The Ghost was waving his arms now. He had Mrs. Emerson's attention. "Don't let her get away!"

But Jazz was already at the gate. She grabbed the card from the startled Mrs. Emerson and pulled the gate closed after herself. Then she dashed along the bike trail paralleling the chain link fence that separated the condominium complex from the public beach.

"Stop!" The Ghost, unable to get out, was running along the sidewalk on the inside of the fence, but he was no match for the blur in blue jeans running as fast as her almost eight-year-old legs could carry her. "Come back!" the Ghost called out when he reached the end of the property, but Jazz turned left and ran across Pacific Coast Highway toward Main Street.

She weaved between the cars on the highway and ducked into Jerry's Surf Shop, panting like she'd just finished a marathon. She caught her breath in the Hawaiian shirt section. The big Coca Cola clock behind the register said it was 4:15. She needed to hide out till dark.

"Can I help you?"

"Oh, hi," Jazz said to a girl wearing a "Guns 'n' Roses" T-shirt. She had bright orange hair and was frowning at Jazz through a face full of freckles.

"I'm gonna get a tuna sandwich at the juice bar in back," Jazz said.

"Where's your mother?"

"I don't need my mom to get a sandwich."

"Do you have any money?"

"What a stupid question." She had thirteen dollars in her back pocket.

Jazz bought the tuna sandwich and had a glass of Jerry's special tropical juice blend to go with it. She nursed them for the better part of an hour. Then she ordered carrot cake for desert. She had to stay out of sight till her mother returned, because with her father arrested they might not let her stay with Gay anymore. They might put her in a foster home. She needed somewhere to hide, then she thought of the movies.

* * *

"I wish Jazz would hurry up and come back." Sonya was sitting on the edge of her mother's bed while Gay changed from the clothes she wore at the salon into jeans and a San Francisco Giant's T-shirt. Jasmine had been gone for almost an hour. She saw the sun, an orange ball going down over the ocean. It would be dark soon.

"Me too, but I wouldn't worry. She knows her way around." But Gay was worried. She didn't like it when the girls were out together after dark, much less one of them alone.

"I wish she could come and live with us," Sonya said.

"Two wishes, you only get one more," Gay said.

"She likes it better over here and I bet her mom wouldn't even miss her."

"She's just next door." Gay zipped up her jeans, studied herself in the full length mirror on the closet door. She pushed her long, curly hair back, then started for the living room.

"Not after her mom gets married again. She'll move away then."

"Maybe."

"Definitely," Sonya said. "Her mom told her."

"I didn't know that," Gay said.

"You could talk to Margo, tell her Jazz could live with us," Sonya said as she trailed after her mother.

"I'm sorry, sweetie." Gay sat on the sofa and Sonya took the love seat across from it. "If Margo moves, then Jazz is going to go, too. There isn't anything we can do about it."

"But Margo doesn't care about her. If you said something, I bet she'd let her stay with us."

"I doesn't work that way, honey," Gay said. "I wish it did, but it doesn't." She sighed, because she meant it. In a way her daughter was right. Ever since

Margo had come into the money, she'd been drifting away from Jasmine, growing closer to her fiancé and those church people.

* * *

Two hours after ducking into the theater, Jasmine went outside to a dark night. She was out of money now. The sandwich and cake at the Surf Shop and the movie had taken it all. But she couldn't think of a better place to hide then the fourth row center. Besides, the movie took her mind off her father.

She crossed Pacific Coast Highway at the Main Street light, and continued on to the bike trail that ran through the beach. She still had Mrs. Emerson's key card, so getting in would be easy.

"Hey, look out!" Jazz jumped aside as a couple of older kids flew by on mountain bikes.

"Watch where you're going!" she shouted after them, but they didn't hear. She watched till they were out of sight in the dark, then she was alone on the bike trail. Spooky. And there was no moon. Real spooky.

She'd lived by the beach all her life, and she'd been on the trail lots of times after dark, but never alone. When she was alone, she always came home the front way, straight across PCH at Main Street, then past the guard shack. She looked through the chain link fence when she reached the condos. Everything inside seemed normal. No sign of the Ghost. And no sign of her dad. It looked safe. She ran her hand along the fence till she got to the gate. She keyed the gate and slipped in without a sound.

She dashed to C building and was about to take the stairs up to the clubhouse when she heard footsteps. She leaned back against the building, arms at her sides, palms against the stucco wall. Her hands were cold, her feet sweating in her running shoes. She inched along the wall till she was under the stairs.

Someone was just the other side of the building. Then all of a sudden that someone was in front of her, standing at the foot of the stairs. The outside light from an apartment on the second floor shone down on Gay, making her face glow like an angel's.

***

Gay dropped to her knees and held her arms out. Jazz burst into tears and ran into them. "It's okay. I'm here." The child looked like she'd been living on the run, like a homeless waif. She was scared.

"Don't let 'em take me away. Please don't let 'em." Jazz was trembling, covered in cold sweat.

"Don't worry." Gay hugged her tight, killing the shivers. But could she kill her fears?

"He's horrible, promise!"

"I promise, Jazz." Gay hated to say it, but she agreed with Jasmine. Her father was horrible. She wondered what Margo had ever seen in him.

"You mean it?" Jazz pulled back, looked into Gay's eyes. "Really?"

"Really. Now, let's get inside and get you into a hot bath." Gay broke the hug. "Okay?" She led her to the safety of her living room. Sonya was waiting, sitting on the couch. The TV was on, a video, The Lion King, but the sound was off.

"You're staying with us till your mom gets back. No one's gonna take you away." Gay was worried about how long Margo was going to be. She said she'd be back Saturday before noon. The woman was a cuckoo clock without springs, but she was usually punctual.

"Not even my dad, you promised."

"Especially not him." Bruce Kenyon didn't stand a chance in hell of getting the girl, no matter how long Margo took to get back.

"Thank you." Jasmine jumped up on the sofa next to Sonya, the bath apparently forgotten.

"But I gotta tell you, I'm worried about your mom. She said she'd be back this morning."

"No way," Jasmine said. "She's starting back at midnight. She said so, so she could be home in time for church."

"I could have sworn she told me before noon."

"She probably did," Sonya said.

"Yeah," Jasmine said. "That's my mom, sometimes she messes up."

She messes up a lot, Gay thought, but she wasn't going to say it. She crossed her fingers, something she hadn't done since she was a little girl.

"Why you doing that, Mom?" Sonya said.

"For luck, wishing Margo a safe journey home." The girls crossed their fingers, too. Both hands.

Chapter Five

Maggie opened her eyes and was surprised to see the dance floor was crowded. A slow song was playing, the Beatles' 'Yesterday.' She saw Horace with the ferret face dancing with a woman wearing a long dress. Except for a quick memory flash of his large friend, she didn't think anything of it. The Lounge was crowded as it was every Saturday, like all the popular pickup places in the Shore.

"You ready to go?" Gordon pushed away from Maggie, met her eyes. "It doesn't look like Nick's coming." Maggie saw tension wrinkling his forehead. His lips were tight. His hand was quivering.

"What's wrong?"

"Nothing?" he said.

"Don't give me that, you're the original Mr. Poker Face. Besides, you've been Mr. Smooth all afternoon, what's up?"

"Mr. Smooth, Mr. Poker Face." Gordon laughed.

"That's better. Now, what is it? You're worried about something. What? And why all of a sudden?"

"The thought of taking Fred down to the pet store just flashed through my mind. It kind of gave me the shivers for a second there."

"I can understand that, Ricky loved that bird. You probably feel that giving it away is like giving away a part of him."

"Maybe." He sighed loud enough for her to hear over the music. "You wanna get outta here now?"

"Yeah." Maggie looked at the Budweiser clock behind the bar. It was almost 7:00. They usually left when it started to get crowded. Maggie liked to dance. Gordon did too. So that's what they did while Nick, who thought dancing was something pygmies did in Africa somewhere, played at being Mr. Important at the bar.

She usually walked home laughing and joking between the two of them, but not tonight. Was Nick out someplace with that redhead? Was she making that drug buy? Did he have a film crew with him? Or was he in another bar somewhere buying her a drink? Was that why he didn't come back to the Lounge as he'd promised?

She linked an arm with Gordon and started for the door. Outside the darkness covered her mood like early evening fog. The sun had been blazing when she'd gone into the Lounge. Now it was gone. There was no moon.

"We really went to town tonight," Gordon said. "It kind of made me feel young."

"You are young," she said. He wasn't, but he didn't seem old. She started down Corona Avenue toward the beach. She wanted to tell him about the baby, but she'd already made her mind up about it, so there didn't seem to be any point.

He squeezed her arm as they turned at Ocean Avenue. The gentle surf, tamed by the breakwater, lapped up onto the sand on the other side of the street. A car went past, slow cruising, then another. At first Maggie didn't get it, then she saw the Whale up ahead.

"I'm going to go in alone tonight." Gordon was tense. He seemed eager.

"Really?" She was uncomfortable and now she knew that it wasn't just giving away Ricky's bird that had him tense earlier. He'd been thinking about going into the Whale by himself.

"Ricky's been gone for over a year, it's time."

"Sure you don't want me to come in for a bit?" She'd been in so many times with him she was a regular. Often she'd been the only woman in the bar, but she hadn't felt threatened. She'd have a drink or two with Gordon, meet some of his friends. Maybe dance to a couple of slow tunes. But tonight he wasn't going in for a drink and to meet friends. He was after something more, and it bothered her. It shouldn't, but she couldn't help her feelings.

"No, I'll be all right."

"If you say so."

"I do." He smiled at her, started for the bar, turned back at the door. "I'll be fine, really." Then he was inside and she was alone with the night.

"Damn," she muttered. She was more than uncomfortable. She was jealous and that didn't make any sense. She stared at the door, half expecting him to come back out, but he didn't.

She should go home, she told herself, but she couldn't. She didn't want to face an empty house if Nick wasn't there, and she didn't want to face him if he was. Thoughts of the baby filled her head, then the thought of it dead crept in. Abortion, she sighed, the coward's way out. Was she going to give up on her baby the way she gave up on racing?

She wrapped her arms around herself, hugged herself and told herself it was the chilly night making her shiver and not the thought of losing the child. But she didn't believe it, couldn't and never would be able to convince herself.

The sound of the soothing surf on the other side of the street seemed to seep beneath her skin, drawing her like a wondering child to a magician. She loved the seashore, loved running in the hard, wet sand, loved the way the runner's high cleared her mind, and if ever she needed a clear head, now was the time.

* * *

"The guy's going into that faggot place." Horace put a hand on Virgil's arm, stopping him. "The way they been acting I thought they were lovers, dancing cheek to cheek, walking so slow, whispering." Wrong about that, not lovers. Something else.

"She didn't seem like the kinda woman would go around with them."

"How do you know what kind of woman she is? God damn, Virgil, sometimes I think you are a retard."

"Don't say that."

"Sorry." Maybe he wasn't a retard, but he wasn't Einstein either. "But you gotta think more before you talk."

"Yeah, okay," Virgil said and Horace chuckled. He didn't have to see his brother's face to know he was smiling. He was always smiling.

Up ahead, the woman was standing outside the fag place, like she was unsure what to do next. Then all of a sudden she started across the street toward the beach. Horace held Virgil back until she was a safe distance ahead, no homes on that side of the street to give them cover.

"I wish we had the van," Horace said.

"I could get it."

"Maybe." Horace grimaced at the thought of Virgil driving his van. It wasn't that Virgil wasn't a good driver, but the van was new. It usually took Virgil a while to get the hang of a new vehicle. However the van had been in the Safeway parking lot since noon. How long before they'd tow it away? He thought about it for a second and decided not for awhile. The supermarket was open till nine, so it was probably safe till then. Still, he'd feel a whole lot better if it was close by.

The woman bent over, pulled her shoes off, then tossed them onto the sand like she was throwing a Frisbee or something. Then she tucked her shoulder bag into her side, like a football, stepped off the sidewalk and started to run.

"Stupid woman." Horace sucked his mustache into his mouth, chewed on it. "She's gotta come back for the shoes." Horace spoke the words the instant the thought came to his head. "Think you can get to that store and get the van back before she does?"

"Really?"

He handed Virgil the keys. "Go."

"I'm gone." Virgil took off at a dead run.

* * *

Maggie took quick breaths. The sand, starting to cool now, sluiced between her toes as she found her rhythm. She was a runner. Throughout the course of the afternoon she'd had five or six drinks. Not that much considering she'd eaten, but too much for her. She'd always been a lightweight, a cheap date.

The water lapping against the beach seemed to be calling her name and she turned toward it. She ran at the very edge of the surf, feet splashing through the water as it rolled up onto the beach. Cold water, cool breeze, gentle waves, almost paradise.

She passed the enclosed Olympic pool on her right and was closing on the Belmont Pier when she stopped to catch her breath and do a few stretching exercises. Here, with the pool complex blocking off the cars on Ocean Avenue on one side and the Pacific on the other, she could imagine she was alone on a Caribbean island, but a horn honk in the distance reminded her she was pretending. She sighed. She couldn't escape the city any more than she could escape her own depression.

"Damn him," she muttered. "He's with that redhead." She bent down, legs straight, grabbed onto her toes. She held the position, the back of her legs burning. "How could he?" She bent lower, feeling the burn. She straightened up, sucked in a deep breath. All of a sudden she was angry. Mad at Nick. And he hadn't done anything. Not really. She was the one who'd strayed. The one who got pregnant. No good blaming him. But where was he? Where had he been tonight?

She bent to the ground again, finished her stretches. She saw two lights far out at sea, green and white, a sailboat on a starboard tack. It had been four years since she'd been on a sailboat, the last time she'd seen her father alive. They'd let her mother's ashes fly in the wind. Two days later he was dead by his own hand. He just couldn't live without her.

"Oh, Dad, we could've worked through it."

She'd been too depressed to spread his ashes. Instead she left the job to his brothers. She was depressed now, like she'd been then and it was taking her down. She raised her eyes to the stars. "Oh, God, I want to keep this baby."

But she knew she couldn't, and it made her heart ache.

She sighed.

Metal against metal clanged up ahead. A city truck was parked at the end of the pier. They were locking the gate, keeping the Belmont Pier safe from the homeless who might spend the night out there. She used to fish the pier with her dad till all hours of the night when she was in high school. Now no children fished with their fathers at night. The pier was locked off. The fish, like the pier, safe till morning.

She sucked in a lungful of air, one more deep bend, knees straight. She dug her palms into the sand. Her legs screamed. She exhaled and eased out of the bend. A chill rippled through her, she felt herself being watch, she stood still, an elk exposed, looking for the wolf. Slowly she moved her eyes around the night, then bit back a gasp as something moved under the pier. There was someone there. She'd been right, somebody was watching her.

She grabbed another quick breath, then sprinted back the way she'd come, legs pumping, determined to run till exhaustion pushed all thought from her mind.

* * *

Ripples curdled up Horace's spine as he stood on the beach and watched the woman run toward the pier.

Something sinister churned his stomach. To do a woman whose only crime was being in the wrong place at the wrong time, it seemed a sin, evil.

But she'd seen his face and maybe Striker's too, certainly his car. That's what really worried the man, and there was nothing Horace could do about that. Striker called the tune, paid the bills. Horace held a hand out in front of himself. Not so steady.

Any minute Virgil would be back with the van and he'd have to make a decision. He was supposed to kill the woman, make it look like an accident. It was going to be hard enough doing her. Horace fought the vomit that threatened when he thought about it. But how in the world he could do it with Virgil around was anybody's guess.

"Stupid," he muttered. No way should he have his brother with him, but Ma had insisted. She thought he was a process server. Maybe if she knew what he really was, she'd have kept her darling at home. But she didn't and she didn't. Virgil needed to spend time with his brother, she'd said. He needed to know what it was like to work for a living. The man was thirty-nine years old for fuck's sake and now she wants him to see what it's like to have a job.

He closed his eyes. A cricket chirped in the distance. It reminded him of Yuma, where he'd grown up. He used to make up games with big brother Virgil outside in the dry desert air. Make something up, that's it. An idea started to take shape.

He opened his eyes, looked around, felt the night. The gay bar across the street was quiet. Every now and then cars came by, but their occupants wouldn't be looking out to the beach, not at this time of night, and they'd most likely have their radios on or a CD in the player.

Tires screeched around a corner.

DEAD RINGER

Horace turned toward the sound. Damn, Virgil had the brights on. Was he trying to wake up every cop in Long Beach? The breeze picked up, tickling the back of his neck. The blue-grey light of a television flickered in the house next to the bar. The porch light came on as Virgil pulled up to the curb.

"The fuck's the matter with you?" Horace said when he got in the van.

"You said you were in a hurry."

"Turn off the brights."

"Yeah, sorry."

"You made so much noise, you got some couch potato across the street to get off his ass and turn on his porch light. Probably watching us right now."

"I won't do it again. I'll be careful. You'll see."

"Okay, okay." He paused. "Look, I gotta get the woman with her husband so I can serve them the subpoena at the same time, otherwise it don't count. But she knows that, see. That's why they never get together." Horace was making up his story as he went along.

"So what are we gonna do?"

"We're gonna grab her, handcuff her and put her in the van. I got cuffs in the glove box. Then we drive to her husband's place where I serve them the subpoena."

"Isn't that kidnapping or something?"

"Not really. Process servers got special powers. We're allowed to do stuff like that, because we're acting for the law. Without us, nobody could ever get sued, then where would America be? All the lawyers would be out of work."

"How we gonna get her?" Virgil didn't even think of questioning what Horace said. He believed it just as if he'd seen it on TV.

"You get down to the water and scare her so she goes the other way. Think you can keep up with her?"

"She's a girl, Horace."

"Right. Chase her back to the pier. She's gonna have to turn right after she passes the pool. I'll be waiting there with the van. Then we got her."

* * *

The effects of the alcohol seemed gone now. Sweat rippled through her hair, down her neck. She was a train, her bare feet on the wet sand the wheels going over the tracks, her breath a steam engine chugging through a canyon. She could go forever.

Someone was up ahead. A man. She noted his size as she closed the distance between them. The white of his T-shirt stood out like a beacon even on this dark night. All of a sudden she knew who it was. She flashed on the image of the big man in the supermarket. Ferret Face coming into the Lounge was no coincidence.

Maggie stopped, panting. Breeze cooled her sweat, prickly rivulets of cold. She looked around. A pair of joggers were behind the man, going the other way. She could scream out. But why? The man hadn't done anything. She remembered him from the store. He'd seemed slow. Anyway she could out run him if he started anything. But what if he had a gun? And where was Ferret Face?

The big man started to move. Coming toward her at a walk. He was still quite a distance away and she couldn't see his face yet, but she knew it was him.

Maggie backed up a step and the man stopped. She stopped too. Had he come here for her? Why? He'd certainly known her in the store. Or at least he thought he had. What was it he'd said? *Saw you in the newspaper.* She'd been afraid then, a little. That's why she'd left the cart.

Again she thought about shouting out, but the joggers were farther away now. Almost out of sight, out of hearing distance.

"Wanna come to the van?" the big man called.

"I'm outta here," she muttered.

"What?"

Maggie spun around and poured on the speed. The man was nuts, she thought as she ran back toward the pier. She looked up toward Ocean Avenue on her right. There were people up there. A two minute sprint across the sand and she'd be safe. But Ferret Face might be up there, too. Waiting.

She kept on, running strong. She looked left, out over the sea. She saw the lights on that sailboat. It was inside the breakwater. She was a strong swimmer, but could she get into the water before the man was on her? She didn't think so. She kept on.

There was a country and western bar at the foot of the pier, just past the pool. There'd be people there. Rednecks. A shout for help and that guy would be toast.

Maggie was fast, but the man behind was gaining, wheezing his breath in and out. He was a train, too. She pumped her arms faster, forcing her legs to match the rhythm. But still he was gaining. His breath, louder now, churning up the tracks.

She felt like she was going to explode as she pumped her arms still faster. She was sprinting all out toward the dark stretch of sand between the pool and the pier. She couldn't let him catch her there. She turned and started chugging up the sand toward the bar, sucking air, lungs about to burst.

The pool was a thing out of a horror story, Dark glass and concrete climbing three stories out of the sand, blocking out Ocean Avenue, blocking out help. She was alone in the world with her pursuer, the distance between them shrinking.

She saw the bar. She was going to make it. The door opened on a black van parked under a streetlight in front of the bar. She was about to shout out for help when Ferret Face stepped out of the van.

He had a gun.

Virgil was almost on her.

She dropped to the sand.

"What?" Virgil shouted as he tripped over her.

She scrambled to her feet and was off, sprinting like she was running the hundred yard dash back in high school. She was so exposed, her back a wide target. She made for the pier. There was someone under there. Scary probably, but someone.

"Get her!" Ferret Face shouted out.

The space under the pier was a dark tunnel to the sea. Waves whipped around the pylons, echoing through the blackness like a hurricane swirling through her soul. She kept her speed up, dodging the pylons till she stumbled over something.

"Hey," someone shouted as she fell. She hit her head on something hard, but she didn't have time to worry about what it was, because she was tangled up with a man. Rancid breath, hairy. She pushed away from him and sprang to her feet.

"Lady come here to be safe." Laughter. Maggie turned. It was a black man, wiry hair akimbo, beard to his chest. He smelled like he hadn't bathed, ever.

"Men after me." Maggie panted. "One has a gun."

"We know," the man she'd tripped over said. He was white, but you could hardly tell through the dirt that covered his face. His hair stuck out like he'd been electrocuted, his great beard was matted. There was a smell here, Maggie could easily imagine it coming from that beard.

"Come on out of there," Virgil said. "We ain't gonna hurt you."

"Yeah, right," Maggie muttered.

"Get under there and get her," Ferret Face said.

"I ain't going under there."

"Come on."

"You go," Virgil said.

"Come on in. We be waiting." The black man's quiet voice was like a gunshot through the night.

"Shit," Ferret Face said.

"Bring yourself on in. We haven't eaten yet," the white man said.

"Fuck, there's two of 'em," Horace said.

"Let's go," Virgil said.

"Yeah."

Maggie held her breath for what seemed like forever.

"They're going," the black man said.

Maggie exhaled. "Thank God."

"A lady shouldn't be alone after dark," the white man said.

Maggie laughed. "But I'm not alone. You're with me."

"You look like you could use a drink." The black man handed her a bottle.

"Thanks." Maggie took a swig. "Shit, that's awful."

"Ain't it though." He laughed as she handed it back.

Maggie dusted the sand from her Levi's. "Thanks, you guys were great."

"Darley." The black man extended his hand. "Darley Smalls." Maggie took the hand. Hard, calloused, but gentle too. He didn't have anything to prove any more.

"Theo Baptiste," the white man said. "It's French." He held his hand out as Darley had.

"Maggie Nesbitt." She took it. He had a firm grip, but not as firm as it could have been. He could have crushed her with his giant paw.

"You weren't afraid. Those men had a gun." Maggie backed a step away from them.

"Gun or no, they were cowards," Darley said. "We weren't worried."

"How could you tell?"

"They were chasing a woman," he said. "Real men don't have to do that."

"No, they don't." Maggie took another half step back.

"They were gonna hurt you," Theo said.

"Yes, they were." Maggie stopped backing up.

"They had that van parked and waiting. It was you they wanted," Darley said, "not just any pretty woman happened to be out after dark. They set you up."

"I saw them earlier today, then the one with the gun later, at the Lounge up on Second Street. I thought he was a policeman because I saw the gun."

"He was no policeman," Darley said.

"I guess not."

"You live with that news guy. Maybe he was poking his nose in a story where it don't belong," Theo said.

"How do you know who I live with?"

"We rest here after dark," Darley said, "but we have to be gone by sunrise or the lifeguards run us off. So we spend the days wandering the alleys, poking through the trash, checking out what people like you toss away. You'd be surprised what we find and what we know. Show us a face and we can put it together with an address. We're not your average bums."

"How do you live?"

"We got places to sell the stuff we find," Theo said. "We get by."

"I gotta get my shoes." All of a sudden Maggie wanted to be home. These men were dangerous. She backed out of the dark.

"You get in trouble. You remember us. We don't take to men chasing after a woman," Theo said.

"Not at all," Darley said.

"I'll remember," Maggie said. Then, "I gotta go."

"I think we'll walk you back to those shoes," Darley said and the two men followed her out from under the pier.

They walked the distance in silence. Maggie's first impression was that the men were dangerous, but they didn't seem so now, not exactly safe either, but she didn't feel threatened by them.

"That them over there?" Darley pointed to the shoes on the sand up by the sidewalk.

"That's them."

"You'll be okay now," Theo said. "They're gone." And without even a goodbye, they turned and started back toward the pier.

Chapter Six

Maggie walked into the Whale out of breath. She took a quick look around, spotted Gordon sitting in one of the booths by the pool tables, playing chess with one of the two men sitting across from him. It was obvious the two were a couple. Good. Gordon hadn't found anyone yet.

"What happened to you?" Jonas, the Swedish bartender, was a big man, sometimes gruff and closing on sixty. But despite the appearance he tried to give off with his plaid shirts, work jeans and lumberjack boots, his heart was as big as he was and it kept his wallet as thin as a beggar's

"I fell down while I was running on the beach."

"Bummer." He pierced her with his water blue eyes. "Nick go home early again?" Sometimes on their walks home from the Lounge, Nick came in with Maggie and Gordon, sometimes not, as he had to get up early on Sundays for his magazine program, *Newsmakers with Nick*.

"I'd rather not talk about Nick. Just give me a rum and coke and let me wallow in my misery." She climbed up on a barstool, reached for a bowl of pretzels, pulled it to her, took one out and licked the salt off it as she stared into those blue eyes that saw everything and missed nothing.

He nodded, ran a hand through his thick hair. Like most Swedes, he was blond and old as he was, he had no grey. He pulled a bottle of Bacardi Select off the top shelf behind the bar. Reaching the bottle would have been a problem for Maggie, not Jonas. He was a tall man.

Maggie looked around the bar while he made the drink. There were twenty-five or thirty men in a place that held maybe three times that number. Poster size black and white photos adorned the walls. John and Bobby Kennedy, Martin Luther King, Mohammed Ali, others. Jonas owned the bar and it was clear where his politics lay.

Both pool tables were busy. Five or six men clustered around the two pinball machines. Real machines, mechanical, the kind you could get to know, not the computer kind. Gordon loved 'em. Maggie was starting to.

"On the house, because you look like you need it." Jonas set the drink in front of her.

"Do I look that bad?"

"You look like you went ten rounds with him." Jonas pointed to the picture of Mohammed Ali. "If that's what running does for you, maybe you ought to seriously think about giving it up."

"I'll take that under advisement." She looked over at Gordon. "He doing okay?" She wanted to change the subject.

"As good as can be expected, for Gordon anyway. A couple of good looking guys hit on him, but he blew them off." Jonas picked up a glass, dried it, did another. He had several to go.

Gordon turned, as if he knew they were talking about him. He waved, then came over. "What happened to you?"

"You too? I must look pretty awful."

"Go wash your face, then come back out here and tell me about it."

"What about your game?"

"It'll take ten or fifteen minutes for them to figure out what they want to do next. Go clean up. I'll be here when you get back."

She nodded, went to the woman's restroom and gasped when she saw herself in the mirror. She looked like a street urchin from some third world country. Her hair was dishevelled, her face blotchy with dirt and she had an egg-sized welt on her forehead. She ran water in the sink, grabbed some paper towels and washed the dirt, gingerly dabbing the area around the bruise.

Her T-shirt was dirty and damp. She couldn't do anything about that. It might even be ruined. She tried to straighten her hair, but gave up after a few tries and went back to join Gordon at the bar.

"I had no idea I looked like that." She picked up her drink, took a sip.

"You don't seem any worse for the wear, except for that bruise. What happened?"

She told them about Horace and Virgil and how Virgil grabbed onto her shopping cart in the Safeway.

Then how she'd seen Horace with the ferret face dancing in the Lounge.

"And that didn't bother you?" Gordon interrupted.

"Not really, I didn't think about it. I see the same people all over in the Shore. It's not like it was a great coincidence or anything." Then Maggie told how Horace and Virgil had come after her and how the men under the pier had frightened them away.

"Big black man, the other crazy looking, dirty beard out to here?" Jonas held his open hands about half a foot from each side of his face. "Looks like Rasputin, starved and wild-eyed?"

"That's them."

"Darley and Theo."

"Yeah, that's their names."

"You're lucky you got away from that pair in one piece."

"They were plenty scary, but they didn't threaten me in the least, in fact they escorted me back to where I'd left my shoes."

"Well, it sounds like an out of the frying pan and into the fire kind of story to me," Gordon said.

"I don't think they're dangerous."

"That's why you came straight here instead of going home," Jonas said. "Because you feel safe and secure?"

"I'll bet there's a story behind those guys, something that Nick could use."

"Don't even think about it," Gordon said.

"Why not? They could be a great story. Two men who roam the back alleys of Belmont Shore by day, living on what John Q. Public tosses in the trash, sleeping under the pier in the cold and damp by night. If he did it right, it'd be a great human interest piece. He could trace their lives, show how they got to be where they are. It could really tug at the heart strings."

"It is the kind of stuff he likes to do," Gordon admitted.

"What if one of them had been successful, then gone bankrupt?" Maggie sighed. "What if one of them was a Vietnam vet? What if one was laid off after twenty years on the job? The homeless are everywhere now. Nobody notices them anymore. They've become part of the background, the same as a lamp post or a tree. If Nick did a story on them it could help change all that. Really wake Southern California up."

"I don't think they want to wake up," Jonas said.

"I think he's right," Gordon said. "Nobody wants to know about the homeless."

"Your friends are calling," Jonas said.

Gordon turned. One of the young men in front of the chess set was waving. "Gotta make my move." Gordon started for the back of the bar and the chess game.

"That'll take him about a second," Jonas said.

"He's really good," Maggie said. "I won't play him anymore."

"The best this bar's ever seen. It's good to have him back at the game again. In the old days, before Ricky passed away, guys came from all over to play him. He was great for business." Jonas picked up a wet rag and wiped the counter.

"So you think I should be afraid of those characters under the pier?" Maggie picked up her drink, finished it.

"Absolutely. I'm a big man. I used to box in Sweden, trained for the Olympics. Not much scares me, but I'm afraid of them." Maggie took in his broad shoulders, the rippling biceps the long sleeved shirt couldn't conceal. He was in great shape, despite his age.

"Maybe you're right." She watched as Gordon picked up a piece, moved it, then started back for the bar. He didn't even sit, spent less than a minute looking at the board.

"What'd I miss?"

"I convinced your girlfriend to stay away from Darley and Theo," Jonas said.

"That calls for another drink." Gordon smiled at Maggie, but he had a warning look in his eyes as he reached for his wallet. She knew the look, he was telling her to be careful.

"No, sir. Your money's no good tonight," Jonas said and he set them up with another round. "I'm gonna have one, too." He poured a draft Coors for himself. "Here's to ya, Harvey." He raised his class to one of the giant photos on the wall, then took a long pull.

"Harvey who?" Maggie stared at the picture.

"Harvey Milk," Gordon said. "He was assassinated."

"What'd he do?"

"I can't believe it," Jonas said. "All the times you've been in here and we never talked about Harvey Milk. I toast him every time I take a drink."

"I've never seen you drink," Maggie said.

"Yeah, well I don't usually during business hours."

"So there you go," she said. "Now tell me, who's Harvey Milk?"

"He got elected to the San Francisco Board of Supervisors," Jonas said.

"He was a cut above the rest of us." Gordon stared up at the photo. Harvey Milk smiled back. He was a handsome man, dark hair, smile so wide his eyes were squinting. He was sitting, one leg over the other, by the side of a brick building, wearing Levi's, work boots and a plaid shirt, kind of like the one Jonas was wearing. His arms were folded over his knee, newspaper dangling from his hands. He looked like he needed mothering. He looked fragile.

He was in another photo with a young black woman. Milk's white skin contrasting sharply with her dark face. Her Afro wild, her smile serene. Maybe Maggie didn't know who Harvey Milk was, but she knew all about Gaylen Geer. An in your face black feminist who raged against everything. Maggie was surprised she hadn't noticed the photo before, but then the walls were covered with black and white shots of the '60s and the '70s.

Milk was in a third photo, sitting on the top of a car, legs dangling through the sun roof, right hand raised in a fist, in his left he was holding up a sign. *I'm from Woodmere, N.Y.* it said. He was wearing a white T-shirt, a garland of flowers hung from his neck. His mouth was open wide, he was yelling something. A crowd of people were marching behind the car. He looked like he was about to be swept up by a hurricane.

"Gay pride parade, he wanted folks to know gays come from everywhere. My sign said I came from Stockholm." Jonas took another pull from his beer.

"Mine said I was from Thief River Falls, Minnesota," Gordon said.

"Was he the first gay elected to the board of supervisors?" Maggie said.

"He was the first openly gay man elected to anything on the planet," Jonas said. "He brought us into the human race."

"You should know that," Gordon said.

"When was he killed?"

"Nineteen seventy-eight."

"I was eight years old."

"You know about those other guys," Gordon pointed to the photos of John, Bobby and Martin. "You weren't even born when they were killed."

"I know about George Washington and Abe Lincoln, too. Come on, guys, it's not the same."

"It is," Jonas said.

"If it isn't, it should be," Gordon said.

Maggie wanted to protest further, but she saw they were serious, so she bit back her words.

"Harvey Milk faced death every day. Back then gays weren't just discriminated against, they were persecuted. We were beaten, defiled and jailed. Sure, Martin Luther King was hated by a lot of stupid people, but it wasn't against the law to be black."

"Harvey said in his will 'If a bullet should enter my brain, let that bullet destroy every closet door,'" Gordon said. "He knew it was going to happen, but he kept on anyway, stayed in front of the public and the cameras, showing the whole world it was possible to be gay and do your job."

"He told me he expected it to happen one day," Jonas said, "but he didn't dwell on it."

"He was my friend and I miss him," Gordon said.

"Me too," Jonas said.

"So you two guys go way back?" Somehow Maggie didn't have a hard time picturing Jonas and Gordon together.

"We do," Jonas said and Maggie wondered if they'd been a couple in the past or would be in the future. She knew Jonas lived alone, though she didn't know why. She grinned. They might be good for each other.

"What?" Gordon said.

"Nothing. I think I'll go."

"Go where?" Gordon's arms were crossed, eyes scolding now. He was acting like a parent.

"Home, where else?"

"Not alone you're not."

"I'm a big girl, Gordon. Besides, you've got a game to finish."

"I'll drive her," Jonas said. "I need a break anyway."

"No you won't," Maggie said, adamant. "I'll jog on home. Nothing's gonna happen."

"They could still be out there," Gordon said.

"Who?" Maggie said.

"That guy with the ferret face and his big friend," Gordon said.

"Or Darley and Theo," Jonas said.

"The first two are long gone," Maggie said. "And Darley and Theo are under the pier where they've probably been every night since I've lived in the Shore. They've never bothered me before, they're not going to start now."

"You've had too much to drink to walk home alone. I'll get my keys," Jonas said.

"No," Maggie said. "I've had a little to drink, but I'm gonna run. I wanna work up a sweat and clear my head before I see Nick."

"Not gonna go down by the beach?" Gordon said.

"No. I'll stay on the sidewalk all the way home. Satisfied?" Maggie pushed her unfinished drink toward Jonas. Then, "Your boys are calling you again."

Gordon turned toward the back booth.

A man at the end of the bar raised his hand for another drink.

"Okay, you guys, I'm outta here." Maggie went to the door and started running as soon as her feet hit the sidewalk.

A couple minutes later she slowed to a jog as she neared home. In front of her duplex she did a few quick stretching exercises, then keyed the door and jogged up the steps to her second floor apartment. She was eager to tell Nick about her night, but she'd come home to an empty house.

Inside she was instantly hot, but Nick was gone. Though he'd mostly grown out of the asthma that had plagued him as a child, sometimes the sea air would bring on an attack and he'd grab his inhaler on his way to the thermostat. The contractions in his lungs could go on for three or four days and during that time he kept the apartment dry and as hot as the Mojave desert at high noon.

She wondered why he was out. It was unlike him. If he was going through one of his bad periods, he should be home in his hot as Hades bedroom, under the electric blanket, heat cranked up to the max. But he wasn't home. It must be a heck of a story if he'd rushed out without turning off the lights.

Maggie opened the door to the balcony, stepped outside to free herself from the heat. From her angle of view she saw both the pier and the Olympic pool. Cool shivers rippled up her spine as she thought about being alone in the dark with Darley and Theo as she huddled in fear, hiding from that slow witted Virgil and Ferret Face with his gun. Why were they after her? She'd done nothing to anybody to warrant such behavior. Could Darley and Theo be right? Could they have been after her because of something Nick had done?

And she thought about what Jonas had said about the two men who lived under the pier. He'd said she was lucky to get away from them, that she should fear them, but he was wrong. They were gentle and kind. Down on their luck, sure, but they'd certainly been no threat to her, on the contrary, they'd saved her from a fate she didn't even want to contemplate.

She shivered. She saw that pier every day, had fished on it with her parents, had taken photos of it, had eaten at the restaurant on the end of it, but she'd never suspected someone lived under it.

She looked out over the ocean. That sailboat was still out there. She sighed. So much had happened to her in the last hour, it was as if her life had been on fast forward, but to the people on that boat, nothing had happened at all. They were lazily moving through the water, powered by a slight breeze. She sighed again. She used to sail with her dad. She missed him.

And her mother. Now more than ever she needed her wise counsel. But they were gone. There was nobody for her now. Nobody she could talk to, confide in, ask advice from. Certainly not Nick. She could talk to him about most things, but not this, not about the baby.

She'd thought about Gordon. But she could never bring herself to tell him she'd betrayed Nick. It would be like one of the Musketeers had deserted, gone off with the enemy. He was a man, after all. He'd take Nick's side.

Oh, why did there have to be sides? The three of them were so close. Maggie wished they could sit down together and talk it out, but she knew that would never happen. This was her problem, her fault. Nobody was going to help her but herself, and she felt woefully inadequate.

A cold breeze blew in from the sea, chilling her. She came in from the balcony, shutting the double doors after herself, plopped down on the sofa, sweating in the heat. For a second she thought about opening the door again and turning the thermostat down, but that wouldn't be right, not if Nick was sick.

She picked up the remote, clicked her way through the channels, clicked it off. As usual, *beaucoup de* channels, but nothing worth watching.

Something smelled. She sniffed, frowned. It was her.

She pushed herself up, went to the bathroom, stripped, got into the shower and stayed till there was no more hot water. With her hair shampooed and rinsed, she put on a robe and came back out to the sofa. She couldn't sleep and the thought of watching television till Nick came home didn't appeal to her.

The phone rang. "Hello."

"It's me." It was Gordon. "Where were you? I called and got the machine."

"I took a long shower. I guess I couldn't hear the phone."

"What are you doing now?"

"Sitting on the sofa feeling sorry for myself."

"What have you got to feel sorry about?"

"Nothing." She paused, almost blurted it out, decided against it. "Girl stuff, you wouldn't understand."

"You want me to come over? Do you have something you want to talk about? Is it Nick? He's not home, is he?"

"What are you, the question man?" She laughed in spite of the way she felt.

"Just the answers, ma'am, just the answers," he said, imitating Jack Webb from the old *Dragnet* TV series.

"No, I don't want you to come over. No, I don't have anything I want to talk about. No, there's nothing wrong with me and Nick. And yes, I mean no, Nick's not home. There, satisfied?"

"No, I'm not satisfied. Where is he?"

"I don't know. Probably still working on that stupid drug story. Now that's something I don't get. How could he be so excited about drugs in high school? That kind of story's been around since I was a kid. It's hardly earth shattering. I mean, even if you filmed it live, who cares?"

"So you're upset because Nick isn't home?"

"I didn't say that."

"Yes, you did. I'll leave now and we'll talk about it."

"No, Gordon, don't do that. I'm in my pajamas and I'm going to bed. You have a good time. I'll see you in the morning."

"You're sure?"

"I'm sure, see ya."

"Yeah, bye." He hung up.

A half hour later Nick still hadn't come home and she hadn't moved from the sofa. Anger was gradually easing away her depression. Where was he? Still out with that ass wiggling bimbo? She had to do something. What? She couldn't sleep and she didn't want to sit on the sofa worrying and waiting.

She got up, went to the bedroom, threw on a clean pair of faded Levi's and a tank top, grabbed her keys and a corkscrew from the kitchen, then went out the back and padded barefoot down the stairs, skipping over the squeaky step, to the garage. She keyed the lock, hit the lights and went straight to the walk-in wine cellar, where she grabbed the last bottle of sixty-eight Heitz. It was her all time favorite. If you could get it now, it'd cost a fortune.

She locked the garage, walked between the duplex and the apartment building next door, crossed the street to the beach. The cool sand tingled her toes as she started out toward the pier. Soon she was at that place where the Olympic pool blocked out the cars on

Ocean. She slowed her pace, eyes on the pier, thoughts on the men that lived underneath it as she approached.

Her heart thumped a quick tattooed rhythm as she got closer. Earlier, with those men chasing her, she'd run right on under. Now, with no one after her, she found she was afraid of the two men under there. Maybe it was stupid, this idea of bringing a bottle of wine out to share with them. She didn't belong here, not now, not after dark. This was their place. She was intruding.

She was about thirty feet from the dark under there when she stopped. She willed herself to go on, but her feet froze in place. She wanted to call out to them, tell them she'd brought them something, but she couldn't. All of a sudden she was more afraid than when she was running from that big Virgil character.

In her rational mind she knew it was nonsense. Those men under there had helped her, saved her. But deep down she was shaking. She took a step backward, another. Then a few more. She moved a good way away before she turned, head down, and walked along the edge of the water, the ocean sounds soothing her fear. But now the depression was back.

She dropped the bottle of wine, dropped to her knees, and sat Japanese style, staring out at the dark sea and cried. Quiet tears at first that welled up into great racking sobs.

She was alone.

She was going to kill her baby.

All of a sudden she was back in the Borneo rain forest, driving as fast as she could on a muddy track with Sara shouting out the turns as Maggie concentrated on the driving, squinting through the rain, doing her best to see through it, trying to see what Sara told her should be there, then all of a sudden the child was there, eyes wide in fear as Maggie drove the car into him, cutting off his scream.

She'd killed him.

Snuffed out his life.

And she was going to do it again.

She was going to kill her baby, let some abortion doctor rip it from her womb, throw it away as if it were no more than a bloody tampon. A thing not wanted. A thing better off forgotten. But she'd never forget. She'd remember for the rest of her life. She'd cry every December. Christmas would forever be ruined. How could she ever celebrate the birth of Christ if all she could think about was the death of her child?

If only she had the courage to face up to what she'd done. If only she had the courage to tell Nick. But she didn't. She couldn't even drive past the speed limit. No, there was no way out for her save abortion. She was such a coward. She bit her lip, wiped the tears away with cold hands. After a bit she felt she could stand. She reached out for the bottle of wine.

It was gone.

Chapter Seven

"Fuck, what are we gonna do now?" Horace put the right blinker on as they passed the Edgewater Marina. "You coulda gone in there after her."

"Not me. It was scary under there, and there was those men." Virgil was wringing his hands in his new T-shirt.

"Yeah, you're right." Horace really couldn't blame the big guy. Did you blame cows 'cuz they couldn't fly? "Besides, there coulda been more than two of 'em."

"Coulda been a gang," Virgil said.

"It don't matter anyway. She's scared, so she's probably gonna go straight home." Horace turned right off of Second Street onto Pacific Coast Highway. "When she gets there, we'll be waiting."

"I don't think I like your work." Virgil was rocking back and forth in his seat now.

"Stop that! And put your seatbelt on!"

"Sorry." Virgil stopped the rocking, belted up, rolled his window down.

"Not gonna smoke in the van, are you?" Horace said.

"Can't help it." He unwrapped the pack from his sleeve, pulled his Zippo from the left front pocket of his jeans. He lit the cigarette, took a deep drag. Virgil had arms like an ox, it was a wonder the cigarettes weren't crushed between the tight fitting T-shirt and the bulging biceps.

"You didn't give me back my knife," Virgil said.

Horace handed it over.

Virgil loved that knife. It was the best thing Horace had ever given him. The big guy spent hours flicking the blade. Horace was surprised it still worked. He'd picked it up in Tijuana for almost nothing and expected it to last about a month, but Virgil had been abusing it for a couple of years and it kept on flicking.

"Try to keep the smoke outside." Horace shook his head.

A car honked. Horace snapped his attention back to the road. He'd started to drift over into the oncoming traffic. He jerked the van back to the right. "Fuck head."

"Want me to drive?" Virgil said.

"No." Horace frowned.

"So, we gonna go home now?"

"No, I still gotta serve those papers, remember?"

"You should get another job."

DEAD RINGER

"Somebody's gotta pay the bills. If I didn't do what I do, we'd all starve."

"Maybe I could get a job. I can do stuff, maybe work at a gas station."

"That's a thought, but right now I gotta finish what I promised to do. You can understand that, can't you?"

"Yeah, I suppose. So what are you gonna do?"

"I'll think of something." But Horace wondered what. If she went to the cops about what happened earlier, they'd give her 'round the clock protection. He'd never get to her.

Fifteen minutes later they were in Huntington Beach, passing the Sand and Sea Condos where Margo Kenyon lived. Horace turned left on Main Street, made a U-turn and parked in front of Jerry's Surf Shop, facing PCH and the condos on the other side of the street. It was a little before nine, and though the stores were closed, the restaurants were open. People were about. Spring Break was almost over and there were a lot of kids determined to wring the last drop of pleasure out of their vacation before they went back to school.

It was quiet in the van.

Virgil lit another cigarette. Horace wanted to tell him to put it out, but he bit back the words. Instead he said, "She's got this fag boyfriend she don't want anyone to know about, that's where she's been all week. That could be good for us, she might think we were a couple a crazies that chased her just 'cuz she was there. She might think she's safe when she gets back home."

"She is safe, all you're doing is giving her those papers, right?" Virgil said.

"Well, la de da," Horace said, ignoring his brother as a red Porsche convertible turned into the

87

condominium complex. "And they say lightning don't strike twice."

"What's that mean?" Virgil said.

"It means we get a second chance and we better not blow it this time or I'm gonna get fired." Horace opened the door, changed his mind, closed it again. "And put out that damned cigarette."

"What are you gonna do?" Virgil stared at the driveway into the Sand and Sea Condos, took a drag, then tossed the cigarette out the window.

"The guard rail's propped up," Horace said. "The guard just waved her on in."

"Maybe he knows her."

"Maybe he's lazy." Horace watched as the woman stuck her hand out the window, pointed it at a sliding fence gate and waited while it opened. "Look, she's got a clicker to open the gate into the parking lot, that's why the guard didn't hassle her. You can't get into the lot unless you got one of those. We need to get in there."

"Maybe we should just go home."

"We can't to that." Horace was thinking a mile a minute. He'd have to get the girl, cuff her in the back of the van, then drop Virgil somewhere. Where? Then he saw the theater across the street from the condos. "You wanna see a movie?"

"Yeah, boy!"

"After we get the woman in the van, I'll drop you at the theater. Then I'll take her to her husband's, serve the papers and come back. How's that sound?"

"Great!" Virgil wiggled in his seat. A dog waiting for a bone.

He started the car, drove past the condos, made a U-turn, parked on the ocean side of PCH. "Now all we gotta do is follow the next guy in." And as if the devil heard, a few minutes later a black Ford Taurus passed them and turned into the driveway. Horace had the van behind him in an instant, hugging the Ford's tail. There were two guys in the guard shack, an old black guy and a much younger white guy. They were talking, probably changing shifts. The fence gate opened for the guy in the Ford. Horace followed him in. The security guys didn't even notice.

"Piece of cake." Virgil laughed. Everything was a game to him.

Horace pulled into a vacant spot next to her car and looked down into the Porsche. The top was down. There was a bag of groceries on the passenger seat. "She must have done some shopping before we saw her at the Safeway, 'cuz she sure didn't buy anything there." It was a detail that bothered Horace. Why was she in the Safeway? Did she forget something and come back for it? He tried to remember how much stuff was in her shopping cart. Couldn't.

"So?"

"So, we wait. She couldn't carry everything in one trip. She's gotta come back for the rest. She's also gotta put the top up. Nobody leaves a Porsche open, even if it is in a secured lot. You never know who could get past a pair of dopey guards like that."

"What are you gonna do when she comes?"

Horace reached past Virgil to the glove box, took out the handcuffs. "You're gonna get out. I'm gonna get in the back. You're gonna grab her and toss her in. Then we're gonna cuff her to one of those eyebolts above the back wheel wells." Horace had the eyebolts put in for his dirt bike, no way could the woman pull one out, no one could.

"I don't think I wanna do this." Sweat ringed Virgil's forehead, glistening even in the dark.

"Don't be a baby."

"I don't wanna," Virgil said.

"I'll tell Ma you wouldn't help."

"You wouldn't?"

"I would, so just do your part." Horace clenched his fists. This was stupid. Maybe he should abort.

"I'll get out soon's she passes," Virgil said. "I'll tap on the door just 'for I grab her, so you'll know to be ready."

"That's more like it." Horace gripped the steering wheel so hard he thought he was going to break it. It was still a stupid plan. He should have hit her back when he'd had the chance, but he'd been too softhearted. Now, luck had given him a perfect opportunity. Perfect except for Virgil. He had to go for it. Besides, fortune had always favored him, no reason she'd let him down now.

"She's coming." Virgil was squirming in his seat again.

"Calm down, it's gonna be all right."

The woman was wearing hard soled shoes. Her footsteps clicked on the pavement, echoing through the night. Horace was breathing fast, ice shot up his spine. He climbed in the back of the van as Virgil got out. Any second they'd have her inside. It was going to happen.

Virgil slapped the door and the sound ricocheted through the van as he slid it open. She was wearing different clothes, a green skirt and blouse. She must've changed the second she got into the house. Horace took his eyes off her clothes and went eyeball to eyeball with her. Recognition filled her face. Now she knew who he was. Virgil had a hand over her mouth. She chomped down on it.

"Owww!" Virgil let her go. Then hit her, a blow to the head and she went down.

"Get her in the van," Horace said.

"Blood?" Virgil was looking at his hand where he'd been bit. Horace was looking at the girl's face.

"Move, before someone comes!" Horace jumped out of the van. "Come on." He grabbed her around the ankles.

"She dead?" Virgil grabbed her wrists. They lifted her from the asphalt and slung her into the van.

"No, just knocked out. Let's go." Horace slid the door closed.

Sweat dripped icicles under Horace's arms as he drove to the gate. "Shit, we got no opener," but the gate opened automatically. "Guess you only need it coming in." The guards, both still inside the guard shack, didn't even glance up at them as they left the property and turned right onto Pacific Coast Highway.

"I didn't mean it." Virgil sat crosslegged in the back, the woman's head in his lap. He was crying now.

"Stop it! She's gonna be fine."

"We killed her."

The woman moaned, opened her eyes. Horace risked a quick look into the back as he slowed for the light at Beach.

"See, what'd I tell you?" Horace handed the handcuffs back to Virgil. Now take these and hook her to one of those eyebolts."

"But she's hurt."

"You don't wanna do it, then I can't drop you at the movies. You'll have to come along and watch her till I serve the papers."

"I can't." Virgil tossed the handcuffs aside.

Horace grabbed another quick look into the back of the van. Virgil was stroking her cheek while he rocked back and forth. She seemed to be unconscious.

"Why don't you smoke a cigarette? That always calms you down."

"I don't like this, Horace."

"You said you could do it!" Horace knew he shouldn't lay into him. He couldn't help what he was. Shit and Shinola, the bastard was getting to him.

"Don't be mad."

"I'm not mad." Horace turned on the overhead and adjusted the rearview so he could see in the back and still keep his eyes on the road. "Stop that rocking! Smoke a cigarette and I'll take you to the movies."

"Can't. Cigarettes are on the dash."

"All right." Horace grabbed the Marlboros, tossed them back.

Virgil grabbed the pack out of the air, tapped out a cigarette, stuck it in his mouth. He was sitting crosslegged, not rocking now. He snaked a hand into his pocket, fishing for the Zippo, pulled it out. The switchblade came too, clanged to the floor.

Horace sighed as the lighter fluid smell permeated the van, followed by the nauseating smell of burning tobacco. Only idiots smoked. Again he glanced in the mirror.

"Virgil!" he screamed.

But he was too late.

The woman had the blade. She thumbed the button, flicked it open and shoved into his brother's belly.

Horace sliced the van across the highway, cutting off traffic in the slow lane. He stomped on the brakes even before the van was on the shoulder, pulled the Beretta from the holster, spun his arm around, muzzle seeking the woman, finding her as she jerked the knife up Virgil's belly, stopping at the rib cage. Horace fired the automatic point blank. The round slammed between the woman's tits, shoving her against the wheel well. Horace kept firing. Eleven rounds in the magazine followed the one in the chamber as rapid fire thundered through the van.

"It hurts!" Virgil had his hands on his belly, trying to hold his guts in. Fuck, the bitch had hari karied him sure as if she'd been one of them samurai guys.

Horace dropped the Beretta, jumped between the seats, was at his brother's side in an instant. Blood was everywhere. Virgil's big heart pumping it out his belly wound as if it were a fountain. The woman's blouse was soaked in it.

"Fucking Cunt," Rage roared through him. "Cunt, cunt, cunt!" He grabbed a fist of her bloody blonde hair, jerked her head up. She was still alive. Not for long. "You know me?" He shrieked. "Do you know me?"

Her eyes flamed as she glared up at him. Then the fire went out.

Horace slapped the woman with an open palm. He raised the hand into a fist. Hit her again, was about to go for her a third time when he got a grip on himself.

The bitch was beyond punishment.

"Horace." Blood trickled out of Virgil's mouth as he croaked the name.

"Don't talk." Horace slid over, cradled his brother's head in his lap.

"Hurts plenty." More blood. He coughed, gurgling it out.

"Hang on, I'll get you to a hospital." Horace knew he was lying as the words left his lips. There would be no hospital for his brother, just the morgue.

Virgil gripped his wrist. One more gurgle. A gasp. His body shook. Eyes dilated. His bowels cut loose, the stink of shit overpowering the smell of gunfire. It was over. He was dead.

A terrible silence ruled the van.

He crawled over the bloody bodies, got into the front, slid behind the wheel. A quick check ahead and in the side mirror told him nobody had stopped. Maybe nobody had heard, the ocean was on the right, closed stores across the street on the left. Horace leaned his head out the window, dragging in good, clean air.

First things first. He was being paid to deal with the bitch, make it look like an accident. Anything else and the DA might look harder into the Fujimori shooting. Striker didn't want that. Horace didn't want it either. But a sex murder might be just as good. Especially if she was found behind that faggot place. Cops would think some gay guy raped her, popped her and dumped her.

Horace laughed.

Then he cried.

"God damn, Virge, you shoulda used the handcuffs."

Horace started the van, pulled away from the shoulder. He made a U-turn at the next light, driving through the Beaches—Huntington, Bolsa Chica, Seal—without seeing them. Virgil was a problem. He couldn't toss his body out any old place. And he damn sure didn't want it connected to the bitch. He thought on it, but nothing satisfactory came to mind.

A cop car passed, going the other direction and that jarred him to the task at hand. He followed the policeman in the rearview till he was sure he wasn't going to do a U and come up behind.

When Horace got to the Shore he made a left on Second Street. He slowed to a crawl as he approached the Menopause Lounge. There were people out front. The pickup places in the Shore were doing a brisk business, matchmaking for the evening. Horace thought about Sadie, but quickly pushed her from his mind.

The dashboard clock said 11:00, still early. He made his left down toward the beach. The street was quiet, tall trees brushed by the breeze flitted in the pale moonlight. Dark shadows danced across his sight. He knew they moved only in his imagination, but he tightened his grip on the wheel anyway.

He passed a couple strolling arm in arm as he made his right onto Ocean. Rage lashed at him, a whip across his back. They looked young. They were gonna go somewhere and fuck. He wanted to smash them.

The flashing neon whale on the gay bar brought him back to reality. He made his turn at the corner before it. The alley was dark as he pulled into it. He stopped behind the bar. It was quiet save for the soft sounds of Simon and Garfunkel drifting through the walls. It didn't seem right. Faggots were supposed to listen to Barbara Streisand and show tunes. S & G were singing about Mrs. Robinson and Horace laughed. It was the soundtrack from *The Graduate*. That counted.

The sliding door opened with a screech, Bob Dylan's harmonica on a bad day. He sniffed the night, worried he might draw attention to himself, but after a few seconds he decided it was okay. Either he was gonna get caught or he wasn't. Fifty-fifty. Time to get on with it.

He climbed in back with the stink. Virgil lay between her and the door. Horace slid it closed in case someone came out to dump the trash. Fifty-fifty maybe, but one couldn't be too careful.

He scooted toward the front, grabbed Virgil by the foot, pulled him away from the bitch. The stink engulfed him. He thought of himself as a hard man, but he gagged, fought the vomit, held his breath. He took up Virgil's knife, cut the clothes off the bitch, tossed them aside.

Next, he took off the shoes. Paused. Had to breathe. Sucked in a short one. Retched all over the bullet holes in the bitch's breasts. On his knees, he fought for oxygen, a drowning man with no choice, he sucked in more of the stench. Heaved again. Stomach clenching. Nothing left but spittle. Dry heaves.

He pressed his back against the door, as far from the dead as he could get. His mind screamed, *Get out. Run.* But he squashed the urge. He had a job to do. He stood, slipped in blood, landed with his ass on her stomach. A gurgling sound erupted from her throat, a cattle prod up Horace's ass.

He yelped, scrambled to the door, yanked it open, bailed out of the van. Clean air. He sucked deep. A quick look around. The alley was empty. In a hurry now. Knife still in hand. Reach back in the van. Wipe the blood off the blade on the bitch's skirt. Flick it closed. Shove it in the back pocket. Grab the bitch's feet. Pull her out of the van.

Her head made a popping sound when it thumped on the pavement, a thunder blast to his heart. The world surely heard, but no one came running. Horace shot a look around. All quiet. Hands still wrapped around her ankles, he dragged her toward the trash dumpster, dropped her in front of it, scurried back to the van.

His eyes lit on Virgil as he closed the back. Poor dumb bastard dead in a pool of blood and shit. Back in the driver's seat he started it up. He took a quick look in the rearview as he turned out of the alley. No lights came on. He was in the clear.

Maybe.

He couldn't be safe till he logged some miles between the body and himself. The freeway called to him. In minutes he was on it.

Chapter Eight

Gordon Takoda slid out of the booth. The game had run over three hours. They were a nice couple, James and Paul, but they were poor losers. Every time he took a piece, they wanted to replay the move, discuss how they could have played it. And to their consternation, Gordon let them do it over, and he still creamed them.

"Good game," James said.

"Yeah, we learned a lot," Paul said.

Gordon gave them a smile before he started for the bar. Those boys didn't understand, chess was like life. In the real world you don't get to take it over.

"Coffee coming up." Jonas started for the pot.

"Black and strong." Gordon inhaled the aroma as Jonas poured. "Uh oh, trouble." A uniformed police officer had come in and was making his way to the bar.

"Problem, officer?" Jonas said. As a rule the police were rare in the Whale.

"There's a body in front of the dumpster out back. Female. She's nude, full of bullet holes."

"We haven't had a woman in here all night." Jonas set the pot down.

"That's not true," Gordon said.

"It couldn't be Maggie," Jonas said. "She said she was going straight home. You called her there."

But Gordon wasn't listening. He was off his stool and out the door before the cop could protest. An icy dagger wormed into his spine. Spasms racked his chest. He was in shape, but a heart attack wasn't out of the question. He was the right age.

He stopped at the mouth of the alley. Jonas and two cops were already there. They'd come through the kitchen. They were standing over a bloody body. The light from Jonas' kitchen gave the alley a kind of black and white look, surreal.

"You don't want to see this." Jonas came toward him, blocking his view.

"Get out of my way."

Jonas stepped aside.

"You know her?" the cop who had come into the bar said.

Gordon sank to his knees with a thud. He dropped his head into his hands.

"Sir, we have to ask you to step back," the policeman said.

Gordon pulled his hands from his face. Tears covered his cheeks. "Get something to cover her with."

"I'm sorry we can't do that. Not yet."

"Come on, Gordon." Jonas put a hand to his shoulder.

"I won't leave her."

"Please, sir," the policeman said.

"Do what you have to. I stay." Gordon took her hand. There was still some warmth.

"Sir, please don't touch the body."

"Just her hand," Gordon said. "I'll be careful of any evidence that may be under her fingernails."

"I'm going to have to insist," the officer said.

"Or what?" Gordon looked up at the cop. He bit into his lip to stop the quivering.

"Just the hand then." The young officer's face was pasty white, he looked like he was about to be sick.

There were some people behind the cop. A small crowd was gathering, despite the hour. There should be more cops. Probably on the way. "Keep them back till your people get here," Gordon said. "I won't disturb anything."

"Yes, sir," the cop said, and with Jonas' help they moved the crowd back.

Gordon ached to wipe the hair from her eyes. She hated that. "Oh, Maggie," he whispered. So much blood.

A couple more uniforms pushed through the crowd. They saw Gordon, one started to speak, but the first officer raised his hand and the man held his tongue. More cops, arriving in pairs. The alley was cleared of civilians save Jonas and the uniforms.

Gordon stroked the back of Maggie's hand with his fingers.

"It's Wolfe," one of the cops said.

"Fucking ghoul," another said.

"He gets the job done," still another said.

Gordon looked up to see a man in his mid-thirties push through the crowd. He was wearing faded Levi's, a threadbare sportcoat over a white Dodgers T-shirt and a blue Dodgers baseball cap over a shaved head. He didn't look like a ghoul.

"Clear everyone out. I need a few minutes," Wolfe said, voice barely above a whisper.

"I heard about you. I know what you need," one of the uniforms said, and the cops started to move back, taking Jonas with them.

"Come on," the cop said to Gordon.

Gordon met Wolfe's eyes. They were pale blue, but sad, like they should have been brown. Gordon tightened his grip on Maggie's hand.

"He can stay," Wolfe said. "Give us fifteen. If the lab van comes, tell them it's me, they'll understand."

Then the alley was empty, save for Gordon, Wolfe and of course, Maggie.

"Your wife?" Wolfe whispered.

"I'm gay."

"How would I know?" Wolfe's voice seemed to carry years of pain. More than a whisper, almost a rasp. Sad, begging empathy. He squatted down to Gordon's level.

"I don't know. Some people seem to."

"Everybody cries," Wolfe said. "Everybody hurts."

"Not just that."

"People are what they are." He reached over and took Maggie's hand from Gordon. He studied her face. "Who is she?"

"Maggie Nesbitt," Gordon said. "She lives upstairs from me. We're friends."

"More than friends, I think," Wolfe said.

"Yeah, we're close." Gordon didn't want to admit she was dead.

"She have a husband? Someone we should notify?"

"Nick Nesbitt."

"The news guy?"

"Yeah, that's him."

"He at home now, you think?"

"He wasn't earlier. Maggie was upset about it." He paused. "Why'd you clear the cops out?"

"I have to spend some time alone with the dead. Get a feel for them. Her." He nodded toward Maggie. "It makes them real. I need that for me to do my job." He handed her hand back to Gordon, then brushed the hair from her eyes. "She was beautiful."

Gordon turned away from her, sad that he had to see her this way, afraid this was the way he was going to remember her. "You're going to get him, this monster?"

"I am. Now, before they come back, tell me all you can."

And Gordon did, finishing with Maggie coming into the Whale and telling them about the two men, Virgil and Horace with the ferret face, that chased her, and the homeless men under the pier that rescued her, Darley Smalls and Theo Baptiste.

"She remembered their names. Both the ones from the store and the men under the pier?"

"Yeah."

"And you remembered too?"

"Yeah, I remembered too."

"Most people would have forgotten the second they heard it."

"I'm a bright guy." Blood rushed to Gordon's face.

"Sorry. Don't take anything I say personally. I have to ask. You understand?"

"Yeah." Gordon took in a long breath, calmed back down. "My IQ's off the chart and I have a photographic memory. Show me a page in book and I can read it back a month later."

"That'd be great for my line of work."

"For me it was a curse. I learned to hide it."

"Why?"

Gordon was still holding onto Maggie's hand. The warmth, what there had been, was gone now. She was getting cold. Gordon shivered. "Being gay wasn't a good thing when I was growing up. It's easier now. I was in the closet and didn't want to draw attention to myself. If people knew how bright I was, they'd want to know why. They'd snoop, find out."

"You think?"

"I know. There was this guy in San Francisco. An ex-marine. He knocked the gun out of Squeaky Frome's hand as she was popping caps at President Ford. Saved Ford's life. A hero for a day, till the press found out he was gay. Dragged him out of the closet."

"I didn't know that."

"Truth."

Wolfe looked back at Maggie, nude, lying broken by the trash. "What did you think of her story?"

"I believed it. Every word. I wanted to go home with her, but she didn't want me to leave my chess game. Jonas wanted to drive her, but she insisted she'd be safe. She was going to run straight home, not leave the sidewalk. She made it there. I know, because we talked on the phone. She said she was going to bed, but she must've changed her mind, gone back out for some reason."

"Who do you think did this?"

"Not those characters under the pier. If they were that kind, they'd have done her there and sent her body out on the tide."

"I'll have to talk to them, but I think you're right. It was the two that chased her. Virgil and Horace with the ferret face."

"Your head, why do you shave it?"

"Is it relevant?" Wolfe said.

"It is for me."

"Chemo. I had cancer. It's in remission. I keep it off now because I don't want anyone to know if it comes back. I was lucky, it was diagnosed early. I took a year off, told my work I needed time to get my life together. They don't know."

"So you know what it's like to be in the closet."

"No, I don't live in fear. If they find out, I lose a job. It wouldn't be the end of the world."

Gordon looked into Wolfe's eyes. "She's cold." He rested her hand on the pavement.

"I'm good at what I do. I'll get the ones that did this."

"Gordon Takoda." Gordon held his hand out.

"Billy Wolfe." Wolfe took the hand, shook it.

"No partner?"

"No."

"You got one now." Gordon forced himself to take a quick look at Maggie, brushed a hand against her cheek. He stood, dusted off his pants.

"I work alone." Wolfe's rasp was cold, final.

"I'm not just some guy that fell off the turnip truck. I put in twenty years with the FBI. I know my way around an investigation."

"How'd you do that?"

"Except for a gay pride parade in San Francisco in the '70s, I was in the closet. I quit right after my twenty was up, for the pension. I came out the next day."

"Why didn't you tell me this straight off?"

"I wanted to know what kind of man you were. If you were a jerk who shaved his head for some stupid macho reason, you know, like Kojack, I woulda had to find this prick myself." Gordon turned away and started toward the crowd at the end of the alley.

* * *

Horace looked at the gas gauge. He'd spent a quarter tank driving. Stupid. He was almost into L.A. Somehow he'd wound up on the Santa Monica Freeway. He took the Vermont off ramp and got back on heading south. Where was his mind? Nowhere.

"Gotta keep it together," he mumbled.

He popped a Meat Loaf CD into the player, cranked it up loud. Keeping it together wasn't gonna be easy. Not with that smell back there.

He kept the van in the right lane, chewing up the interstate. He cruised onto the Long Beach Freeway, tapping his finger on the wheel as Meat Loaf made love by the dashboard light. He punched the repeat button. He loved that song.

He got off the freeway in Lynwood, drove to one of those car washes he knew about where you do it yourself. Something had to be done about the smell. He backed the van into the middle stall so nobody could see in when he opened the back doors.

Chopped Harleys lined the curb in front of the biker bar across the street, but Horace wasn't worried about them. They'd be sucking 'em up till last call and then some. He had plenty of time.

He got out of the van, fed quarters to the coin box. He turned the knob to extra soap, then opened the back doors. His brother was covered in blood and stunk like shit. Horace shook his head. Poor bastard.

He went for the hose. It had a gun-like handle with a yard long nozzle. Horace held it like a range shooter, arm extended, and imagined he was picking off rattlers in the desert. Virgil loved that. Not anymore.

Horace climbed into the passenger seat, dragging the hose. On his knees, facing into the back, he held the hose out.

Virgil was lying head toward the back door, feet facing Horace. A jerk on the trigger, soapy spray shot out of the hose. Aiming at his brother's shoes, he blasted the soles, moved up to the legs, shooting blood, shit and the woman's clothes out the back of the van.

He kept it up till the money ran out, then surveyed his handiwork. Virgil lay on his side, Moby Dick, whiter in death, way white contrasted with the metallic black paint on the inside of the van. Black floor, roof, walls. White Virgil, white and dead.

Across the street a couple of bikers wearing Angels' colors came out of the bar. Time to wrap it up. Horace put away the hose, picked up the shoes and clothes, tossed them in the trash. One of the Harleys rumbled to life, then another. Horace started the van as they roared off in the direction of the freeway.

* * *

Gordon waited at the end of the alley while a police photographer shot a couple rolls of film. The lab men filled baggies with blood samples and bits of evidence from around the site, a lot of it irrelevant, but they were leaving nothing to chance. The coroner's wagon backed up the alley. There were more people out now. It was a quiet crowd, but somehow the neighborhood knew, as if death's quiet voice traveled from house to house, waking them, letting them know he'd come calling.

DEAD RINGER

"You wanna take a ride with me?" Wolfe took Gordon by the elbow, moved him away from the gawkers. He led him to a nineteen eighty-something Chevy, opened the passenger door, closed it after Gordon got in.

Gordon watched the night roll by as Wolfe drove. He picked a teddy bear off the floor. "Yours?"

"My boy's. He tossed it up from the car seat in back. Got an arm on him like Sandy Koufax used to have."

"Dodger fan?"

"That your IQ at work?"

"You ever see them play in the Coliseum?" Gordon looked in the back seat. There was a baby's car seat back there. It looked like a permanent part of the car.

"Before my time."

"What are you, thirty, thirty-five?"

"Old enough to vote. Look, I'm supposed to be the one asking the questions." Wolfe was on Second Street now. He pulled up in front of the twenty-four hour coffee shop across the street from the Lounge, shut off the engine.

"This isn't the police station."

"You are sharp." Wolfe got out of the car.

The restaurant's apple pie flavor seemed out of place in the Shore. Two hours before sunup and the place was doing a brisk business. Gordon had never been in before, probably a mistake, this many people didn't come to a place this early unless it was good. He ordered the country breakfast, he was going to need his energy. The cop ordered eggs over easy, bacon and toast.

"Tell me about yourself," Wolfe said.

"You interrogating a suspect?"

"No, interviewing a partner."

* * *

Horace snuck into the house at 3:30 in the morning, shoes in hand, so as not to wake Ma. Virgil had always been her favorite. No more back rubs for Ma. No more pedicures. No more whatever else Virge did for her.

"Why do you sneak into this house like a thief in the night?" She was up. Horace squinted, eyes getting used to the dark. She was sitting straight backed on the couch with that quilt she'd made when they were kids wrapped around her. She looked like a squaw.

"I didn't want to wake you."

"We keep decent hours here."

"Sorry, Ma." He had to be careful here. A wrong word could bring on one of her fits. She'd had the epilepsy her whole life, but the tumor made it worse. Any little thing could set it off.

"Where's your brother?"

"He didn't come home?" Horace felt his asshole tighten up. Nothing he could do about it. He didn't want to hurt her. The lung cancer and the brain tumor were bad enough, she didn't need to know Virge was never coming home. She didn't have long, and the end was gonna be painful enough without that. "He got a girl."

"Really?"

"They went to the movies. She had a car."

"What kind of girl?"

"A teacher at Long Beach State. I didn't get to meet her, you know how Virgil is about stuff like that."

"That's nice." She started drumming her fingers in her lap, like she did when she was happy. "He's a good boy, it's about time." Then, "Where you been?"

"Looking for a girl myself."

"Jealous of your brother?" She was smug. If she only knew what he'd had to do to get the money for her doctor and the hospital. It wasn't right. It shouldn't cost so much money to die.

"A little, I guess." It couldn't hurt to let her think that. He sighed. Now he could see pretty good in the dark room, she was wearing that satisfied smile she used to wear when she could see. He turned away, padded toward his room in stocking feet.

"That man's been calling," she said.

"What man?"

"That so called friend of yours that calls whenever he wants. Don't he know better than to call in the middle of the night?"

"I hope you were polite." Horace hustled into his room, grabbed the phone, pushed buttons. That's all he needed, Ma talking to Striker.

"Yeah." It was Striker.

"I did the Kenyon woman." Horace wanted to get out the good news before Striker had a chance to complain about how long it took.

"Is it gonna come back on us?

"No way." Horace talked low, hand cupped over the mouthpiece so Ma couldn't hear. "I couldn't do it like you wanted, so I made it look like a sex crime. She had this faggot boyfriend nobody knew about. I dumped her behind this gay bar he was at." It didn't sound too bad the way he said it, maybe Striker wouldn't mind.

"Just so there's no come back."

"You call the tune, I do the dance." He wanted to ask about the money, but Striker might take it as an insult.

"I got another job for you. Can you get over to Catalina in that plane of yours?"

"Any time you want."

"Sunup."

"Tell me about it."

"It's an old woman, should be a piece of cake."

Horace almost puked again as he listened to Striker tell him. Christ, another killing, and it was another woman, an older woman. But there was nothing he could do right now except close his mind to it.

He went to the bathroom and stripped off his bloody clothes. The shirt was ruined now, the pants too. He rolled them up, went naked and barefoot out to the kitchen. No one to see, Virgil wasn't coming home and there wasn't any reason to dress for Ma. She was already in her room anyway, happy like a rat in the trash. Her boy got a girl. Ma was nuts. He got a garbage bag from under the sink, stuffed the clothes in it, then stuffed the bag in the trash can outside the back door.

Back in the bathroom he got in the shower, turned the water as hot as he could stand it. Steam filled the bath. Striker wanted him to do another woman, the thought busted into his head. He didn't want to do it, didn't know if he could. In the end it was the anger that got him through the Kenyon bitch. She'd just stabbed Virgil, after all. Killing her didn't feel premeditated. He turned the water even hotter, punishing himself.

When he could take it no longer, he got out of the shower, changed into another pair of baggy pants, a denim work shirt and slipped on his leather bomber jacket. He faced the mirror, closed his eyes and forced the thought of the old woman he was supposed to do to the back of his mind. Time to be cool. He opened his eyes and looked at himself. "Cool to the max." He turned away from the mirror and left the house.

The van still smelled, not as bad, but the taste of shit lingered on the air. He'd have to get one of them air fresheners in the morning. It started to rain when he entered the on ramp, a slight drizzle. God's tears, Horace thought, then he cried. Snot drizzled down his nose, mingled with salty tears on his lips. Horace didn't get control of himself till he got off the freeway on Lakewood Boulevard by the Long Beach airport.

He turned into the airport, drove to Condor aviation, passed the flight school and drove onto the line. He parked next to his Cessna 172, with the van's sliding door facing the passenger door of the plane.

No one challenged him, the place was deserted, the planes lined up like soldiers in the night. He shut off the engine and listened to the quiet. Off in the distance rolling tires hissed by on damp pavement as late night travelers journeyed home.

Out of the van now, he slid open the door, then opened the passenger door of the plane, glad he had sun protectors covering the windows. The body had moved during the trip. Now Virgil was on his back. Horace pulled the body to the door.

He squatted, slid his arms under it, careful to keep the belly wound away from the expensive bomber jacket. The body was limp and that surprised him. He'd expected rigor to set in like in the movies, but it hadn't. With strength he didn't know he had, he stood, got his balance, then staggered to the open door of the plane and slid his dead brother into the passenger seat.

Trying not to look, he pulled on the shoulder harness, cinching the seatbelt tight. Finished, he closed and locked the door. Now all he needed was a motel room so he could get some rest away from Ma for a couple of days and some cement.

Chapter Nine

Maggie rolled over, rubbed her eyes against the light sneaking in the bedroom. She pulled the blankets up to her chin, scrunched herself up in their warmth, pulled her knees to her chest.

"Nick," she mumbled. Again, "Nick." She wanted him to pull the shade, the way her father used to come and turn out the light when she was a little girl and too comfy to get out of bed and do it herself. Her father had always been there, but Nick wasn't, and all of a sudden last night came pouring back.

She ran her tongue over dry lips. She was thirsty. She had to pee. And Nick still hadn't come home. She pushed the blankets away, forced herself to sit up. "Ouch." She put her hands to her temples. Her head hurt. She felt like she could drink gallons. She felt like she could pee gallons.

She checked the digital alarm clock on the nightstand. Quarter to seven. The last time she'd looked it said 4:45. Great, she'd only managed to get two hours of fitful sleep and now she had a hangover. And Nick hadn't come home at all. He'd never done that before. Then it hit her. Yesterday was Saturday. How could he film a high school drug bust when there wasn't any school?

"If it's that redhead." She dropped her legs over the side of the bed, stood and closed her eyes to keep the room from spinning. "Never again."

She took a deep breath, steadied herself, padded into the bathroom. The toilet seat was down. There was the proof. He really hadn't been home. Bastard. She sat, peed, then at the bathroom sink she lowered her head and drank.

The water was a river in her mouth, flooding thought the cracked desert of her lips and tongue. So cool. She sucked it down, animal-like, greedy. She stopped after a bit, wanting more, but she'd get sick if she continued.

She studied herself in the mirror. She slept in the nude and nude she was. So, she hadn't been so drunk she couldn't get undressed. She put a finger to the welt on her forehead. It looked like it should hurt. She poked it. It did.

She cupped her hands under the running water, splashed some on her face. It wasn't enough to make her feel human, so she stepped into the shower, ran the water cold, to wake.

Images from last night rushed thought her mind.

Those two men had been after her. They'd recognized her in the Safeway and had been waiting for her on the beach. If it hadn't been for those homeless men under the pier, who knows what could have happened? That Virgil man was big.

She faced into the spray, drank more water. She needed a clear head. She needed to run. She shut off the shower, dried off, jumped into Levi's and a sweatshirt. She stuffed twenty bucks into a back pocket, in case she was hungry as she jogged by the donut shop. It happened sometimes.

But once outside she decided to jog down to the beach where she could run full out. She started as soon as she hit the sand, and she poured it on when she got to the place where those men, Horace and Virgil, had tried to trap her the night before. She glanced at the pier, thought about stopping, remembered the disappearing bottle of wine and decided against it. She took a look at the pool. The glass walls glowed orange, reflecting the rising sun. It was no threat now.

Past the pool she saw the country and western bar. She ran up to it, ran past it, through the Safeway parking lot, then the sprint home. In front of the duplex she doubled over, hands on her knees, dripping sweat. The headache was gone. She was still thirsty, but this was an honest thirst, her body craving the water she'd lost as sweat.

She turned on the garden hose, drank, then sat on the front steps. It was Sunday, still early. The neighborhood was quiet save for a cat across the street. She watched while it prowled under a car, looking for God knows what. Then it crossed the street, slinked under Gordon's old Ford and all of a sudden it was out of sight.

Gordon's car reminded her of the garage out back. Part of their rental deal with him was that they got the garage, Gordon parked out front. He didn't seem to care. Besides, nobody in their right mind

DEAD RINGER

would ever think of stealing his car. What could they get? Maybe fifty bucks.

Nick stacked the old newspapers in the garage. Every other month or so he called somebody to come and collect them. Till then he kept them stacked by paper, filed by date. He said he kept them that way in case he ever wanted to go back and check a story, but Maggie knew it was because he was an obsessive organizer.

The big man named Virgil had said something about her being in the paper. Maggie felt as if she were back in the frozen foods section. Goosebumps shivered up her arms.

The garage seemed huge without cars. Nick still had her Mustang. The newspapers were stacked up against the wall that butted up to the house. Maggie skipped over the *Times*. She read it faithfully. If what she was looking for was there, she'd have seen it. But she never even glanced at the *Long Beach Press Telegram*. Nick hardly did either. Still, it was a newspaper, and as such Nick felt he should subscribe. He was a newsman, after all.

She took the top paper off the stack, leafed through it, leaving it in a pile on the cement floor when she was finished. To heck with Nick. Thirty papers followed. She gasped when she opened the thirty-first, because the girl staring out at her from the second page had her face.

She'd half expected it. Had been hoping for it most of her life, but had given up thinking about it after she'd married Nick.

She read the caption under the photo,

> This time Huntington Beach resident, Margo Kenyon struck out in her petition attempt to keep convicted

> child molester and murderer Frankie Fujimori behind bars. Ms. Kenyon declares, Fujimori is sure to kill again.

She devoured the article, learning that Margo's ex-husband, attorney Bruce Kenyon, had defended Fujimori seven years earlier. A month after an innocent verdict he raped and murdered a four-year-old child. Fujimori was declared mentally incompetent. Two years ago Margo had started a petition campaign that gathered over a hundred thousand signatures and convinced the parole board that Fujimori wasn't ready for society. However, on his next attempt at parole, the board ignored Margo's petition and released him.

"Margo," Maggie whispered.

She closed her eyes and pictured her birth certificate. Box number 5. Twin, born second. She had an older sister. Dead just days after her birth, lost to the deep when the small plane her mother had supposedly taken her on had crashed into the ocean halfway between San Diego and Los Angeles. But somehow, like Maggie, her twin hadn't been on that plane.

She sighed and flashed on the Sunday before high school graduation. She'd gone down to Huntington Beach with a bunch of friends to celebrate. They'd been playing in the sand and the surf since noon, but her fun had been dampened because she'd been worried about her best friend's blouse. She'd borrowed it, washed it with her red sweatshirt, and the once white blouse, was now pink. She'd been waiting all day to tell her, and just as she was about to a hunk came up to her, kissed her on the cheek, and said, "Nice suit, Margo." Then, "See you at the dance tonight." He took off before she'd had a chance to say anything, running down the beach with a football and a gaggle of friends.

That chance meeting was like something out of a science fiction novel, because Margo was the name of her twin sister, and she was buried at the bottom of the Pacific in that plane with her mother and those Marines, somewhere between Catalina and the coast.

She'd wondered about it off and on for years. Such a strange coincidence, a boy she didn't know calling her that. Sometimes, late at night when she was caught in that world between sleep and not sleep, she'd imagine Margo was alive. But then she'd put it out of her mind, because it hurt so much to feel so incomplete, a sailboat set adrift with no sails, no anchor.

She wanted to cry, she was so happy. Margo was real and now. Maggie was looking at her picture and Margo had her face. She was alive. A kind of pleasure rippled through her. Maggie felt good all over.

She got up from the cool cement floor and went into the house. Straight to the living room and the phone books. She picked up the Orange County edition and found an address. 913 Pacific Coast Highway, #1310. And a phone number. Maggie picked up the phone, put it down and went for the door. Nick had her car, but she knew how the busses worked.

Still in Levi's and sweatshirt, she caught the bus in front of the Safeway, rode it to Seal Beach where she changed and took the Orange County Bus to a stop only a block past the Sand and Sea Condos.

She stepped off the bus to a cool morning breeze. It was 8:30 and there wasn't a cloud in the sky. It was going to be another hot day. But it was chilly now. She held her breath against the diesel fumes as the bus pulled away. The place where Margo Kenyon lived was so close. Maggie's heart thudded as she let the breath out. She walked slowly toward the condo entrance.

"Didn't see you go out, Ms. Kenyon," an elderly guard said.

Maggie ignored him as she followed a sidewalk that wound between the condos and the beach. There were several buildings, each with four units in them, two upstairs and two down. The smaller buildings were clustered about a larger one that was home to several units. Maggie was checking the numbers on the doors when she heard a child scream out.

"Mom!"

Maggie turned to see a little girl scramble down the steps from the main building. She stood, frozen in place as the child jumped the last two.

"Margo!"

Maggie spun around and saw a big man moving toward her, not running, but walking fast.

"Mom!" The child charged across the green lawn. Instinctively Maggie went to her knees, arms open. In an instant the girl wrapped Maggie in a strong hug. "Don't let him take me."

The man was getting closer. He would have been handsome if he didn't have the acne scars. Not what you'd call a pockmarked face, but close.

"Promise you won't ever leave me again," the girl said.

Maggie turned back to the man. He looked determined.

"Promise!" the child said again.

"I promise," Maggie said.

"I was worried, Margo," the man said." You went away without telling the cops. They took it out on me." Maggie recognized him from television. Bruce

Kenyon the lawyer, Margo's husband, the defender of Frankie Fujimori.

"Really?" Maggie said for time.

"Arrested me. Assholes. I was out before they had a chance to book me. They're going to regret it."

Bruce Kenyon had the prettiest blue eyes and shocking blond hair, but neither was able to soften his look. He was a man consumed. Maggie didn't want to get on his wrong side. She was about to tell them who she was, but the child's grip was tight. The girl was afraid of him, so Maggie held her tongue.

"Are you all right, Jasmine?" Bruce Kenyon said.

"You can't take me. Mom's here now." The girl squeezed Maggie even tighter.

"No one's taking anybody," Maggie said. Was he really here to try and take the girl?

"We need to talk," he said.

"Not now." Maggie knew the way to deal with lawyers was not to talk to them.

"I came all the way out here."

"It's Sunday. It'll keep." You had to be firm, otherwise they walked all over you.

"What happened to your head?"

She touched her forehead, winced when she touched the bruise. "Bumped it."

"Come on, Mom." The child eased out of the hug, pulled on her arm.

"Margo?" Bruce Kenyon implored.

"Tomorrow!" Maggie turned and let the child lead her away from the man.

"Fuck it." He sounded disgusted. "I'll call you." Apparently there wasn't any love left between Margo and Bruce Kenyon.

Maggie followed Jasmine to a condo that faced the beach. The door was marked 1310. Margo's house. Jasmine opened the door and Maggie followed her inside.

"We're gonna be late for church if we don't hurry," Jasmine said as Maggie studied the place. The living room was bright, with light beige carpets, rattan furniture with floral print cushions, two lamps with glass bowls stuffed full of sea shells for bases, tropical prints on the walls. Maggie guessed Hawaii.

"Let's skip church today," Maggie said.

"That's a sin."

"I think God will forgive us."

"Can I go to Sonya's then?"

"Sure."

"Thanks." Jasmine was out the door before Maggie could say another word.

Alone now, she walked around the condo. She went to the bedroom, saw a Queen size bed, rattan end tables, a painting of a palm tree swaying in a storm above the bed. Margo was a water woman. An island woman. Maggie smiled, because she was too.

She turned and gasped. For an instant she thought she was face to face with her twin, but it was only her reflection in the floor to ceiling mirrored closet doors. She frowned, pushed the hair out of her eyes. She was dripping with sweat. What a way to greet her sister for the first time. Before she could stop herself, Maggie slid open the closet. She had to know more about her twin, and what better way to know a woman than by her clothes?

"Yuck." Maggie ran her hands through the hanging suits. What kind of woman lived by the beach, decorated an apartment so wonderfully, than dressed like that? Old lady lawyers. Not real people. Maggie closed the closet and went back to the living room.

The timer on the VCR under the TV said, 8:45. Fifteen minutes till Nick's Sunday show. He didn't come home last night, but wherever he'd slept, he'd be out of bed for that. If she'd been thinking clearly, she'd have realized it earlier. He was always at the station an hour or more before the show. She could have called him there.

She went to the kitchen where she saw a handbag and two bags of groceries that begged to be put away. In less than a minute she was as familiar with the kitchen as if it were her own. She put away the groceries. Ten minutes till *Newsmakers with Nick*. She found coffee and filters for the Mr. Coffee.

Back in the living room with black coffee, she turned on the television. She took a sip and watched as Carry Ann Close, Nick's co-host, came on the screen. She apologized for Nick's absence.

"It is this newswoman's sad duty to report that Nick Nesbitt's wife, Maggie, was found murdered last night. Her nude body was discovered, battered and broken, behind a gay bar in Long Beach. It's not known yet if she'd been sexually assaulted—"

Maggie stared at the set, stunned as Carry Close cut to a live camera outside of the Whale. The whole thirty minutes was spent on the murder. It was those men, Horace and Virgil. It had to be. They'd mistaken her for Margo yesterday. They must have followed her and Gordon. Then somehow they found the real Margo, killed her and dumped her there.

Her first instinct was to call the police. She looked around the room. No phone. But there was one in the kitchen. She got up, sat back down. What about the promise she'd just made to the child. What would happen to her if Maggie called the cops?

What was the matter with her? It was her sister. It could have been her. She got up, went out to the kitchen, picked up the phone, dialed 911, then hung up before it had a chance to ring. Margo was dead. Nothing she did could bring her back.

And she'd promised the child, Jasmine.

That stopped her. She'd promised not to let her father take her away. What was she, eight? Ten? He must be awfully bad if a kid like that was so afraid of him.

Her hair was in her eyes again. She pushed it back, went back into the living room and slumped down onto the sofa. The TV was still on. Carry Ann Close was talking about how dangerous it was becoming for a woman in Southern California. What planet was she from? It had been dangerous for a long time. Maggie picked up the remote, clicked off the TV. Let Carry Ann tell it to somebody else.

She wanted to bury her head in her hands. She'd found a sister, only to lose her before she got to know her. Life was so unfair. Tears welled in her eyes. They would have been close.

"Come on, Maggie," she said to herself. "You don't have time to cry." She wiped the tears away. She needed to find out as much about her sister as she could before Jasmine came back from her friend's.

There was a bookcase, rattan to match the furniture, next to the TV. Maggie went to it and ran a finger along the books. Three different Bibles. Who had three Bibles? Several of the other books, no, most of them, were on Christianity. They were all hardback, all expensive. One titled Born Again stood out because it had a well used look about it. Most of the others were new, as if they were for show, or they'd only been glanced at before being stuffed into the bookcase.

Born Again. Maggie pulled it out, opened it. "To Margo, the brightest light in our church. I hope you enjoy the book," read the inscription on the inside of the first page. It was signed with a flourish, "Yours in faith, T.J. Goodman." Maggie frowned, she knew about Goodman. He was one of those who claimed to have a personal channel to God. She checked the cover. Yep, it wasn't just a gift. Goodman wrote the book.

So, Margo was a born again Christian who dressed like a prude. Maggie went back into the bedroom. She'd only glanced at the stuff in the closet earlier. Margo must have had something a normal person might wear. Nope, not a pair of Levi's anywhere to be found. Not a cut off sweatshirt, no old, comfy T-shirts, no broken in running shoes. Everything looked new.

She spied a checkbook on the nightstand next to the bed. Checks, three to a page on a three ring binder. Was Margo in business? A quick scan told Maggie no, but she had a little over forty thousand in her checking account. Once a week she wrote a check to Goodman Ministries for a thousand dollars. That explained the autographed book.

Her mortgage was twenty-five hundred dollars a month. She deposited the same amount around the first of every month. The notation on the stub said, "Jack-child support." The ex-husband couldn't be all that bad if he was shelling out that kind of money.

In the drawer under the checkbook Maggie found a savings account booklet, simple, the kind any child might have. She whistled when she saw the figure, three hundred eighty-six thousand dollars and seventy-five cents.

She also found a schedule of classes. Margo was a student? Apparently. She was taking a full load, going five days a week, but they were freshman classes. What kind of thirty-one-year-old woman had a third of a million dollars, dressed for power, and went to college? What was she studying to be?

Numb, Maggie went back out to the kitchen, picked up the purse, took it to the sofa. She dumped it out. Another checkbook, a normal one, a little over seven thousand dollars in the account. Walking around money? A pink wallet. Pink? A little over three hundred dollars in it. She put it back, took out the driver's license.

Margo Sue Kenyon. Height 5´7˝, Eyes. Blue. Hair. Blonde. DOB. "Oh my God!" Maggie gasped. She should have been born on May 10, but she wasn't. March 5 is what the license said, two months before Maggie. Something was wrong. If that was true, they weren't twins, they weren't even sisters. It wasn't possible.

Maggie looked at the photo, a mirror image of her own. Margo's husband, Jasmine, the wrongful identification of the girl found dead. They all pointed to the fact that Maggie and Margo were twins. There was no other explanation. Therefore the birth date was wrong. Had to be. Why?

Did Margo know she had a twin? Did she get fake ID to hide it? She would've had to have done it years ago, before Jasmine. Before the husband. Again, why?

Maybe she didn't. Maybe she didn't know. Maybe she was kidnapped at birth, stolen from the hospital, maybe. The new parents, the fake parents, could have gotten a phony birth certificate, raised the child as their own. Maybe.

Maggie slipped the license back into the wallet, dropped the wallet back into the purse, gathered up the other stuff—lipstick, too red, make up, too light—blush, mascara, mousse. Made up, she must

Dead Ringer

have looked like Dolly Parton. She looked up at the bookcase. There were some photo albums on the bottom shelf. She'd been so put off by the Goodman book, she'd failed to notice them.

She moved over to the bookcase again, sat on the floor and took out one of the albums. She shivered at the first photo on the first page. Margo in a cheerleader's uniform. Maggie had been a cheerleader. She closed her eyes. She had her own photo albums in Long Beach. Most she could live without, except the one that documented her own high school life, the one with the pictures of her parents in it.

She looked at more pictures. Margo at the beach in a yellow bikini. Margo with a young Bruce Kenyon in a Marine Corps uniform. An officer. Margo and Bruce on an island somewhere. The Caribbean? Hawaii? Margo pregnant. Margo in the hospital. Margo holding a baby, smile a block wide, a glow in her eyes that radiated out of the photo. Margo, Bruce and a baby girl, a Christmas tree behind them. Maggie looked across the room, saw where the Christmas tree had been. Margo had lived here a long time.

Maggie turned the page, almost dropped the book. Margo on Second Street, standing in front of the candy store next door to the Lounge. The pink sign by the entrance was less than a year old. Maggie could have been inside the Lounge with Nick. They could have met. Known each other.

All of a sudden a sadness welled up in her. She was sitting crosslegged on the floor. She bit her lip to stop the feeling, but it didn't work. Quiet tears streamed down her cheeks. She was powerless against the emotion.

"Mom!" Jasmine said, almost a whisper. Maggie looked up, face wet. Jasmine was in the middle of the living room with another girl. Cafe au lait skin, wide brown eyes. "What's wrong?"

"I don't know," Maggie sobbed.

"Get your mom," Jasmine said and the other girl left at a run.

"It's okay, I'm okay," Maggie said.

"You don't look okay."

"What's going on?" A woman's voice.

Maggie looked into a dark face, knowing eyes, high forehead. "I know you."

"Of course, I live next door."

Maggie put her hands to her head, ran her fingers through her hair as she studied the other woman. The Afro was gone, but it was her. "You're Gaylen Geer."

"Girls, go next door!" Gaylen had the kind of voice that commanded respect. The girls obeyed. Then to Maggie, "My name is Sullivan."

Maggie wiped her face with her hands, then stood. She looked into the woman's eyes. "No it's not."

The black woman met Maggie's eyes, shook her head, then left.

Maggie closed the door, slumped down on the couch. "Well, you certainly handled that well," she said. She stretched out. She was so tired. She cried for her sister. She cried for her baby. She cried for Nick, because just maybe she'd found a way to keep her baby and keep her promise to Jasmine, but it meant she'd never see her husband again.

After awhile there were no more tears. She was spent. She stared at the ceiling, imagined stars and planets floating there, imagined herself at peace. She needed to turn off, to rest. In college when she was up at all hours, studying and partying, she'd learned to grab sleep whenever she could, and she did it now. She closed her eyes, made her mind a blank and in seconds she was asleep.

Chapter Ten

Horace Nighthyde shut off the engine in the Condor Aviation parking lot. He'd spent the later half of the night at a motel on Lakewood, near the Traffic Circle. Better there than going home. Ma would've waited up for her darling. Sometime around 2:30 she'd have started pacing, wearing out the linoleum in the kitchen. He couldn't bear to see her gnashing her teeth as she worried about Virgil.

It was gonna be hell for her. That was a major downer for Horace. She shouldn't have to spend the time she had left worrying about a son who was never coming home. But it was better if she thought he ran off with a teacher from Long Beach State, than if she knew what had really happened. Far better.

He got out of the car, slung his flight bag over his shoulder, went to the trunk and got out the bricks, closest thing to cement he could come up with. Not quite the same, but they'd have to do.

"Hey, Horace, how's it going?" Startled, he turned to see Sara Hackett, the race car driver, getting out of her Jap Jeep. "Going up today?"

"Yeah." He nodded.

"Bummer." Sara was taking flying lessons and had rented Horace's plane through the flight school on several occasions. She liked it better than the others at Condor. Horace didn't like renting his plane out, but he couldn't afford to keep it otherwise.

"Sorry," he said.

"What's with the bricks?" Sara was close enough to smell.

"Samples for a friend in Big Bear," he lied.

"They don't have bricks up there?"

"At three times the price. I'm driving up in a couple of weeks. It's a chance to make a buck."

"So you're flying up now?"

"Right."

"You want company?"

"What?" Did Sara Hackett just ask if she could fly up to Big Bear with him? There and back would take all day.

"I need more cross country time. If you don't mind riding on the right while I fly, I'd like to come along. I'd pay, of course."

Horace bit his lip. She was gonna pay too. But he shook his head. "Sorry, I've gotta stay overnight."

"I could get a motel, come back with you tomorrow."

He bit into his lip again, harder. "Sorry, I'd like to, really, but I might need to stay longer."

"All right then, some other time."

"Sure." Sweat trickled under his arms. All he could do was stand, feet lead, and watch as she made her way into the Condor building to rent somebody else's plane.

Turning his attention away from Sara Hackett, he looked out at the wind sock. There was a gentle breeze blowing straight down Two-Five-Right. A Piper Cherokee was starting its take-off roll. There were clouds over the ocean, but they were at altitude, no problem flying under them. It looked like a good day for a VFR flight out to Catalina.

He started toward the plane with a brick in each hand. His Cessna was at the end of the line, closest to the runway, farthest from the hanger. At the plane he set the bricks down and looked around. Nobody within viewing distance. He opened the passenger door.

The smell attacked him first. Meat. Not rotten, but getting there. Steeling himself, he wrapped a hand around Virgil's wrist. Cold. He gave a gentle tug. Stiff. Rigor.

He picked up a brick. He was loath to touch the corpse again, but he had no choice. The feet were hard to push apart when he moved them aside for the bricks. Once they were in place between the legs, he pulled a couple short lengths of rope from his flight bag and tied one to each ankle. Finished, he stood, studied his work. He was good with ropes and knots, they wouldn't come loose.

"Best I can do, Virge."

A fly buzzed by, then another, then more. They went for the eyes. Inside the plane there had been no way for the insects to get at the body. They'd come in droves now, making up for lost time. Horace shooed as many away as he could before closing the door.

He was careful about flying. Usually he did a complete preflight, talking to himself, so he wouldn't forget anything, as he worked his way around the plane. Not today.

He pulled off the sun protectors, no choice, but he was far enough away from prying eyes. He was just a plane getting ready to go. Satisfied he was safe, he called ground control and got permission to taxi to Two-Five-Right. Then a shudder rippled through him. There was a chance they'd train binoculars on him from the tower. Would they be able to see his passenger was dead?

On the runway he did his run up, then set the radio for the tower frequency.

"Long Beach Tower, this is Cessna 27 Yankee seeking permission for a straight out over the harbor."

"Hold, 27 Yankee. There's a Piper Cherokee on final, another turning base and a Bonanza in the downwind, you're cleared after the Bonanza."

There was nothing for it but to sit and wait.

"Damn, Virge, you look bad." He shuddered at the sight of Virgil's waxy, translucent like skin. Looked into his sunken eyes. Virgil's lips were stretched tight, as if he were about to bare fangs. That and the blue hands made Horace think of vampires. He shuddered again. If only he could feed his brother some blood, if only he could make him live.

A couple of flies landed on the dead eyes to lay eggs that would never hatch, because shortly Virgil was going to be resting in the arms of Davy Jones. Horace loved his brother too much to let him become bug food. He waved a hand at the flies, shooing them from the face.

The tower cleared him for take off.

"Here we go, boy." He taxied onto the runway, turned into position, stomped on the brakes, pulled out the throttle, let the revs climb. Feet off the brakes and the plane started down the mile long runway, Horace keeping it on the center line.

A fly flew into his mouth, down his throat.

He gagged. Revulsion rippled thought him as he choked air up from his gut, trying to get it out. Another fly in his eyes. Fuck. He pulled a hand from the controls, swatted it, smacking himself in the face.

"Watch the center line, 27 Yankee." The voice from the tower jolted Horace. He'd almost revolted himself off the runway. He swallowed the fly and eased the plane back to the centerline.

A quick look at the wind speed gauge. Fifty miles an hour. He'd almost really fucked up.

"You okay, 27 Yankee?"

Horace grabbed the mike, thumbed the talk button. "Swallowed a fly. I got it together now."

"I hate that," the tower said. Then, "You have a nice day now, 27 Yankee."

"You too." Horace hung up the mike. Speed 70 MPH. He started his takeoff roll, felt the thrill as he did every time the wheels left the ground. At two hundred feet he eased off some of the back pressure on the yoke. He preferred a flatter climb than most. He loved looking out, watching the houses, yards and pools gradually shrink in size. In the plane he was like a kid.

Virgil loved the takeoffs, too. He'd get all excited, pointing out places he knew, the Taco Bell, the car wash, the graveyard by Signal Hill where they'd buried their dad. For Virgil, Dad's ghost haunted that hallowed ground. Twice, sometimes three times a week he'd take his brother to Dad's tombstone. Not anymore. Horace would never go there again.

He banked left over Long Beach Harbor, climbed up to five thousand feet. Over Huntington Beach he banked right and headed out over the ocean. A slight detour before heading out toward Catalina and as usual a slight shiver shimmied up his back. It happened every time he flew over the water. Blue sea below, white clouds above, but he wasn't worried about the weather, as the visibility ahead seemed endless.

The weather was the least of his worries. He was flying with a dead man as co-pilot. He grabbed another look at his brother, who believed in ghosts. Horace didn't suffer that affliction. When you were dead, the light went out. That was it. Nothing, just nothing. No god like Ma said. No ghosts like Virge believed. It was over. Just plain over.

Still, he had to struggle with his nerves when he reached over Virgil's stiff body and fished around in the pouch on the passenger door. Virge kept a lot of junk in there—cookies, comic books, his juggling balls. Virgil had been slow in the head, but he was agile of body. On more than one occasion Horace had to yell at him to stop the juggling when they were on final. Imagine trying to land a plane with them balls flying around the cockpit. Fingers moving through the crap, Horace found a CD. Music was necessary, Virgil wasn't going out to the drone of a prop.

He shoved the disc into the player. Bruce Springsteen filled the cockpit. "Born in the USA." Horace screamed along with the Boss. Virgil loved that song. Horace hit the repeat button. It would play for him for the duration of his last ride.

Billowy cumulus clouds loomed ahead. Shit, where'd they come from? Horace wasn't instrument rated, but it looked like he could skirt them. He made a slight turn to the right. More clouds. "Born in the USA," Horace ranted as he climbed to avoid them. Turbulence shook the plane, cloud vapor wisped by, cotton trails blurring his sight. Then he was up and over, still climbing, still banking right. More ahead, darker, grey. Storm, squall, Horace didn't know, didn't care. He just wanted to get over it.

Dancing around clouds was something he enjoyed, was good at. More turbulence, there was plenty of rain in them. Still in the right bank he saw a hole and climbed up through it and found Heaven. Blue sky above, rolling white cotton below. He hung in the air as if suspended by the hand of the god he didn't believe in.

A quick look at the altimeter, Eighty-five hundred feet. He'd climbed farther then he'd thought. There was a cloud bank ahead. More Cumulus fluff. He checked the oil pressure, the compass, the radios, the VOR needles. Off course, but he knew that.

He was cold. The sweat under his arms, chilly rivulets dripping under his shirt. His teeth chattered. "Born in the USA." He leaned over the body, pulled off the harness and seatbelt. He unlatched the door. Still leaning, he pushed on the body's shoulder with the palm of his hand. Virgil tumbled sideways, half in the plane, half out. The plane went into a downward right turn, the open door acting like flaps.

It was the rigor. Virgil had dropped onto his right side. His body from the waist up outside the plane, but his legs were still bent, like he was sitting. He couldn't fit through the doorway.

Horace pulled the wheel to the left, countering the drag on the right. He checked the altimeter, he was losing altitude. The cumulus in front didn't seem so innocent now. The sweat under his arms seemed frozen. Icicles stabbed his heart.

He pulled back on the wheel, added power, slowed the descent and grit his teeth as the plane slipped into the soup. He was flying blind, still losing altitude. The stall warning sounded, buzzing loud. He pushed the nose downward to avoid the stall. He had to get the body back in the plane.

With his left hand on the controls he stretched, grabbed onto an arm and tried to pull it back in. No joy, it was stuck in place, and the altimeter said he was dropping at two-hundred and fifty feet a minute. He had to get Virgil gone.

He pulled off his harness and seatbelt. More cold sweat. He took his feet off the rudder pedals and the plane turned more to the right. He spun around in the seat. Using the door on his side as a back brace, he pulled his feet up onto the seat, planted them on Virgil's ass and pushed.

Nothing. Virge was wedged in. Back solid against the door on his side, Horace tucked his legs to his chest, then lashed out, slamming his feet into his brother's rear end. Movement. Some. It was gonna work. He pulled his knees back again, slammed them into Virgil's rear again and Virge moved a little more, but he was still stuffed tight in the doorway.

Breathing hard, head spinning, fighting panic, Horace pulled his knees to his chest, grabbed a great breath, heaved it out, screaming like a kung-fu fighter as he hammered his feet into Virgil's rump.

Virgil popped out of the plane like a Champagne cork, pulling the bricks after himself as he disappeared into the clouds. "Born in the USA." And Horace slid after, his feet dangling out of the plane. He spun around, hands flaying for something to grab onto. Frantic fingers found the seatbelt. He grabbed onto it. The plane was in a spiraling descent now, any second it was going to go into a spin.

Horace felt his hands slipping from the strap, but a quick vision of an uncontrolled plunge into to the water below gave him the extra strength he needed to pull himself up toward the seat. He grabbed onto it, pulled more, got his legs out of the sky and into the plane. He grabbed onto the wheel, turned it to the left as he struggled into place. Panting, he got a foot onto the left rudder peddle as he pulled on the seatbelt.

"Holy shit," he muttered over and over as he tried to find the right combination of rudder and aileron to take him out of the turn. If he wasn't careful he'd pull the wings off the plane. He eased back on the wheel, sweat dripping from his forehead into his eyes. He blinked it away. He was still going down, still in the soup, still blind, but he was out of the rotation.

He reached over, latched the door, checked the level control. He'd done some flight time under the hood, all he had to do was concentrate. He could get out of this. He could.

The altimeter said sixty-five hundred feet. He had the wings level. He eased back a little more on the wheel, stopped the descent. But now he had other problems. Up or down, back the way he'd come, or continue on toward Catalina?

He cursed himself for not getting the morning's aviation weather. Really dumb. He'd never flown without it before. "One fucking time," he muttered. He hit the button on the player, popped out the CD. Between the Boss and Virgil, his thinking got so messed up he almost went out the plane, too.

He decided to drop under the cloud cover. Keeping his eye on the gauges, he tried to pretend he was back with a flight instructor doing his instrument training. Halfway through he'd dropped out. Who wanted to fly in bad weather anyway, he'd reasoned. But he'd learned enough not to panic.

Using the gauges, he kept the wings level as he trimmed up for a controlled descent at a hundred feet per minute. Then he set the auto pilot for Catalina and took his hands off the controls.

The altimeter said he was flying at forty-five hundred feet. He was tense, almost frightened. It was important he calm down, so he snaked an arm back in the pouch on the passenger door and came out with a couple more CDs. Billy Joel, *Goodnight Saigon*, Virgil loved that one, but it was guaranteed to heighten Horace's apprehension. The other, Mozart's *Concertos for French Horn*. He popped it in, turned up the volume. Now it was just him and the master till he broke through the clouds. His fate was in Mozart's hands now, Horace wouldn't be touching the controls till he saw the water below.

At three thousand feet, he closed his eyes as a horn solo soared through the cockpit. This was what made him exceptional, the ability to remove himself, to take himself away till the crisis passed. If there wasn't anything he could do, then there was no reason to stress himself out. He pictured Sadie in his mind. Sexy Sadie. Would she remember him if he called? No woman had ever affected him like that and he'd only spent a couple of dances with her, knew nothing about her.

He felt the light and opened his eyes to a bright sun. The cloud mass was behind, the altimeter said seventeen hundred feet. Catalina was dead ahead. He set the autopilot for straight and level flight. He'd always been lucky. He hummed along with the horn.

Then he thought about the old woman he was coming in to do. It was typical Striker. Getting someone to behave the way he wanted by attacking his family. Horace bit his lip, chewed on his tongue. It didn't seem right, the poor woman probably never hurt a fly and she was gonna get killed just for being some asshole's mother. It was as if someone was gonna kill Ma because they were pissed at Horace.

It wasn't fair. But that Kenyon bitch killing Virgil wasn't fair either. Also it wasn't fair Ma sitting blind in her rocker, a tumor swelling in her brain while cancer ate up her body. No, life wasn't fair. It sucked.

He heard some chatter on the radio and it jerked his mind back to the controls. He took the plane off auto and flew it himself. The small airport on Catalina Island was atop a mountain. The wind sock told him he had a slight headwind. Piece of cake landing.

On the ground he took a cab down to Avalon. It was after 10:00. He was hungry enough to eat raw fish. Fortunately he was able to get a quick burger and fries at one of the many seaside restaurants. He would have liked to linger, to watch the girls stroll by, but he had a job to do, distasteful as it was, and he wanted to get back to the mainland before dark.

He found the house without trouble. Striker always gave precise directions. He pulled a pair of surgical gloves out of the inside pocket of his bomber jacket, put them on. A light knock on the door. Calm, not even a foot tap to the music in his head. Bruce Springsteen again.

No answer to the knock. Maybe she was hard of hearing. He tried the bell. The door opened. She was old, like Striker said.

"Can I help you?" She had a thin lipped smile, happy grey eyes. She probably never had a bad day in her life. Well, she was about to have one now.

"Yeah." Horace stepped into her, pushed her back into the house, closed the door. He had the Beretta in her face before she had a chance to think. "Where's the children?"

"They're not home." She had panic in her eyes now.

"Here's the deal, lady. You swallow these pills and if you're dead before they come back from wherever they are, they get to live."

"Why?"

"My boss needs to distract your son."

"How do I know you won't harm them?" she said. Horace had to admire her. She was worried about her grand kids, not a care for her own safety. She was a plucky lady. She wouldn't whine.

"There's no reason to do the kids. Besides, alive they're a bigger distraction, but I'll do them if we don't get on with it." He held up the bottle.

"How long will it take?"

"It'll be quick." Horace didn't know what the pills were. But Striker had said she'd be out of it fast.

She stared at the bottle. For a second he thought she was going to resist. "Don't scream."

"I wasn't going to." She held out her hand, took the bottle, opened it. She swallowed the pills.

"If it means anything, I don't feel good about this," he said.

"How could you?" She backed up, sat on a wing chair that was covered with a quilt. Kind of like something Ma might have made.

Horace took a seat on a sofa that looked like it had been around forever, curly wooden legs, some kind of Frency design, he didn't know about that kind of stuff. He looked around the room. It was a grandma's house, no denying that.

"What's your name?" she said.

"Why you want to know?"

"In case someone asks."

"Who would?"

"God."

"No such thing." Horace shook his head. She was as nuts as Ma, trying to lay a guilt trip on him like that.

"Then tell me your name." She was starting to nod off. Those pills were fast.

"No."

"It doesn't matter. He'll know you when it's your time." She closed her eyes. Her head slumped to the side.

In a hurry now, Horace found the bathroom, put the plug in the bath, ran the tap. He adjusted the water to warm. It had to be done right, it was the details that would keep it a suicide and not murder. No one about to kill herself would climb into a cold bath.

Back in the living room, the woman was breathing like she was in a deep sleep. He glanced around the room. The old lady was a neat freak. He walked around the house, checking it out. Everything had a place, even the shoes were lined up in a row in the closet. In the hallway he found a hamper. Now he knew how to do it.

"Gonna handle you with care," he said, and he meant it. She deserved that much. He undid the buttons on the woman's blouse and pulled it off. She was wearing a camisole under it and he pulled it over her head. Her bra was next. Old lady tits, Horace tried not to look. Then he pulled off her shoes, jeans and panties.

"Gotta make it look real," he muttered. He put the shoes in the closet, lining them up like the others there. Then he dropped the clothes in the hamper before he picked her up and carried her into the bath.

He laid her out in the tub. She looked so peaceful, just sleeping. He ran his eyes over her old lady body, tits all but gone now, waist he could wrap his hands around, legs no more than sticks. But she was made up nice, hair cut short, styled neat, professional. An old lady with money, class.

He fished the blades out of his shirt pocket, took the cellophane off. He picked up a wet hand and used her thumb to slide out a single edged razor. Squeezing the blade between the thumb and forefinger of her right hand, he drew the blade down the inside of her right arm, from wrist to elbow. Then he repeated the procedure with the other hand, letting the blade fall into the tub when he was finished.

She was breathing peacefully as she bled out.

It looked real.

He opened the medicine cabinet above the sink and put the blade dispenser on the top shelf, next to a bottle of aspirin. A neat lady like this wouldn't leave them lying around for the kids to get hurt with.

An hour later he took off. The sky had cleared and he could see Long Beach Harbor from over Catalina. He popped Mozart back into the player. The french horn he loved so much filled the cockpit, but it brought him no peace. He took it out, shoved in the Springsteen.

"Born in the USA!" He'd be hearing that damned song for the rest of his life.

Chapter Eleven

"Wake up!"

Maggie opened her eyes, met Gaylen Geer's stare. "What time is it?"

"I didn't think you knew who I was." Gaylen put her hands to her hips. "How come you never said anything?"

Maggie rubbed sleep out of her eyes. From her position on the couch Gaylen looked formidable. She pushed herself up. "How long have I been asleep?"

"Three or four hours. We kept checking on you. You must have had a hard night, because thunder wouldn't have wakened you."

"You wanna sit?" Maggie said.

"Sure." Gaylen took one of the chairs opposite the sofa. Maggie had admired Gaylen Geer since high school and now she was sitting right across from her. And Gaylen thought Maggie was Margo Kenyon. What further proof did she need? Margo had been her twin, no matter what that driver's license said.

"Are you going to keep staring at me?" Gaylen said.

Maggie didn't know what to say. She was still in kind of a sleep fog. Should she tell her? Could she not? Just a short time ago she'd been thinking about stepping into her dead twin's life. Was her own life so bad she'd leap at the chance to get out of it? No, but it was a chance to keep her baby. She'd been weak, about to get rid of it. As Margo she could keep it, would be able to support it. But she couldn't do it alone. If Gaylen could help.

"Come on, say something."

"Margo's dead."

"What?" Gaylen threw her hands to her breasts as if she'd been struck with a mallet.

"I'm her sister. Her twin." Maggie clasped her hands in her lap and her thumbs went to war with themselves. She was powerless to do anything about it.

"I didn't know she had a twin sister." Gaylen barely got the words out.

"She didn't either."

"How?"

Maggie told everything, starting from when she saw Virgil and Horace in the Safeway and finishing with her seeing the story about her own murder on television.

"So you were going to take over her life, like a pod person from the *Body Snatchers*?" Gaylen said after Maggie had finished.

"No, not initially. I didn't know she was dead till after I got here. Not till I saw on television that I'd been murdered." She paused. "I thought about how Jasmine was afraid of her father and the idea sort of came to me as I was dialling 911."

"So why tell me?"

"I used to worship you. I wanted to be like you. You've got that strength most of us are missing, so I guess I thought if you helped me, maybe I could pull it off."

"I think you might have taken me a little too seriously. I know I did."

"You helped change history. Things are better because of you."

"What you're asking is wrong."

"How well did you know Margo? Can you tell me about her?"

"Didn't you just hear me say it's wrong?"

"If you don't help me, that horrible man's gonna take away that frightened child. She's my family now. I can't allow that, so I'm asking for your help." She paused again, met Gaylen's eyes straight on.

"I can't do it," Gaylen said.

"Maybe I'm asking the wrong person. The Gaylen Geer I used to see on television all those years ago, the one who said there was supposed to be a brass ring for everybody, regardless of color or sex, that Gaylen Geer would help me."

"That Gaylen Geer's gone."

"I don't think so."

"I'm Gay Sullivan now."

"You'll always be Gaylen Geer. You can't change what you are."

"I did." A whisper. Gaylen broke eye contact, looked down at the carpet. She seemed ashamed.

Maggie decided to back off a little. "I promised Jasmine I wouldn't let that man take her, ever. I need your help to keep that promise."

"Oh my God!" Gay said.

"What?"

"Margo's car. It's in the lot. She'd been gone for a week. I've been watching Jazz. She must've come home last night."

"There were groceries in the kitchen when I got here. I put them away."

"This is scary," Gay said.

"The killer must have grabbed her here. Then dumped her behind a bar I'd been in earlier. That doesn't make any sense."

"I just thought of something."

"What?" Maggie said.

"She saw a murder." Gay told her about Frankie Fujimori and how Margo was in the store when he was shot and about how Margo's ex was Fujimori's lawyer and how he was there too, hoping to catch Margo harassing the child killer, so he could get a court order against her.

"The guy sounds like a sleazeball."

"He was. The world's better off with him dead."

"I was talking about the ex, Bruce Kenyon."

"Oh. Yeah, well I guess he is too." Then Gay told her about the long-haired cops, the albino and the Mexican, and how the girls called the albino one the Ghost. "They had Margo up at the Long Beach PD looking at pictures. She was supposed to go again, but in typical Margo fashion, she left Jazz with me and took off for a week without telling them a thing."

"Typical Margo fashion?"

"She didn't want to find the killer's picture in any book, so she took off on a religious retreat. That's why she left, it's just like her. Out of sight out of mind."

"Was she afraid of the killer?"

"Heck no. She thought he'd performed a public service. No way would she have turned him in. I wouldn't be surprised if she'd seen the shooter's photo in one of those mug books and passed over it." Gay clutched her hands together in her lap. "I think the killer saw you in that store and thought you were Margo. I think he followed you to that bar, then chased you on the beach. When you got away, he came here hoping to catch you and got the real Margo instead. Then he killed her and dumped her behind that bar, God knows why. But I think that's what happened. Frankie Fujimori's killer got her so she wouldn't talk."

"But you said she never would."

"The killer didn't know that."

"Those guys in the Safeway thought they knew who I was. One said he'd seen my picture in the paper. He was slow. But the other one, the guy that looked like a ferret. He wasn't slow, and he had a gun."

"Still want to take over her life?" Gay said.

"I promised Jasmine," Maggie said.

"I still think it's wrong and it's probably not safe. I mean if the killer sees that Margo's still around, still breathing, so to speak. He's gonna try again."

"He's gonna try again anyway, because I saw him in the supermarket, then on the beach. If I come forward as Maggie, he'll know I can identify him. So I think we should leave him out of it, at least for now."

"Even if she would've died of natural causes, even if the killer wasn't out there, it'd still be wrong," Gay said, but not with her earlier conviction, she was wavering. "If you want to care for Jazz, then you should come forward and fight for her."

"Do you really think they're going to give a child to an aunt who popped out of the woodwork the day her mother was killed? I don't think so."

"What would you tell Jazz?" Gaylen was whispering, but Maggie saw something in her eyes. A spark.

"The truth."

"No way could she keep it secret. She tells my daughter everything. Now you've got four people in on your secret and two of them are eight years old. How long till they slip and tell someone else? If you to do this, I don't think you can tell Jazz, at least not yet."

"So you'll help me?"

"I didn't say that."

"But you will. How well did you know her?"

"As well as anyone, I suppose, but she was a hard person to get to know. Most of what I could tell you, I've learned through Jazz. She practically lives at my place."

"Then I'm going to have to tell the children."

"Children?"

"If Jazz is going to tell your daughter anyway, she might as well hear it from me."

"You wouldn't tell Jazz to keep it from her?"

"I couldn't ask her to do that. Not if they're as close as you say."

"You've got that bump on your head. You could tell them you had an accident and you've got some kind of amnesia that makes you forget stuff. You could say you need their help remembering. You could even tell them if they slipped up and told anyone, the police would think you're not able to take care of Jazz and they'd take her away to live with her father. That way if they do screw up and blab, you won't have the cops descending on you."

"No one's going to believe a story like that."

"The girls will. They're eight. It'll be a grand secret adventure."

"Thank you," Maggie said.

"For what?"

"For helping me."

"I think I'm doing it as much for me as for you. I kind of miss the old Gaylen. The last ten years have been happy, except for the bad time when I lost my husband. He was a big Irish man with a smile to die for and a heart the size of Chicago. But he was a man, you see, and he was white. What would the world have thought if Gaylen Geer married. A black guy would have been bad enough, but a white guy? Nobody would have listened to me anymore. So, to avoid the humiliation, I dropped off the face of the earth. At first I hated myself. It was like I was selling out, but then, on my thirty-fifth birthday, I found out I was pregnant and a whole new world opened up.

"Were you gay?"

"Is that what you thought?"

"No, I saw a photo of you last night. Harvey Milk had his arm around you. You had that Afro."

"Ah, Harvey. I haven't thought about him in a long time. All he ever wanted was for everybody to get along." She sighed. "God, he had that dopey smile. So courageous. Most people don't know." She sighed again. "No, I wasn't gay, but I believed in Harvey and what he stood for."

"So what do you do now?"

"I work at a beauty shop up on Main Street. My sister-in-law and I run it. Own it actually. None of the customers know about me. I'm just one of the women they give a ten dollar tip to if I do a good job on their head."

"I've never tipped ten dollars in my life."

"Then you haven't been to Huntington Heads."

"Huntington Heads?" Maggie laughed. It felt good.

"Best head job on the Coast. That's our motto." Gay laughed too.

"Then you could cut my hair. And I bet you've got black hair dye in your medicine cabinet." Maggie stopped laughing.

"Why would you want to cut your hair?"

"Anybody who sees me as Margo will notice the haircut and a dye job, but anybody from my old life might pass over me. They think I'm dead, so if they see a woman with short dark hair, they might not give her a second look, might not take the trouble to notice the resemblance."

"I'll get my stuff." Gay got up. "And I'll order a pizza for the girls. That and a video should keep them entertained for a few hours."

"So what don't you remember?" Jasmine was sitting in one of the rattan chairs next to Sonya. Both girls stared with saucer eyes, blue and brown pools of wonder at Maggie's new hair cut. The once shoulder length blonde hair was now cropped close and it was as black as Gay's.

"I don't know," Maggie said. "But I remember you, and Sonya and Gay. That's enough for starters, don't you think?"

"Yeah," Jasmine said. "I guess so. Then, "Your eyebrows look funny."

"What?"

"Your hair's too dark for them."

"Eyebrow pencil," Gay said.

"Good idea," Maggie said.

"So, I understand how you can forget stuff because of the bump on your head, but why'd you change your hair?" Jasmine said.

"I needed a change," Maggie said. "Besides, I think it makes me look younger, more like a college student, don't you think?"

"Maybe."

"No, it does," Maggie said. The shock of the hair cut and the new color was wearing off. When the girls first saw it, all they could do was gape.

"You don't want to look like an old lady when you go to class," Sonya said.

"Right, exactly," Maggie said. "I felt uncomfortable with all the kids." She hated lying. She wanted it to stop.

"So you remember about school and that kind of stuff," Jasmine said.

"Some," Maggie said. "Not enough, but enough to know that I want to blend in more."

"But you guys have to remember something," Gay said, rescuing Maggie. "If anybody finds out Margo has amnesia, then Jasmine's dad is going to swoop down here like white on rice, and he'll scoop Jazz up and take her away, and she might never be allowed to come back, even after Margo gets all her memory back."

"Swoop and scoop," Sonya said. "We won't tell."

"Yeah, we can keep a secret," Jasmine said.

"Just not from each other," Sonya said.

"It's just like one of those Jack Priest scary stories you're always reading," Jasmine said.

"Jack Priest?" Maggie said.

"Writes horror stories, your big vice," Gay said.

"Yeah, you love spooky stuff, don't you remember?" Jazz said.

"I do now." But Maggie wondered why there weren't any horror novels in that bookcase. "When's the last time I read one?"

"A long time, I think," Jasmine said.

"Why?"

"You started reading that other stuff. You know, the church stuff."

"When did I start doing that?" Maggie said.

"I don't know, before Christmas, I guess," Jasmine said.

"I see." And Maggie did. Somehow Margo got born again after she came into the money.

"See how easy it's going to be?" Gay said. "We just remind her and she remembers. It's not going to be hard at all."

They spent the next couple of hours talking, Maggie gently probing, seeking information about her twin, but also seeking information about Jasmine. She wanted to know everything about the child, what she liked, disliked, friends, how she got on in school.

Jasmine and Sonya told how Mrs. Roberts, their third grade teacher, wasn't coming back after Spring Break, because she got married. The girls were wondering what the new teacher was going to be like when they were interrupted by someone rapping at the door.

"I'll get it." Jasmine jumped up.

"Jasmine, we missed you in Sunday school." It was T.J. Goodman, *God's Good Man*. He looked the same as he did on television. She never watched, but you couldn't avoid the televangelists when you channel surfed.

"Sorry, I was gonna go. It's not a sin is it?" Jasmine went white, clenched her tiny fists. Maggie couldn't believe it. The child was afraid.

"It is, but you can make it up next week." Goodman was smiling with his mouth, but not his eyes.

Maggie was stunned. She didn't know a lot about the televangelists. Some seemed sincere, others slicker than eel shit, as Nick would say, just out for a buck. T.J. Goodman reminded her of the worst of the lot. A smooth salesman with every hair in place. He was still local, with a church in Garden Grove. Every time she'd seen him on television, he'd been promising the world if you'd just send in money. Financial independence. A faith healing. Romance. Just send in the cash, it could all be yours. God knew who sent in the prayer gifts.

"I kept her home." Maggie pushed herself off the couch. She was burning for a fight, but she bit back her anger. This was the man Margo gave a thousand dollars a week to. Maggie didn't want to forget that. She was also afraid the man would see through her.

"Why?" Goodman looked into her eyes. His were pale grey and they were smiling now, along with that mouth she wanted to put a fist through. He broke eye contact, stared at her hair.

"Something came up."

"It must have been important." He was back at her eyes. He seemed to be looking right into her.

"It was."

"Can you tell me? If you have a problem, maybe I can help. It's what I do." He frowned, but didn't break eye contact again. He was trying to intimidate. Maggie relaxed, smiled. She'd expected to see a question in his eyes, instead she saw he was annoyed. The arrogant bastard didn't have a clue.

"No."

"I didn't think we had secrets. I'm your pastor, remember?" He paused, looked beyond Maggie to

DEAD RINGER

Gay and Sonya. "Ah, it's private." Now he gave a knowing look to his eyes. Maggie wondered if he practiced it, talking with his eyes. "We'll talk later."

"That would be good." Maggie felt the rage about to erupt. She didn't want to let it out.

"But we did miss your offering?"

"That little thing." Now it was Maggie's turn to clench her hands into fists. Any second she was going to haul off and belt him. The arrogance, coming here for money.

"You could write the usual check. God's work, you know."

"I think I'll pass this week," Maggie said. "After all, I missed the sermon, so I wouldn't be getting my money's worth, would I?"

"I'm sorry, but it doesn't work that way, you made a commitment to the Church, to God." The jerk hadn't even heard the sarcasm dripping from her voice. Could he be that self-centered?

"I guess I'll have to work it out with God."

"What about the Bible fund? The money's due tomorrow."

"Bible fund?"

"Eleven thousand, you promised it today."

"You came over here to collect a check for twelve thousand dollars?" She was about to erupt.

"Two checks." He wasn't getting it. "One for the church and the other for the fund."

"Get outta here."

"What?" He laughed. He still didn't get it.

"You heard me." She pushed him through the doorway, slammed the door in his face.

"You're not going to pay, are you?" He shouted from outside. Now he got it.

"No!"

"Margo," he pleaded from the other side.

"Go away!"

"Mom, you pushed him." Jasmine was shaking. "We're gonna go to hell for sure." She was ashen, lower lip trembling. The poor child was afraid of God. What had her mother done to cause that?

"No we're not." Maggie knew in her heart she was going to have to go slow with the girl, but this was something she had to take care of right now. She dropped to her knees. "Listen to me. You're not going to hell. No way. In fact I bet God's already got your wings picked out. Yours too," she nodded to Sonya.

"How do you know?" Jasmine said.

"When I hit my head," Maggie touched the bump with a finger, "I forgot a lot, but I also remembered something I knew a long time ago. Something I wanted to tell you."

"What, Mrs. Kenyon?" Sonya said.

"Please don't call me that. Call me Maggie." Oops, a slip.

"But that's not your name," Jasmine said.

"It's kind of short for Margo. My mom used to call me that."

"It's another one of those things you remember, isn't it?" Gaylen was smiling.

"Yeah, it is," Maggie said.

"What did you want to tell us?" Jasmine said.

"Ah, that. I wanted to tell you that you don't have to go to church or Sunday school to find God. You don't have to say prayers before you go to bed to talk to him. And you don't have to get A's on your report card or dress up to please him."

"We don't have to get A's?" Sonya said.

"Not for God. He's not impressed by a good report card. He just wants you to do your best."

"But that's the same thing," Sonya said.

"Then you're lucky." Maggie laughed. "But if you do your best and only wind up with a C, then God's just as proud of you as if you got an A, and I will be too." Maggie paused for effect, took a deep breath. "I want you to listen to this part very carefully, because these next two things are important. One, God never, never sends little girls to Hell. Two, You should never be afraid of him. No matter what anybody says, you should never be afraid of God. You guys got that?"

Jasmine and Sonya nodded their heads.

"Okay, girls I want you to go next door and play," Gay said. "Margo, I mean Maggie, and I have some things to talk about."

"I had no idea she was giving money to Goodman," Gay said once the kids were gone.

"A thousand a week."

"I knew she came into some money when her father died, but I didn't think it was that much."

"It was enough."

"And she was giving it away. Buying her way into Heaven, poor thing."

"I don't like the idea of spending any of it. By rights it belongs to Jasmine, but I don't have much choice. I can't exactly go to my old bank and make a withdrawal. I can't get my car either. That's a bummer, I really liked that car."

"What kind of car?"

"Mustang."

"You have a Porsche now, you'll get over the Mustang. If you live to enjoy it."

"It's just a matter of time before the killer gets caught," Maggie said. "I got a good look at him. I'll tell the cops what he looks like, maybe I'll find him in those mug books you were talking about. Once they get him, it'll be smooth sailing."

"I hope your right." Gay got up, went to the window and looked out. "Oh shit." She stepped back from the window. "It's your significant other. And he's walking like he's got a hockey puck up his ass."

"My what?"

"Greg something or other. He's like a fiancé, but he hasn't given you a ring yet. Too cheap."

There was a loud knock on the door.

"What's he like?"

"Cut from the same cloth as T.J. Goodman."

"I'll handle it," Maggie whispered. "You better get out of sight."

Another knock.

"You sure?"

"Yeah, it's better this way. I know what to do."

"Okay." Gay stepped into the hall, went into Jasmine's room.

Maggie opened the door. "Come in, Greg."

"What did you do to your hair?" He was out of breath.

"I felt like a change." She closed the door after he came in.

"I liked it better the old way." He was still breathing hard. He must've run all the way from the parking lot.

"I like it this way."

"I didn't see you in church," he said, apparently no longer interested in her hair.

"And." She sat in one of the rattan chairs, motioned for him to take the other.

"T.J. called me. He said you weren't gonna pay for the Bibles."

"That's right." She spoke with a soft, but deliberate voice. "I decided I needed to save the money for Jasmine's future."

"Those Bibles are important. They'll save souls right away, not years from now."

"How do you feel about abortion, Greg?" She spoke even softer now, almost a whisper.

"What's that got to do with anything?" His voice, however, went up an octave.

"Please, Greg, just answer the question."

"You know how I feel. It's murder."

"I'm pregnant."

"What?" He jumped out of the chair. "How could you? We've been saving ourselves for marriage. We've never—"

"It was a kid at school. It didn't mean anything. I'm sorry." Maggie couldn't believe her luck, it was going to be easier than she thought.

His eyes turned to slits. "You tramp."

"It was only one time."

"So what do you want me to do?"

"We could get married right away," she said. "No one has to know."

"What, me raise someone else's kid? Not even for all your money."

"You don't mean it. Think about what you're saying. We'd have lots of time for more children. All our lives." She was out of her chair now.

"You ignorant slut." He raised a hand.

"Better not," she said.

"I'm gone." He dropped the hand, went out, slammed the door after himself.

"Are you all right?" Gay said, coming out of Jasmine's room.

"Fine."

"Boy, you sure know how to end a relationship." Gay shook her head. "We could get married right away," she imitated Maggie. "No one has to know." She laughed. "He won't be back. And I think I can safely say you've seen the last of T.J. Goodman and his ilk as well."

"You think?"

"Oh yeah, you said the A word like you were actually thinking about it."

"Yeah, I've seen enough of his kind to know that would set him off." She rubbed her stomach, faced Gay. "Well like it or not, a woman's got a right to choose. And I choose to keep this child."

"Good for you," Gay said. Then, "What child?"

Maggie told her.

Chapter Twelve

Maggie got up at 4:30, started the coffee. She sighed as she waited for the machine to do its magic. It was still too much to believe, one day she was Maggie Nesbitt, pregnant with no hope, the next she was Margo Kenyon with an eight-year-old daughter and a future for her unborn baby.

She went to the cupboard, got a cup. Then she decided to check on Jasmine. Peeking in her room, she saw the girl was sleeping the sleep of the just, but she'd thrown her covers off during the night. Eight, what a perfect age. Maggie had a perfect life when she was eight. The only problem she had then was boys and how icky they were. Maggie entered the room, pulled the covers up over the child.

A lump welled up in her throat. Maggie willed the tears away. Margo was gone, she was here. She was going to have to do the best she could for herself and Jasmine. The child moaned in her sleep. A dream maybe. Maggie wondered if she could ever tell her the truth about her mother, the truth about herself. If she did, would the child hate her? Could she do anything but? Maggie backed out of the room. She didn't want to think about it anymore.

Back in the kitchen the coffee maker buzzed and she poured herself a cup. Black and strong. After a hot sip she went to the cupboard below the sink and pulled out a pack of trash bags. Another sip and she went out to the living room and that bookcase by the television.

T.J. Goodman's book begged to be first. She spread open a bag, pulled his book out and dumped it in. Too many books to count followed, Bibles included. It took four trips to the dumpster out in the parking lot to get rid of them all.

Another cup of coffee and she started in on the papers in the nightstand. She found a broker's number, a list of stocks, an owner's manual and insurance papers for a Porsche 911 Cabriolet. Also insured were a pair of diamond earrings, a diamond pendant, a pearl necklace and a Rolex. And she found a birth certificate. Same DOB as on the license. Parents Gilbert and Debra Murrant. How could that be?

She found the watch, the diamonds and pearls in a jewelry box on the bureau. A diamond solitaire, about half a carat, an elegant pearl necklace. Diamond earrings, about a quarter carat. She took out the Rolex, put it on, a part of Margo. Then she closed the box, sat down on the bed, took a sip of the coffee, warm now.

Margo was rich, but she still dunned the ex for child support, lived in a small condo, and was starting college. She had inexpensive rattan furniture, Hawaiian prints and ordinary flatware in the kitchen. True, she had some jewelry, but it was simple, not showy. There was the car, but who wouldn't splurge on a new car if they'd suddenly come into money?

Maggie flipped through the checkbooks. The big one started seven months ago, when the checks to Goodman's church had started. The one in the purse was older, but a large deposit had been made about the same time. She went back to the car papers. The Porsche was seven months old.

Coffee cold now, Maggie went out to the kitchen to warm it up.

Next she went to the breakfast table with a fist full of canceled checks and started practicing Margo's signature. It wasn't hard, a flowery M followed by a K and a kind of squirrelly slash that dipped for the Y in Kenyon. Obviously Margo had been left handed as she was. After an hour Maggie was convinced the signature would pass even the closest scrutiny, she had it down perfectly. Probably because they were twins.

That taken care of, she went through Margo's notes for her U.S. History class. The handwriting was remarkably like hers, a little more flourish on the loopy letters, the Ls and Ts above the line and the Ps and Ys below it. Maggie tended not to loop anywhere near as much above and she didn't loop at all below.

Finished, she scooped up the evidence of her work and dumped it in the trash under the sink.

"Mom?" It was Jasmine.

"Here."

"What'd you do? The books are gone." Jasmine was wearing flannel pajamas, white with pink and yellow flowers. She looked worried, little frown lines went out from her eyes.

"Spring cleaning." Maggie wanted to hug her, but would Margo have done that? She resisted the urge. "I threw them out."

"All of 'em? Even the Bibles, the kids' Bible stories too?"

"All of 'em."

"How am I gonna study for Bible class?"

"I think maybe it's about time you worried about just being a kid."

"What's Mr. Weiner gonna say?"

"Who?"

"The Bible school teacher."

"Whatever he says, it won't affect you."

"Why not?"

"No more Bible school," Maggie said.

"But, Mom—"

"No buts, remember what I said yesterday."

"Yeah." Jasmine scruched up her face. A frown, almost a smile, a frown again, than a smile, the real thing. "No more Bible school." She said it as if she were trying out the phrase. "No more Bible school." She obviously liked it.

"No more," Maggie said.

"But what about when you get all your memory back? Are you gonna change your mind then?"

"Not a chance."

"Promise?" Jazz opened the refrigerator, pulled out the milk.

"You can count on it."

"You gotta promise or it doesn't count."

"I promise."

The child seemed to be thinking. "That's good. I never liked it." She opened the milk, sniffed the carton and made a face. "Yuck, sour. No Tony the Tiger today."

"You have Frosted Flakes every morning?"

"It's my fave," Jasmine said. "What are we gonna do for breakfast?"

"We could go to Denny's."

"Really?"

"Yeah, I feel like a treat. How about you?"

"Yeah! I'll get my school stuff, you can drop me after we eat."

"Do I drive you everyday?"

"Is this one of the things you don't remember?"

"Yep."

"You drive me, then after you go to your school."

"Thanks, kiddo." But she was talking to air, because Jasmine had flown to her room to get ready.

Alone in the kitchen, Maggie rinsed out the coffee cup, dried it. She was surprised at how steady her hands were, because she was more nervous than she'd ever been on a first date. Very soon she was going to be stepping into Margo's life, meeting her classmates. Did she have special friends at school? Favorite professors? Someone she flirted with? There were so many ways she could be tripped up, so many mistakes she could make. And on top of all that, there was the killer to worry about.

"I'm ready." Jasmine came into the kitchen wearing a pink jumpsuit and pink tennis shoes.

"What, you don't wear jeans to school?"

"You wanted me to dress like a little lady, remember?"

"That's one of the things I think's gonna stay forgotten. What do you say we go shopping this weekend for some new stuff for you? Jeans, T-shirts, running shoes, stuff like that?"

"You mean it?"

"Yeah."

"Can I borrow some stuff from Sonya till then?"

"Sure."

"Be right back." Jasmine flew from the kitchen.

Maggie put away the cup, plucked what looked like car keys off a key holder by the refrigerator. She studied them in her hand. Probably the last thing Margo had done in this kitchen was to put the keys on that key holder.

She went out to the living room to wait for Jazz. She was wearing the Levi's and sweatshirt she'd worn yesterday. She was going to cut Margo's first two classes and go by the police station in Long Beach, but she was going to school after, and no way was she going to college dressed for the boardroom, or worse, church.

Jasmine burst in the front door. "How do I look?" She was wearing brown shorts and a faded Lion King T-shirt with white sneakers.

"Perfect."

"Really?"

"You're my girl. Let's go."

"You forgot the clicker."

"The what?"

"You know the clicker for the top." Jasmine picked up a small remote from the top of the bookcase. "Oh, I get it, this is one of those things you don't remember. Well, you need this to put down the top before we get to the car."

"A remote control for the top?" Maggie smiled. She couldn't help herself.

"Yeah, neat, huh?"

"Neat," Maggie said.

But a minute later, as they approached the car, Jasmine said, "Mom, you left the top down."

"I must have forgot." Maggie shivered. The killer must have grabbed Margo right here. How'd he get by the security guard?

"And look, you forgot to bring in a bag."

Maggie looked at the bag of groceries in the passenger seat. That was the proof of it all. Margo had brought in two bags. The killer must have followed her in and snatched her when she came out for the last bag.

"Good thing it's only cans." Jasmine stuffed it behind her seat as if she were used to her mother being a scatterbrain, then got in.

Maggie ran her hands over the driver's door. It was red, like her Mustang. It was beautiful. She opened the door, slid into beige leather seats. The car still smelled new. Maggie closed her eyes. Her Mustang was only six or seven months old. She must have bought it about the same time Margo got the Porsche. They were both sports cars. They were both red. Had there been some kind of psychic connection between them?

"Come on!" Jasmine said.

"Okay." Maggie started the car, felt a charge ripple through her as the engine sprang to life. Did Margo feel that same charge?

"Let's go!"

"You don't have to say that twice." Maggie put the car in gear.

"So, can I have strawberry waffles?" Jasmine said.

"What?"

"You know, at Denny's. Strawberry waffles. It's my fave."

"I thought Tony the Tiger was your fave," Maggie said.

"At home it is, but in a restaurant it's strawberry waffles."

"If that's what you want, then that's what you get."

"You're not gonna make me eat oatmeal? Lately whenever we go out for breakfast you make me eat oatmeal. Oops, maybe I shouldn't have said that."

"That's okay," Maggie said. Then, "Do we go out to breakfast a lot?"

"Only on Sunday, after church."

"Ah. Well, we'll still go out for breakfast on Sundays, only no church and you can have whatever you want." Going out to eat was supposed to be special and oatmeal was anything but that. Maggie shook her head. Why would Margo take her daughter out to eat, then spoil it by not letting her have what she wanted?

Jasmine bubbled all through breakfast. Maggie doubted she'd ever seen anyone so happy. She almost wished she didn't have to take her to school. It would have been nice if she could have spent the whole day just getting to know her. But she'd have time for that later, now it was important for her to get on with Margo's life.

* * *

Maggie had promised Gay she'd go straight to the police station after she dropped Jasmine off at school and describe Ferret Face to the cops, but she wasn't ready. Besides, nobody was going to kill her in class and by the end of the day she'd have her story down pat.

She found a spot in student parking, found the bookstore and bought a map of the campus. Margo's first class, American History, started at 10:00. American Government at 11:00. An hour for lunch, then Psych 1A at 1:00, Spanish at 2:00 and Biology at 3:00. A very full load.

DEAD RINGER

She settled into the history class. She may have come in at the middle of the semester, but she'd have no problem in the class. She spent the time listening to the professor drone on without taking notes. He wasn't very good. Maggie thought back to when she was in college, remembered her American History professor. He'd made history come alive, not like this guy. As an instructor, he was a wet noodle.

She gasped when she walked into the next class. The redhead she'd seen with Nick at the Lounge was talking to the professor at the front of the classroom. How could that be? What were the odds? Then she remembered Nick said she was a student at Cal State.

The girl looked up as Maggie took a seat at the back. They locked eyes for a second, then the redhead turned back to the professor, a smallish man in a cord jacket and slacks. She hadn't recognized her. Didn't have a clue. And she was a journalism student. What kind of reporter could she ever turn out to be? Maybe it was the new hair, or head job as Gay called it.

Maggie wondered if Nick spent the night with her, wondered what Nick was thinking right now. Did he have to go to the morgue to identify the body? Was he grieving? Could she find out from the redhead how he was handling it? Would that be smart? Probably not.

She saw the albino on her way to her third class.

"Mrs. Kenyon."

"Officer —," she let it linger.

"Norton," he said.

"That's right." She had to play it cool. It was a good thing Gay told her about the cops.

"We've missed you this last week."

"Sorry." She couldn't think of what else to say. "Where's your partner?" She remembered Gay saying he had a Mexican partner.

"He's on his way to England."

"I don't understand."

"He put in for a transfer a couple of years ago, kind of a cop exchange program. He found out he got accepted this morning. He's on his way to the airport as we speak."

"That sounds kind of fast."

"Apparently he'd been approved weeks ago, but there was some slip up when it came to notifying him."

"Sounds like he was lucky he got the news at all," Maggie said, feeling her way around the conversation.

"Sounds like." Then, "You cut it off, dyed it."

"What? Oh, the hair. I felt like a change," she said.

"It looks good on you." He hadn't had any trouble picking her out of a crowd of students, but then cops were trained to be observant.

"So what are you doing here?"

"You were supposed to come down to the station and look at more photos." He was studying her hair. Any second she expected him to ask why she'd done it.

"Now?" Maggie fought panic. She wasn't ready.

"If it's not too much trouble."

"I've got a class."

"How about after?"

"My last class gets out at 4:00."

"Mrs. Kenyon."

"I'm sorry, school's important to me."

"All right, I'll pick you up at 4:00."

"That's okay, Mr. Norton. I know how to find the police station."

But she had trouble finding a parking spot that evening and didn't get into the squad room with Norton till ten after five. "That's a lot of books," she said when she saw the stack she was going to have to go through.

"We could be here a while," he said. "It's a good thing I live alone."

"Okay, let's get started." Maggie was glad she'd called Gay and told her she might be late. From the amount of mug books on Norton's desk, it could be an all nighter.

Three hours later, eyes bleary, she turned a page and sucked in a quick breath.

"See something?" Norton said.

"That kinda looks like him." It looked like Horace with the ferret face, only lots younger and with longer hair.

"You're sure?"

Maggie looked at the picture for a few seconds. It was Ferret Face. She gulped. Part of her wanted to tell this policeman everything. Another part said to hold her silence and that's what she did. Yes, he and that Virgil character had chased her on the beach, but what if it was only because they'd seen her in the paper? What if they were only going to mug her?

"It's not him," she said.

"You don't look so good," Norton said.

"It's a little warm in here."

"No it's not."

"I'll be all right." But she didn't know if she would be.

"Make real sure it's not him. Look hard."

Maggie did. "It's not him." But it was Ferret Face, however that didn't mean he was the one who did the killing in the mini mart. She couldn't be sure, not for certain. She couldn't name him for that. Besides, she'd look awful stupid if she said it was him and it wasn't. If he had an alibi, like if he was miles away or something.

"Norton, phone," a seedy looking detective from the other side of the room called out. "I'll transfer it over."

"Norton here." He listened. "Oh no!" He sat as if the air had been ripped from his lungs. "I see." He hung up.

"What?" Maggie knew it was bad.

"My mother took her life." He was shaking.

"Is there anything I can do?"

"No." He looked at her, eyes misty. "My ex-wife died last year. A skiing accident."

"I'm sorry."

"We were young, had kids, then divorced. We never should have married, but she got pregnant, you know how it goes."

"Yeah, I do," Maggie said.

"The kids have been staying with my mother in Avalon."

"I've been to Catalina. It's nice. Good place for kids to grow. Safe."

"I'm going to have to take some time, go over there."

"Of course." Maggie wanted to comfort him, but didn't know how.

"I'll have to get my cases reassigned, yours too."

"I understand."

"I don't think you do." He was speaking as if every word was an effort. "A man named Larry Striker is the lobbyist for Nakano Construction. They build all over the county, office and apartment buildings of the ten to twenty story variety. It's rumored they use a lot of Yakuza money. Yakuza, that's like the Japanese Mafia."

"I know who the Yakuza are," Maggie said.

"Striker used to be a cop. Twenty years, rose to captain. He knows everybody. When he left the force he went to work for Congressman Nishikawa as his local administrative assistant. It was Nishikawa who got him the job with Nakano. You see, there's laws, a congressman can only pay so much. With Nakano the sky's the limit for a guy like Striker."

"What do you mean?"

"He was the kind of cop that wasn't afraid of breaking the rules. He wouldn't think twice about lying on the stand, lying to his boss, to the press, to anyone if it furthered his career. I'd imagine he'd be very valuable to a company like Nakano."

"So why are you telling me all this?"

"This guy you almost identified, Horace Nighthyde, he used to snitch for Striker."

"Surely that's a coincidence?"

"Maybe." He stared across the room with a faraway look in his eyes. "Let's look at what we have so far. When we pulled your ex in he acted like the ballbuster he is in court, but as soon as we threatened him with a few hours in a holding cell, he started to make nice. He confessed he was working with Frankie Fujimori. They knew you were following him and were waiting for you to harasses him. Kenyon didn't just want a restraining order, he wanted you arrested."

"Swell guy."

"You married him."

"We all make mistakes."

"Yeah, well, I know about that." Then, "Fujimori wasn't the only Asian in that store when he was killed. Ichiro Yamamoto, ex-employee of Congressman Nishikawa was there too. He was Striker's right hand when Striker was in the Congressman's employ. He stayed on for a year or so, then he was caught in a bar with an ounce of cocaine and sixty-thousand dollars."

"Let me guess," Maggie said. "He said it wasn't his."

"You're partly right. He owned up to the coke, but said the money wasn't his. He wanted to cut a deal, said he had the goods on the Congressman. For something that big we called the DA and Assistant DA Norris Stover came right over. Yamamoto said the money was from Striker and Nakano, a regular payment which Nishikawa distributed among a few other congressmen to get them to vote against anything that has the government interfering in Western Africa."

"I don't get it."

"Yamamoto claimed Nakano was supplying some oil company with weapons and that somehow those weapons were being traded for illegal diamonds."

"I still don't understand."

"Conflict diamonds. Diamonds mined by rebel armies. They use them to finance their wars."

"Oh."

"But the investigation stopped dead in its tracks, because Yamamoto made bail and two days later someone shot Frankie Fujimori dead right in front of his eyes. All of a sudden Yamamoto says he was lying about the congressman and the diamonds. Apparently he'd rather go to jail, then have what happened to Fujimori happen to him.

"You think Nishikawa had Striker send this Nighthyde character to kill him? Nishikawa's a war hero. He wouldn't do that. That's nuts?"

"You're probably right. It's just one of those things that bothers a homicide detective, you know, a coincidence."

"Your Yamamoto character was probably lying through his teeth."

"I admit it's thin, but it's something I would have followed up."

"Do you think it should be?" Maggie didn't want to admit that Congressman Nishikawa might be a crook. She'd met him at several functions. He was kind of a friend of Nick's. He seemed like such a nice man.

"Yeah, but it's not easy questioning people like Nishikawa and Striker without a lot more to go on." He pushed his hair out of his eyes, sighed. "Look, there's this guy, Lt. Wolfe. Billy Wolfe. He's a weird duck, works alone. I can try and get him interested in this. Maybe he'll take it on. He's the only one I'd trust with it."

"What do you mean?"

"Besides having to go up against the brass to get permission to question a congressman, we're overworked, and it's no secret if you don't clear a homicide in the first couple of days, it's almost never solved. We're going on two weeks with this one, so most of the guys would put it on the back burner even if Striker and Nishikawa weren't potentially involved."

"And this Billy Wolfe won't." Maggie fidgeted in her chair.

"He's not like the rest of us. It's not that he's smarter. He just looks at things differently. It's one of the reasons he works alone. The other is he doesn't keep regular hours. He might work forty-eight straight, then we might not see him for a week. Sometimes he works nights, sometimes days, sometimes he sleeps at his desk.

"If he takes a case there's a high probably it'll get solved. He has the highest clearance rate in the state, the nation I'd bet."

"What do you mean if? Doesn't he get assigned cases like any other officer?"

"Nope, he only takes on the ones that interest him."

"How's he get away with that?"

"He doesn't take the easy ones. He gets an open and shut and he passes it on. Makes him very popular among the guys. The brass don't like him much, but they keep him around because he hands them the hard ones on a platter. The press keeps his name out of the papers because he delivers good stories, usually slanted to put pressure on whoever he's investigating, but they're good stories nonetheless. They know he's using them, but they can't help themselves.

"I'll talk to him, tell him what I have. If I can get him interested, we got a shot at solving this. If not, well, once the shooter finds out the case is gathering dust, he might forget about you." Norton got up from his chair.

"Maybe we should just forget about the whole thing." Maggie got up too. "I mean nobody's going to be mourning for Frankie Fujimori."

Norton met her eyes with his pale greys. Was it her imagination or did his faraway look go suddenly sadder? "It's your call."

"You can do that, let a civilian decide?"

"I'm going to Catalina in the morning. If I don't interest Billy in this, ain't no one else gonna run with it. It's the way it is."

"Why are you doing this?" Maggie felt as if the walls were closing in.

"The shooter didn't do you in the store when he could've, so chances are he's already forgotten about you. Hell, he probably just had a hard on for Fujimori like you did. I'm sure you got nothing to worry about."

"That's good."

"But if the shooter was Horace Nighthyde—"

"What's your first name?" Maggie said.

"Abel."

"Abel," she held our her hand. "Maybe you better have that talk with Lt. Wolfe."

"I think that'd be best." He took her hand, shook it." Meanwhile, you be careful."

"I will." She hadn't fooled him at all.

Chapter Thirteen

Maggie inhaled the night as she walked down Pacific Avenue to the Porsche. She faced into the wind, took another deep breath. Late moon, gentle breeze, a nice night for a ride in a convertible. She punched the remote and smiled as the top came down. She'd never get used to that.

A car rounded the corner from First Street, rap music blaring from speakers loud enough to fill the Hollywood Bowl with sound. The car, chromed and lowered the way only a teenager could do it, cruised by and Maggie waved. The kid riding shotgun waved back, then flashed Maggie the thumbs up sign. She gave it back. Four kids having fun. Maggie envied them.

DEAD RINGER

She reached the Porsche as the kids turned onto Fourth Street, taking their music with them. Then the night was quiet again. She got in, started the car and sighed to the sound of its powerful engine.

Going east on Ocean she saw a liquor store on the other side of the street. She needed milk for Jasmine's Frosted Flakes and she didn't want to go to the convenience stores in the Shore because she might be recognized, despite the head job. She made a fast U turn at Atlantic. A quick glance in the rearview told her the car behind did the same. She parked in front of Beach Liquor. The car behind, a shiny black BMW, slid on by panther-sleek as it slowed, then parked in front of her.

She stepped out of the Porsche, eyes on the Beemer. Was it following her? No. Just another person who needed something at the liquor store. She was being paranoid. She shook her head and went inside. Still, with everything that had been going on, maybe paranoid was a good thing to be. She passed the checkout counter, went to the back, to the cooler section, where she got a half gallon of milk.

She started toward the check-out, stopped. There was no one in the store, except herself and a young black kid behind the counter reading a computer magazine. Whoever was in the black BMW hadn't come in yet. Why not? Were they out there waiting for her? That's absurd, she chided herself. But still they'd been out there long enough. There were no other stores open on the block. Either they were here to buy something in the liquor store or they were following her. Nothing else made sense.

Then, as if in answer to her question, a big man wearing an expensive suit came in the front. He appeared to be in his late forties or early fifties, hair cut close, like he was in the military, but he carried himself with all the confidence in the world. Maybe he was an officer, a general or something. The driver of the BMW. Had to be.

She met his eyes and shivered under the cold stare. He appraised her the way no woman likes to be looked at, a leer, almost evil. Instinctively she took a step back. She turned toward the coolers, turned into the next aisle and picked up a bottle of California wine as if she were interested in buying it.

She put it back, picked up another, studied the label without seeing it. He was coming closer. She heard the soft steps of his hard soled shoes on the cement floor. All of a sudden he was behind her.

"BV Private Reserve, 1995. Good wine, but a little young." He had a rich voice. A baritone, almost musical. It terrified her, sent a cold wind up her back. She didn't know why. There was no explanation for it.

"I'm just looking." She couldn't think of anything else to say.

"If you need some help, I'm sort of an expert on California Cabs."

"No, I can manage."

"Really, I don't mind." Now he sounded like a vampire from one of those old black and white horror films. She wished he'd just go away.

"My husband's the wine drinker." She hoped he'd take the husband hint and leave.

"You don't drink God's nectar?"

"No, the milk's for me." She held it up. It was so stupid, but she didn't want him to think she was buying the wine for herself, didn't want him to think she had anything in common with him, didn't want him to think there was any chance, any way, she was going to continue the conversation.

"Milk." He said it as if it were a dirty word, stepped away from her and went to the check-out where he bought a pack of Kools.

Kools? What kind of man smoked menthol? Not the kind that knew anything about California Cabs. Menthol and Cabernet, no way did they go together. He paid, turned and met her eyes while he was waiting for his change.

She looked away, but not before she caught his wink. It curdled her stomach. What was happening to her? Normally she'd be in the guy's face, but instead she was acting like a lamb being led to the slaughter and she couldn't help herself. There was something about the man. Something menacing.

The bottle of wine seemed hot in her hand. She put it back. Stalled for another minute, head down, staring at the labels on the bottles, till she was sure the man had enough time to get back in his car and be gone.

She'd been taking short, rapid breaths. She felt numb, her fingers and toes cold. She took in a deep breath, held it, willing her heart to slow down. She felt wrung out, she was sweating like she'd just done a mile flat out on the sand.

How could someone affect her that way? She thought about all the photos she'd just seen in the police station. Thought about the young Horace Nighthyde. That must have been it. She'd been looking at all those pictures of criminals and it must have made an impression on her subconscious. Down deep she'd been expecting someone to come after her. Especially after being chased on the beach that way. She'd let her paranoia run away with her.

Pretty dumb.

The man in the BMW had probably been just what he looked like. A guy who was out of cigarettes.

He'd seen a woman get out of a Porsche. Saw her at the wine section when he came in. Was intrigued, started a conversation to see where it might go and when it didn't, he left.

She took the milk to the check-out, paid for it and went back out to the Porsche. The Beemer was gone. She'd been right, after all. It was just a coincidence that the guy followed her through a U-turn and then into the store.

She got in the car, pulled on the shoulder harness, thinking about Nick now. He'd probably tell her the man was following her. Of course, he didn't believe Oswald killed Kennedy, thought James Earl Ray was innocent and was convinced the Queen was responsible for the death of Diana. Nick would keep a good eye on the rearview mirror. Maggie decided she would too.

She started back down Ocean, made a U at the next intersection and continued on toward the Shore, Pacific Coast Highway and the ride along the seaside to Huntington Beach and her new home.

She gasped. It was there, parked on the right, the black BMW. She grabbed a quick look as she passed it, then looked in the rearview as it pulled away from the curb and came up behind her. So he was following her, after all.

All of a sudden she wished she was in her Mustang. It had a car phone. A simple call and the cops would be on the creep in the Beemer in nothing flat. But the Porsche had no phone. Maggie was on her own.

Soon she was at the Y junction. Go right and Ocean continued along the beach till it dead ended at the river that separated the counties, Los Angeles and Orange. Go left and you went up Second Street, through Belmont Shore.

She saw the Belmont Pier up ahead, thought about Darley and Theo. The duplex she'd lived in with Nick was only a couple blocks away. He wouldn't be home, but Gordon would be.

She put her right blinker on, but went left at the last second. She didn't want to involve Gordon. She'd call him someday after her new life was running smoothly. Sometime before the baby was born. But right now it was too soon.

Another look in the mirror. The guy had dropped back some, but he was still there. Her life was hanging by a thread and now some clown on a power trip was trying to intimidate her with his suave voice and fancy car. Well, she had a fancy car too. And it was faster than that BMW, she'd bet.

"Get ready to rock and roll," she muttered, but she kept the speed at thirty-five. Up ahead, Pacific Coast Highway. Second Street became Westminster Boulevard when it crossed PCH. A long straight shot into Orange county, slicing through the Seal Beach Naval Weapons Station. Her boyfriend used to race down that street when she was in high school, speeding through the night with her at her side. PCH to Bolsa Chica—Hot Rod Alley. Now she was behind the wheel.

It had been a long time since she'd driven like a hell hound. She felt the adrenaline pumping. If she was going to put away her past, part of it that needed to be dealt with first was that boy in Borneo. She used to be the one of the best racers on the planet. She knew how to drive. It was time she did it again.

She looked in the rearview at the headlights behind as she passed the Edgewater Marina. She slowed for the light at PCH, clutched, dropped it into first, stopped. She drummed her fingers on the wheel, gripped it.

The light changed.

She punched it.

Rear wheels spinning, screeching, the car careening out of control, heading for the traffic light on the opposite side of the street. Maggie jerked the wheel to the right, pulled the car away from the light, back onto the right side of the road. She did it without letting up on the accelerator. Like her boyfriend used to do all those years ago, like she'd done so many times before.

Back on the straight she punched the clutch, slammed it into second. She didn't shift to third till the engine screamed and she kept her foot on the floor till it screamed again, then speed shifted into fourth.

Headlights up ahead. Car coming. Oh shit. Two pair. Some asshole was passing in her lane. The engine howled. She was doing over a hundred.

A quick look in the rearview. The Beemer's brights filled it. He was riding her tail. That guy could drive.

The car ahead, the one passing in her lane, turned on his brights too. He wanted her to pull over, give him room. Slow down maybe. Maggie kept her foot on the floor, gobbling up the distance between herself and the oncoming car. She was almost driving blind.

The bright lights in front were two whirling suns giving out cold light rays, stealing the road, stealing the fence that protected the Navy base from civilians, stealing the night. Maggie centered her concentration on a place between them. The fucker better pull over, because she wasn't going to.

He did, crashing into the side of the car he was passing. Maggie screamed as the side mirror made a shotgun sound and was ripped off. Collision, her first thought, but it was a glancing blow and then she was past. Now it was her headlights chewing up the dark and she had her vision back.

Another look in the mirror. She was pulling away from the BMW.

Eyes back on the road. Oh Fuck. Traffic light ahead. The end of the Navy base. Houses, stores, cars and people on the other side of that light. She had to slow down. She panicked, slammed on the brakes. Locked the wheels and the car started spinning, a speeding second hand on a crazy out of control clock.

She was on one of those wild rides they had at Disneyland, spinning, spinning, spinning. But all of a sudden calm descended. The world revolved, raged around her. She pulled her hands from the wheel. She felt a hand on her shoulder. Death.

She was a top, turning as if controlled by a giant child's hand.

The baby.

She grabbed the wheel again as the car slid into a stop in the middle of the intersection facing back the way she'd come.

Downshift into first. Rev the engine. Pop the clutch. Spinning wheels again, screeching, a banshee wailing into the night and the wail was answered by another, the shrieking tires of the braking BMW. They passed, going opposite directions, missing each other by centimeters as the Porsche sped up and the Beemer slowed down.

Maggie threw it up into second, chirping the tires again as she came upon the wreck she'd caused. She hoped they were okay. She wanted to stop and see, but a quick look in the mirror told her the BMW was back on her tail. She passed the tangled cars doing fifty in second and went up into third.

Ahead she saw a small train start to cross the street. The Naval Weapons Station was cut in half by

Westminster Boulevard. Heavy machinery and weapons were transported back and forth on a rail that crossed the road. What could they possibly be moving after dark? Maggie remembered the rumors of nukes. The Navy claimed they had none at Seal Beach, everybody else knew better.

Was she heading toward an A bomb at seventy-five miles an hour? Could she beat it? She upshifted into fourth, keeping the accelerator to the floor. A horn blared from the train. It had to be loud, because she heard it over the roar of her engine.

Light in her eyes. The BMW was behind her again, brights on, reflecting from the rearview. No time to move the mirror aside, too dangerous to take her hands from the wheel.

The train was at the road, moving left to right, starting to cross. Two cars, smaller than a real train. Some kind of tractor, or crane on the lead car.

It was halfway across. Maggie eased right, onto the shoulder now, driving like she was possessed. Rocks and gravel flew from the tires as she flew by the train, the Beemer on her tail.

"Oh shit." The light on PCH was red. There was traffic, headlights moving in both directions. The BMW was still behind. She busted the light at eighty, barely aware she'd skinned through without hitting anyone.

She was back on Second Street now, the Shore up ahead. It would be crowded. People out. Pedestrians. Even at this hour. Belmont Shore was a college town, people were out till late. She couldn't keep going, she might kill someone.

Downshift to third, tap the brakes, down to second and a screaming left onto the dark road to the marina. A boatyard, boat shops, then restaurants on the right, a hotel on the left, then a side road that fed into PCH. For an instant she thought about taking it, changed her mind and fishtailed into the boatyard parking lot. There would be people at the popular seafood restaurants. Surely they'd scare off her mysterious pursuer. The restaurants overlooking the marina were doing good business, the lots were full and she was rocketing between two rows of parked cars.

She resisted the urge to look right, at the boats in their slips. Instead she grabbed a quick look at the speedometer. She was doing forty, parked cars flying past. She checked the mirror and saw only dark. The Beemer hadn't made the turn.

She saw a couple leave one of the restaurants as she slowed down. Then she heard the BMW, a smooth scream as it sped up the aisle on the left. Damn. She popped the clutch and stepped on the gas. She flew out of the row of cars and the BMW shot out of the next row over. She couldn't go left, she jerked the wheel to the right. The rail, the boardwalk, boats, the sea in front of her, she cranked the wheel right again, to shoot down the next row of cars, but she was out of control heading for the rail in a tire smoking arc.

The Beemer's headlights caught her as she worked the wheel, but the Porsche's tires screamed in protest as the car smashed into the railing between the parking lot and the marina boardwalk five feet below. The rail gave with a blast.

For an instant the car seemed suspended in midair, then the spinning rear wheels found purchase as they hit the boardwalk. The Porsche shot forward and crashed into the sea.

Like a hammer blow to her chest, the wind flew from Maggie's lungs as she slammed forward, body jerked back by the shoulder harness. She struggled for the catch, forced air into her lungs, sucked deep as the car sank into the dark.

Water rushed around her, the car was turning over. Upside down. She found the catch, pulled, yanked off the belt and harness, pushed away from the car as it went over and struck out for the surface, broke through and sucked air.

She looked over to where the car had gone under. Nothing there now to tell the world what had happened, not even a ripple. The water in the Marina was flat calm, but any second the place was going to be crawling with people full of questions she didn't want to answer.

Her acquaintance with the car had been short, but she'd loved it. The next time she met that bastard, the story would have a different ending. He was going to pay. Her emotions were running high, she'd shifted from fear to anger before she'd broken the surface and anger was still fueling her.

She kicked off her shoes, then struck out for the other side of the bay. On her right she saw the red and green lights of a sailboat coming toward her. She stopped, treading water, to let it pass.

She looked back to where she'd gone into the water with the car. A crowd was already gathering and she wasn't surprised. She'd made a heck of a racket. The restaurants must have emptied out. She saw the flashing blue and red lights of the police.

The sailboat was closer now. Maggie moved toward it. A small sloop, thirty feet or so, and it was trailing a dinghy. Maybe they were going out to anchor off the oil islands. Probably going to fish from the dinghy. Or maybe they were going all the way to Catalina.

The boat seemed to take forever to get to her, and when it did Maggie saw an opportunity. Any minute the police were going to light up the bay, looking for whoever they thought might be in the car. She wanted to be as far away as possible when that happened, so she grabbed onto the dinghy and let the boat tow her toward the sea.

Hanging on to the dinghy she felt like shark bait. She hated sharks. A quick scissor kick propelled her out of the water and up onto the rubber tube. She pulled herself inside. The dinghy was trailing the sloop on a long painter, twenty feet, twenty-five. But not so far she couldn't make out the back of the man steering the boat. What would he do if he turned and noticed the hitchhiker?

As if sensing her thoughts, he did.

"Hey!"

She waved. They were in the river that separated L.A. from Orange County now. To the left Seal Beach, Long Beach on the right. She stood, dove into the sea. The sailor probably thought he'd seen a mermaid.

The water wasn't as cold now that she was swimming. Soon she was at the rocks and pulling herself from the water. In seconds she was up on the jetty. The sailboat had stopped.

She waved.

He waved back, continued his journey. A story he'd be telling in sailors' bars for years to come.

Maggie climbed down the other side of the jetty and faced the long beach that had given the city its name. The tide was out, so she had a wide stretch of hard, flat and wet sand to walk on. A mile or so to the duplex where she had lived up until yesterday.

Chapter Fourteen

"Ma, you here?" Horace went through the house to her bedroom. "Blind as a bat and never home." He was talking to the house. Where she was, was anybody's guess. Up and down the block, visiting probably. He sighed, he bought her the best of everything, new furniture, plush carpets, but she was always out. But then if he was her, he probably would be, too. She couldn't see any of it, for her the house must be like a prison.

He went to his room, pulled a suitcase out from under the bed, stuffed it with clothes. He needed space.

Back at the motel he flopped on the bed. He woke with the setting sun, still thinking about Ma. Maybe he shoulda stayed. She was gonna be crazy with worry about Virgil, jumping around like bugs on a waffle iron. He had to go back.

"Where'zzz he?" she hissed from her rocker as soon as he walked in, slurring the words, almost unintelligible. But Horace knew what she was saying.

"Virgil? He's not back?" He tried to sound surprised.

"Don zzzhit me."

"Maybe he's still with her."

"Two dayzzz?" She was rocking with worry and anger. "I think he's dead. He'd be back by now if he wasn't." She slumped down in the rocker, gathered up her quilt. She was old, but it seemed like she'd aged twenty years right in front of him. Her eyes were red rimmed, cheeks puffy. She was defeated.

"You've been crying?" Horace had never seen her cry, not even when their daddy hung himself out in the garage. "He'll come back when he's ready, try not to worry."

"You think?"

"I'm sure of it." Then, "I've gotta go to my room. I'm kind of working right now and I've got some calls to make."

"It's late," she said.

"In my line of work your time is never your own," Horace lied. Then he turned away from her. He couldn't think of anything else to say.

In his room he picked up the phone, dialed information, asked for Sadie's number and was mildly surprised when the operator turned him over to a mechanical voice that gave it to him. So she hadn't been lying to him about being in the book. Maybe she really did want him to call.

Only one way to find out. He pushed the numbers.

"Hello." She answered on the first ring.
"It's me, Horace."
"I was hoping you'd call."
"I didn't know if you meant it."
"I did." She sounded sleepy.
"You wanna get together sometime?"
"I'd like that."
"When?" He said.
"How about Saturday?" She seemed awake now. "We could do dinner and a movie."
"Okay." It had been a long time since Horace had taken a woman to a movie, years. "I'll call tomorrow and you can tell me where to pick you up."
"Cool," she said.
"See ya."
"Yeah." She hung up.

Horace held the phone to his ear for a few seconds, imagining she was still there. Then he remembered the woman in Catalina and called Striker. Like Sadie, Striker answered on the first ring.

"It's me," Horace said. "I took care of the Catalina job."

"How can I believe you?" Striker spoke softly, but there was no hiding the anger there.

"I say it's done, it's done."

"Like the Kenyon woman?"

"Yeah, like that. You got a problem with the way it was handled, I'm sorry, but she's dead and there's no way it can come back on you."

"She's dead all right. I took care of it about half an hour ago. Unfortunately I think she picked your photo out of a mug book."

"What the fuck you talking about? I put a clip into her chest."

"You shot up Maggie Nesbitt. She's married to that guy on television. The one with the grey hair and that fucking dimple stuck in his chin. The one sounds like Kennedy."

"No way."

"Margo Kenyon spent the evening with the Long Beach Police Department. Afterward she drove her Porsche into the bay. The divers will pull her out in the morning."

"You're shitting me?" Horace couldn't believe what he was hearing. It was the Kenyon woman he'd killed. He couldn't make a mistake like that. Couldn't.

"And you've got another problem. That albino fuck's gonna hand the case over to Billy Wolfe. Anyone else would shelve it. But Wolfe's different, dangerous."

"You said if the albino and his partner were out of the picture, the case would die a slow death. What happened?" Horace felt sick. He took a couple deep breaths.

"You there?" Striker said.

"Yeah."

"Wolfe's got a wife and kid. Do the kid before Wolfe gets his teeth into this thing."

Fuck, a kid, is what he thought, but, "Okay, e-mail me the details," is what he said. Then, "About the Kenyon woman, it was her I did. If there was some cunt at the cop house claiming to be her, she was lying."

"The news guy identified the body. It was all over the television. Don't you watch?"

"Not if I can help it." Horace felt like his head was going to explode.

"Never mind. It's taken care of. On this other, check your e-mail, then do it tonight if you can."

"Sure." Horace didn't think Striker had heard, because he'd already hung up.

Horace booted up his computer, logged on. Calm, he told himself as he opened the message. His heart was racing. A pain started in his temples. How in the world could he have killed the wrong woman for Christ's sake? He'd been following her for a bloody week before she'd disappeared. He knew what she looked like.

The message flashed on the screen.

WOLFE AND WIFE SEPARATED. WIFE LIVES WITH 2 YEAR OLD JIMMY AT OCEANVIEW TOWERS. 1701 ON THE SEVENTEENTH FLOOR. ACCIDENT! SEE ATTACHMENT!

Jesus wept, the boy was only two. Horace bit his lip as he opened the attachment. It was a copy of a newspaper clipping. The story about the body behind the gay bar. The woman's name was Margaret Nesbitt. Married to the guy who did the six and eleven o'clock news.

He called Striker back.

"Yeah."

"Something screwy's going on. You got an address for the news guy, Nesbitt?"

"110 Ocean. It's in the Shore. A duplex. He lives on top."

"You had that real fast," Horace said.

"You wouldn't have told me the Kenyon woman was dead unless you believed it. Find out what's going on, but be discrete."

"You got it."

"And don't forget the boy."

"Don't worry." But Horace was worried. Two years old. It was enough to make your stomach turn.

* * *

A twenty minute walk along the dark beach and Maggie was between the sea and the Olympic pool. She looked out toward the pier, dark under there. She thought of those two men. They'd helped her, but she shivered when she remembered that disappearing bottle of wine.

Then she trudged up over the sand toward home.

Only it wasn't home anymore.

It was a risk going there, someone might see her, but not Nick. He'd be at the station. He might miss his Sunday magazine show to identify his wife's body, but the news was sacred to him. He'd be at his desk, wearing that blue blazer. He'd be heartbroken, but he'd do the news.

And then there was Gordon. She hated deceiving him as much as she hated deceiving Nick, maybe more. Nick had his work, his friends, family. Gordon didn't have anyone, except maybe Jonas for a shoulder to cry on, but that was all. She wished there was a way she could tell him.

Close to the duplex, she came up the alley behind, was about to take the stairs when she remembered the newspapers on the garage floor. Nick was a newsman and he wasn't stupid. If he saw those papers like that, he'd know she'd gone through them. He'd want to know what she was looking for and he'd find it.

Maggie tried the door. It wasn't locked. Inside she turned on the light. There were no windows so there was little danger anybody would see. They'd have to be close enough to see light coming out from under the door, a risk she had to take.

The papers were where she'd left them. For a second a flash of anger rippled through her. Nick never failed to park his precious Mercedes in the garage. But her Mustang, that was too much trouble.

Maggie took a breath, pushed her anger away. It was stupid. Her job here was to put the papers back the way they were as quickly as possible and get out and that's what she did.

Outside again, she took the back stairs, careful to step over the fifth step because it squeaked. At the top she found the key under the mat where she expected it. A quick breath and she opened the door. She eased it closed, locked it. The house was dark, but enough light seeped in from the apartment building next door for her to see her way around.

Bedroom first. She stopped at the door. The bed was rumpled. The place smelled of sex. Nick was fastidious, he'd never leave an unmade bed. Not ever. So the girl must have been in it when he'd gone to the station. Where was she now? Would she be back soon?

She closed her eyes for a second and examined her feelings. The affair must have been going on for some time. How come she wasn't hurt? Maybe she hadn't been as much in love with Nick as she'd thought.

She went to the closet and pulled out her flight bag. Then to the bottom bureau drawer, Nick's drawer. She fished under his ski sweaters, found the pistol. She didn't know much about handguns, but she knew about this one, a Smith & Wesson Sigma nine millimeter automatic. Nick's plastic gun. Better than a Glock, he'd boasted. Seventeen rounds in the mag, plus one in the chamber. Just point and shoot. And Maggie knew how to do that, Nick made sure of it by taking her to the range more afternoons than she could count. It was the only gun she knew, but she knew it well.

She checked to make sure he'd chambered a round. He had. She dropped it into the bag. Nick would miss the gun and undoubtedly report it stolen, but that couldn't be helped. She wanted protection now, tonight.

* * *

Gordon Takoda stepped out of the shower, pulled a towel from the rack and dried his hair. Despite the shower, he felt like he hadn't slept in a week. Losing Maggie had been as bad as losing Ricky.

Ricky had been worried about renting the upstairs to a straight couple, especially a TV person, but Nick Nesbitt was willing to pay the high rent and they seemed like nice people. Ricky used to say there were three kinds of straights. Those who hated gays, those who bent over backwards to prove they were okay with it and those who didn't give a shit. Nick and Maggie didn't give a shit.

Nick had been standoffish at first, but he was that way with everybody, he was on television, he had to be careful. Maggie, however, had swept into their lives as if she'd been there forever. They swiftly became fast friends. The three of them did everything together. Then Ricky died. Without Maggie, Gordon would have taken his own life.

At least Maggie never knew about Stephanie. She'd spent the night last night. Maggie not even buried yet and they were sleeping together. There was only one explanation for it. They'd been doing it before Maggie'd been killed. A man didn't jump in the hay with someone the night after his wife was murdered unless he'd been rolling in it for sometime.

A motive?

Not Nick, surely. Gordon couldn't believe that. But the girl? He'd have to give it some thought.

He stepped into his jeans, pulled on a pair of running shoes without socks. He was out of coffee and besides, the walls were closing in. He had a yellow Spooner Hawaiian shirt half on when he heard a noise. He paused. It sounded like somebody was upstairs. He listened for a second. Nothing. Just ghosts in his imagination.

* * *

Maggie went to the closet, pulled out a pair of faded Levi's. Though she wasn't so wet she was dripping, she was uncomfortable. An Angels sweatshirt with cut off sleeves followed. She shucked off the wet clothes. Nick was gonna know someone had been in the apartment anyway, if he noticed the wet spot on the carpet, it'd just confuse the cops. She put on the dry clothes and felt better right away. After wrapping the wet ones inside another sweatshirt, she stuffed them in the grip along with a second pair of Levi's. She was a sweatshirt and Levi's person and there were three more pairs of the jeans and a couple sweatshirts left in the closet, Nick wouldn't notice what she'd taken.

But he'd notice her jewelry box. Too bad.

She hated rings on her fingers or in her ears. Necklaces seemed like a noose around her neck. And even though she hardly ever wore the engagement and wedding rings Nick had given her, she wanted them. She also wanted the gold crucifix her mother had given her. And she wanted the pearl earrings her father had given her when she graduated from high school. She loved the memories associated with her jewelry, the love that went with the giving of it. And besides, despite how she felt about it, sometimes she'd put some on for a dinner party or something.

She remembered she was barefoot and went back to the closet where she found and slipped on a pair of well used Nikes.

Now all she wanted was a photo album from the bottom bookshelf in the living room. She pulled out

DEAD RINGER

the album and flipped through it. She was there as a little girl, with her mother, with her dad, with both during birthdays, graduation, holidays. She closed it, dropped it in the grip.

She was about to let herself out when she noticed all the correspondence on the coffee table. There was plenty enough light coming in from the streetlamp out front for her to go through it.

She sat down on the sofa and started. Condolence cards. Heaps of them. Already? She'd only been dead a couple of days. There was a clipping from the Press Telegram with her photo in it. Not a good one, she thought, but anyone would recognize her. She hoped Margo's friends or classmates didn't see it.

She read the caption and gave a start. She was being buried tomorrow at noon.

Poor Margo. Maggie fought tears. Life was so unfair.

* * *

Horace found the house, an upstairs duplex. The lights were out. That made sense if the guy did the eleven o'clock news. He'd be at the station in L.A. till midnight. He parked in front of the garage in back as if he lived there, got out of the van without locking it.

He paused, took out a pair of disposable surgical gloves, put them on.

There was some light from the apartments next door, but the alley behind was dark. He went for the steps confident he wasn't seen.

A squeak rippled through the night. Horace pulled his foot off the tattletale step as if it were red hot and he'd been barefoot.

* * *

Maggie heard the squeak. Somebody was on the steps out back. Not Nick, he'd have stepped over it as she had. Someone else. She started for the front door. Stopped. If it was the police they'd be out front, waiting. If that was it, then someone had called them. Could Gordon have heard something from downstairs? Was that it?

* * *

Gordon was on his way to the front door when he heard the telltale step. Nick? No, he said he'd be doing the news as usual. Probably that Stephanie.

* * *

Horace stood still as the night. Any second he expected lights, shouting. But it didn't happen. He thought about Virgil. He thought about Ma rocking in that chair. He thought about Sadie. He thought about Striker and Congressman Nishikawa. And he thought about Margo Kenyon back from the dead.

A cool breeze wafted between the duplex and the apartment building next door. Someone put a CD on or turned on an oldies station. The Beatles, 'Yellow Submarine.' Stupid song, but he found himself softly humming along with Paul McCartney's vocals as he ghosted the rest of the way up the stairs.

At the landing he unzipped the bomber jacket, fished a leather pouch from the inside pocket, opened it and smiled as he fingered the picks. Standard lock, probably the one that came with the house when it was built back in the '50s. Piece of cake.

He went to work.

* * *

Maggie forced herself to be still, though her heart was racing. The doorknob clicked as someone tried it. She grabbed the grip. More clicking sounds. Someone was out there trying to pick the lock.

The police didn't do that. They'd bang on the door, wake up the whole neighborhood.

Instinct said run. She rose from the sofa, started for the front door. Stopped. She flashed on Ferret Face and Virgil. What if it was them? One could be waiting somewhere out front.

She inched her way toward the bathroom. A mistake, she realized as soon as she slipped in. There was no way out and the lock on the door wouldn't keep out a child, much less someone able to pick locks. She was about to leave, to take her chances going out the front way, when the back door opened.

Too late, whoever he was, he was in.

She took her hand from the door. It was open a crack. She heard quiet footsteps tiptoeing through the kitchen. She backed up to the bath, sat on the rim and fished in the bag for the gun. She let out a silent sigh when she found it, wrapped a hand around the grip, finger on the trigger as she pulled it out.

* * *

Gordon strained his ears, searching for sound from above. He'd heard the step. Heard the door open. Heard someone ease it closed. Nick never did that and there was no reason why Stephanie would either. He expected to hear footsteps cross the kitchen. And he expected to see the reflection of the upstairs light on the trees outside his windows when it came on. Whoever was up there was taking pains to be quiet and they were moving around in the dark.

He went into the bedroom, reached under the pillow, pulled out his thirty-eight. He took the holster out of the top drawer of the nightstand, clipped it to his belt at the small of his back.

Armed now, he opened the front and back doors, turned off the lights, then stood in the dark, gun in hand, in the center of the living room. Not even God could get out of that upstairs apartment without making some noise and Gordon planned on hearing it. When whoever was up there came down, he would be waiting.

* * *

Horace stopped in the middle of the kitchen. The lights were out, but the house seemed alive. He eased a hand into the shoulder holster, brought out the Beretta. He sipped at the air, but heard no sound.

There was a hallway off the kitchen. He was familiar with the layout, there were a lot of duplexes built to the same plan in the Shore. In his younger days he'd been in several.

He passed the bathroom on the left, checked the bedroom on the right. Empty. Sterile. A guest bedroom most likely. Back in the hall, he started for the bedroom at the end, stopped a few feet from the door. The house seemed more alive now. He had to piss. A look over his shoulder at the bathroom door. It was ajar. If there was anybody home, they'd be asleep in the master bedroom. He'd check it out, piss after.

* * *

Maggie sat on the rim of the tub, elbows on her knees, bracing her arms, two hands wrapped around the butt of the Sigma. She sucked air as if she were taking it through a straw, slow and silent. He was just outside the door. She heard the rustle of the thick pile on the carpet as he started toward the back bedroom. He was quiet, but she was quieter. But of course she wasn't moving and he was.

DEAD RINGER

* * *

Horace stepped into the room gun hand first, Beretta ready to fire. The bed was empty, but he smelled the sex. That must have been what made him think the place was occupied. He wrinkled his nose. What kind of guy fucked around right after his wife died?

Then he saw it. An eight by ten color glossy surrounded by a silver picture frame on the nightstand next to the bed. He picked a miniature flashlight out of his jacket pocket and lit up the photo. It was a wedding picture, groom in tux, bride in white. And the bride was her, spitting image.

How?

Twins, had to be. No other explanation. And he'd killed the wrong one. Wait! Not possible. He and Virge grabbed her from the parking lot in Huntington Beach where Margo Kenyon lived. And the red Porsche, that was Margo Kenyon's car. The woman he did was Margo Kenyon, no doubt about it.

Something strange was going on.

* * *

A bead of sweat ran from behind Maggie's left ear, down her neck. It tickled and itched at the same time. Her senses were all aware. She was running on overdrive. Her lips were dry. She licked them, but there was no moisture on her tongue. Sweat trickled under her arms. She shifted her weight. Her right heel rubbed against the tub. It squeaked.

* * *

Horace froze. There was someone in the house. His first instinct had been right. Oh shit! He hadn't checked the living room. Someone could be asleep on the sofa.

His went cat-quick through the hallway, gun ready. In the living room he pointed it at the sofa, a perfect place for falling asleep while watching television. But like the bedroom, there was nobody there.

* * *

Maggie heard the intruder rush down the hall. She tightened her finger on the trigger, expecting him to come crashing through the bathroom door, but he ran past instead.

Her nerves were lit, the fuse was short, but her hands were steady on the gun. Thank God for Nick and that endless practice on the range. She'd learned how to conquer her fear of the weapon, to hold it still and sure no matter how much her stomach was churning. And it was churning now.

* * *

Gordon heard the ceiling creak as footsteps moved fast through the hallway above. They stopped in the living room. He looked up. The intruder was right on top of him. He aimed the thirty-eight toward the ceiling, almost as if he were going to fire through it, like those action heroes do in the movies. He was breathing fast, panting like a tired dog, and he hadn't strained a muscle. He was in shape, swam a hundred laps at the Olympic pool every morning, but he was ringing with sweat now. Not so cool, he thought, but then he was thirteen years out of the FBI. He was a sixty year old man who'd been living a quiet life in the Shore for the last ten years.

He'd dealt with death during two tours of duty in Vietnam and during his twenty year tour with the Bureau, but now he was what he was. A quiet man, a reader, a chess player. He'd gotten lazy over the years.

He couldn't remember the last time he'd fired the gun, but he still remembered how.

* * *

Horace shook his head. He felt like an idiot. A stupid high school jerk. He was as jumpy as he was on his first date at a drive-in movie. He sighed. Steamy windows, long blonde hair swirling around pink tipped breasts. He smiled at the memory. High school was the best time of his life. It had been all downhill after that. Then he met Striker and things started to pick up.

He was somebody now. He drove a new van, had an airplane, a zillion channels on the TV. He dressed well, ate at good restaurants. He felt good when he left the house.

He slipped the Beretta into the shoulder holster, looked down, saw the condolence cards on the coffee table. He picked up a couple, dropped them. He still had to piss like a race horse. He started for the bathroom.

* * *

Maggie heard him coming. She steadied herself, licked her dry lips again.

She'd expected him to pass by the bathroom as he had twice before, but all of a sudden the door was pushed in and the light came on.

"What?" he said when he saw her. It was Ferret Face.

She pulled the trigger, again and again and again.

* * *

Horace knew he'd done a stupid thing the second he turned the light on, then he caught a quick glimpse of a dark haired woman with Margo Kenyon's face. Another one, he thought, registering the gun. Then something hit him in the side, spun him around. He was slammed out of the bathroom as if he'd been hit by a train, picked up and smashed into the wall. He slumped to the floor amid a hail of gunfire, rapid explosions that took away his hearing as bullets tore through the plaster above.

He curled up like a baby as everything turned to black.

Chapter Fifteen

Maggie ran out the front door, grip over her shoulder, gun in her left hand. She crossed the porch, leapt down the steps to the sidewalk.

"Freeze!" Gordon's voice rang out through the night.

Maggie turned, Gordon was on the porch, in the shooter's position, feet spread, arms extended, both hands on a pistol.

"Gordon, it's me!"

"Maggie?"

"Yeah." She put her right index finger to her lips, the sign for silence. Sirens in the distance broke the quiet of the night. "I need a ride outta here!" she said.

"I'll get my keys."

"Hurry!" Maggie said.

Seconds later Gordon slammed the door after himself, leapt from the porch. "It's not locked."

Maggie jumped in the passenger seat of his old Ford as Gordon slid behind the wheel. "Drive!"

"Whatever you say!" Gordon keyed the ignition, stepped on the gas. The tires screeched, the car shot forward. The Ford was more than it looked. Close as Maggie was to Gordon, she'd never ridden in his car. The Shore was a beach community, they walked everywhere.

He slid the car around a corner, drove like a man possessed. The Shore had stop signs on every other street. He ran them all. Suddenly he hung a right, slowed down, drove normally, turned on Ocean and headed toward downtown Long Beach.

"So, you're alive."

"Yeah." Maggie pulled the flight bag off her shoulder, stuffed the gun into it, then tossed it in the back. "The guy from the other night, the one with the ferret face. I just shot him."

"Annie Oakley," Gordon said.

"I guess," Maggie said. Then, "We have to go to Huntington Beach."

"Gotta make a short stop first." Gordon pulled a pack of cigarettes from the visor above his head, tapped one out on the wheel, pushed in the cigarette lighter.

"You don't smoke."

"Only when I drive." Gordon lit the cigarette, sucked in the smoke, exhaled. He looked at her, smiled. "Tell me about the hair." Gordon took another drag on the cigarette. They were out of the Shore now, in Long Beach. Gordon moved the car into the left lane, signaled when they approached the freeway, took the on ramp.

"I don't know where to start."

"Start from when you left the Whale and keep on going till you get to where we are right now. Take your time, we've got a ride ahead of us."

Maggie wanted to ask where they were going, but she didn't. Gordon had a right to know. She told him. It didn't take so long, just till Gordon turned onto the San Diego Freeway, headed toward the airport.

"Sit back, relax. I'll let you know when we get there," he said.

More than anybody, Maggie trusted Gordon. She closed her eyes, she was so tired. She opened them when Gordon glided the car off the freeway. She wasn't familiar with the area, Imperial or Roosevelt, up by the airport. Inglewood maybe. She was about to say something, but Gordon turned into a warehouse complex. One of those places where you store your stuff when you have nowhere else.

He guided the car to a post in front of a sliding gate, stuck his hand out the open window, punched some numbers on a keypad. The gate creaked open, the wheels needed oil. He drove past a row of warehouses with roll up garage doors and stopped when he came to the last one in the line of the first complex.

"Wait here. This won't take long." He got out of the car.

Maggie watched as he turned the dial on a combination lock. He missed the combination the first time. It was dark, after all. He tried again, pulled the lock open, took it off, pulled up the door.

He went inside, rolled the door down after himself. Maggie saw light creep out from underneath, heard noise, like he was moving boxes around. She looked around the warehouse complex. Dark. Spooky. She was in either the bad part of West L.A. or

Inglewood. Gangbanger territory. She didn't belong here, especially at night.

She hunched down in the seat even though there was no one to see her. Every few seconds a car went by on the street back by the sliding gate, but none stopped. She sighed, no one was coming in after her. Besides, she had the gun. She reached into the back, got the grip and got the Sigma out.

She ejected the clip, racked the slide and pumped out the one in the chamber. She emptied the clip, counted out ten rounds. The gun held sixteen, plus one in the chamber. She'd fired off seven at Nighthyde. She thumbed the rounds back into the clip, shoved the clip back in, then chambered a round. Loaded again, she sat up, gun in her left hand, ready for action.

She heard the creaking sound behind her, looked out the rear window. The gate was opening. A car cruised in. Slow. The headlights went off as soon as the car passed the gate. Whoever they were, they didn't want to be seen. Maggie ran her thumb along the butt of the Sigma. She'd shot a man tonight. She didn't want to do it again.

The car motored toward her. It was one of those gangbanger cars, lowered, darkened windows. It slowed to a crawl. Maggie felt her skin creep as it got closer. For a second she felt like slinking down in the seat, but she tossed off the thought. There were no other cars in the complex. If whoever was in that car was going to check out Gordon's car, they'd see her even if she scrunched down.

The car came closer. A Toyota, similar to the car she'd seen leaving the police station earlier. Kids out enjoying a hot night. She'd waved to them, got a thumbs up in return. Somehow she didn't think the kids in this car were going to be as friendly.

The car slowed even more as it approached, came along side, stopped. Maggie scooted over behind the wheel. The window was down. The Toyota's passenger window came down. She was facing a black youth, seventeen or twenty, she couldn't be sure. He was wearing the red bandanna of the Bloods. He smiled, he had a gold tooth. Top, left front. He ran his tongue across it. Maggie had never seen anything so sinister in real life.

"Hey sister, what'cha doin' out alone on such a dark night?"

"I'm not alone," Maggie said.

"Don't see no one." The kid was smirking.

"I have my nine millimeter friend with me and I've already killed one man tonight." She brought the gun up to the window, pointed it at the gold tooth. "So kissing your sweet ass goodbye would be like icing on the cake."

"Hey, we don't want no trouble." All of a sudden the kid's attitude went away.

"Well, you found it." She was shaking inside, but determined not to back down.

"You ain't the only one with a piece," the kid said.

"No, I suppose not." She smiled at the kid. "So should we start shooting now?"

"Leave the honky bitch," the driver said.

"You one lucky lady," the kid said.

"Luck is my middle name."

"Yeah," the kid smiled back as the roll-up door opened. The kid took one look at Gordon framed by the light coming from the inside of the warehouse and rolled up his window. The car eased away.

Maggie froze when she saw him. He was holding a pump shotgun in his hands, ready to use it.

"What was that about?" he said.

"Nothing, just some kids," Maggie said.

"Wearing Blood colors," Gordon said.

"Kids gotta have friends," Maggie said. "Maybe with a little direction they'll grow up to be fine young men."

"And maybe not." Gordon opened the back door, tossed the shotgun onto the back seat.

"Yeah, maybe not," Maggie said.

"I got some more stuff." He went back into the warehouse, came out with a couple of boxes. He put them into the back as well.

Maggie was torn between watching him and the kids in the Toyota. They stopped in front of a roll-up door in the next building.

"Probably where they stash their drugs." Gordon got in, started the car. "Good spot. Centrally located, safe from the cops."

"What do you mean?" Maggie said.

"They'd need a warrant to bust into one of these places," he said. The gate opened automatically as they approached. You needed the code to get in, anybody could get out. He looked in the mirror, turned and looked out the back window. "Yeah, the kid that went into the warehouse is coming out already."

Gordon drove out of the complex. The Toyota came up behind. Gordon turned left toward the freeway. The Toyota turned right toward the hood.

"What's in the boxes?" Maggie asked.

"Stuff from a former life," Gordon said.

"Former life?"

"I was in the FBI."

"They let you keep shit like that pump action in back?"

"Twenty years, you acquire stuff like that."

"So what else you got?"

"A couple kevlar vests, some Glocks, a twenty-two throw-down, some other stuff."

"So what'd you leave back in the warehouse, a tank?"

"No, it's mostly Ricky's things from before we were together. He had this horrid furniture. I like classy stuff."

Maggie nodded, he did like classy stuff. His apartment was tastefully furnished with restored antiques. Anyone would think he was wealthy if they saw his furniture. And it went with the image of a sophisticated gay man. The shotgun and the stuff in the boxes in back did not.

Gordon was the best friend she'd ever had, but she was beginning to wonder just how well she knew him.

"Police," Gordon said. A black-and-white was just ahead, coming toward them on the other side of the street. "Scoot over here. Act like we're lovers."

Maggie moved over next to Gordon, draped an arm over his shoulder, snuggled her head against him. She felt him turn toward the cruiser as they passed.

"It's okay now."

"What was that all about?"

"I got a beat up looking car. They expect that here, but if they see Joe Whitebread, they might wonder what he's doing in this neighborhood so late." Gordon had his eye on the mirror. "When they looked over and saw an old guy like me smile back with an obviously younger girl clinging to his neck, they assumed you were a hooker."

"How can you be so sure?"

"I told you, I was in the FBI. I know this kind of stuff. Besides, that's the kind of smile I gave them."

"That's so degrading."

"Uh oh," he said.

"What?"

"We have a tail."

"How?" Maggie turned around, saw headlights behind. Then the blue and red lights on the cop car came on.

"Turned his headlights on when he saw the black-and-white." Gordon slowed.

"What are we waiting for? Let's get out of here."

"I want to see how it goes." Gordon killed the lights, stopped in front of a two story white house, reversed and parallel parked between a pickup and a VW bus. He did it fast, like a pro, like a cop.

"I don't think this is a good idea." Maggie thought the house looked like it was once the proud home of an upper middle class family, but the ghetto had expanded, chasing the affluent out of the area. Now the house seemed to be falling apart. She imagined roaches and rats darting among babies crawling on the floor. She wanted to go.

"He must've been waiting outside my place," Gordon said.

"Let's go," Maggie said.

"I checked in the rearview when I was busting all those stop signs and didn't see anything. He was running without his headlights, otherwise I'd have spotted him."

"Should we be waiting here like this?"

"The cop let him go," Gordon said, ignoring her. "That was fast." Then, "Down!"

They ducked.

Gordon popped his head up as soon as the car passed. "Black BMW."

"What?" Maggie was up now, too.

"Your friend from earlier this evening."

"How can that be?"

"Good question." Gordon started the car, pulled away from the curb without turning on his lights.

"What are you going to do?"

"Do you have to ask?"

"I guess not." Maggie settled back, eyes on the Beemer's tail lights. "He's getting on the freeway?"

"Yeah." Gordon slowed, waited till the BMW was around the on ramp and out of sight before turning on his headlights. Then he accelerated through the ramp.

"This car really goes," Maggie said.

"A hot rod in disguise," Gordon said. "Four hundred twenty-seven cubic inches tuned to perfection under the hood. Holly four barrel carb. This old girl can do a hundred and fifty all day long and go from zero to sixty in six flat."

"So can a lot of cars these days, that BMW for instance."

"Yeah, but who'd expect it of a twenty-something year old Ford? Mechanically she's new, but she's ordinary looking, an old man's car."

"Gordon, nobody drives cars like this anymore."

"That car up there is a product of precision engineering, like the space shuttle. It's fast, it's flashy, it screams money. Ricky had a BMW when we met. I hated it, all that computer crap under the hood. Give me an old American car any day, something a human can understand. Besides, there's nothing like the feeling of four hundred cubic inches rumbling under the hood."

"You surprise me."

"What? I can't be macho?"

Maggie laughed as the BMW moved into the fast lane. Gordon did too. It felt good, laughing, but it was serious business they were about, the laughter was short.

"That bastard drove me into the bay." Maggie didn't want to forget that.

"Maybe not," Gordon said.

"What do you mean?"

"He followed you, sure. But that doesn't mean he meant you ill will."

"Sure he did, otherwise I wouldn't be here now."

"You said you noticed him right after you left the police station. How do you know he's not a cop? Maybe he was shadowing you for your own protection."

"In a BMW?"

"Coulda been a cop, you never know. I used a 450SL on a stake out once."

"Gordon, he chased me."

"Sounds more like you might've run. Why'd you do that?"

"I don't know." Maggie clenched her fists. "I just did."

"You could've driven back to the police station, or into a gas station, someplace with people."

"I didn't think of that."

"You will next time."

"So you think it was a cop?"

"In a BMW? Get serious."

"Gordon!"

"I said it coulda been, I didn't say it was. I was trying to make a point. You ran without thinking, and now you don't have a car. You had other options."

"So you don't think it was a cop?"

"No."

They followed the BMW as it got off the Long Beach Freeway at Lakewood Boulevard and they stayed a safe distance behind when it took the Traffic Circle onto Pacific Coast Highway. It stopped at an office building where PCH intersected Anaheim. Gordon drove on by.

"Now what?" Maggie said.

"We go back." Gordon turned, parked around the corner. He opened his door.

"You're not going in that building?"

"I'll be right back."

"I'm coming." Maggie reached over the seat, seeking the grip in back.

"Leave the gun."

"No." She pulled it out, got out of the car. She stuffed the gun between her Levi's and the small of her back, pulled the sweatshirt down over it just like she'd seen Thomas Magnum do so many times on TV reruns when she was in high school. "All right, let's go."

Gordon led her around to the front of the building, tried the door. "Didn't lock up after himself." He pushed through the glass doors.

"Don't these buildings have a security guard or something?" Maggie whispered.

"Five story office building, four or five offices to a floor—I don't think so. Custodian probably locks it around six, it would lock automatically after anyone leaving late, but if someone opened it with a key—"

"And forgot to lock it after himself—"

"Exactly," Gordon said.

Inside they were in a lobby, high ceiling, marble floor. A reception desk to the right of the double glass doors was empty now. Light from streetlamps outside gave the lobby an eerie feeling, like walking through a horror movie. Tingles rippled up Maggie's spine, turned to ice at the back of her neck.

"Look there." Gordon was pointing to a legend on the wall between double elevators.

"Long Beach City Bank, so what?" Maggie said. There was the bank, a travel agency and an Italian restaurant on the first floor.

"Third floor, Hightower, Private Investigators." He turned to her. "I need to know you're safe in the car."

"I'm coming with you."

"No argument. If you don't go to the car right now, we're leaving. Then we'll never know what the guy in the BMW was all about."

"Gordon."

"No, it was stupid of me to even let you get this far."

"I'm coming."

"No!" He was whispering, but he was firm. "I've been trained for this, you haven't. You'd be in the way."

"You sure?"

"Absolutely."

Maggie backed through the doors as Gordon entered a stairwell next to the elevators. She didn't want to go back to the car, but a part of her was secretly relieved. She'd had enough of guns and shooting to last her a lifetime. It was good that Gordon was taking over.

She got in the car.

Safe.

Thank God for Gordon.

She pulled the gun from its place behind her back and put it in the glove box. A car went past, lights splitting the dark. Only now did she realize how late it was. She looked at the dashboard clock. Midnight. How long had Gordon been up there? Maybe she should check on him.

But he'd said to stay in the car.

Ten minutes later she couldn't stand it anymore. He'd been gone too long. She got out of the car, walked to the office building, opened the door and stepped into the lobby. She looked up at the legend. The private investigator Gordon wanted to check out was on the third floor. She looked for the office number, but she saw something else. She took two steps forward, stood between the elevators, stared up and read.

**THE DISTRICT OFFICE OF THE 35TH CONGRESSIONAL DISTRICT
5TH FLOOR, ROOM 500.**

Now she knew where the man in the black BMW had gone and it wasn't to any private investigator on the third floor.

The elevator on the right started to move. She looked to the numbers above it. It was coming down from the fifth floor. She stood transfixed as it descended to the fourth floor, then the third. Any second it was going to open and she was going to be caught. She cast her eyes around the lobby, saw the reception desk and ran toward it.

She heard a bell tingle as she dove behind the desk. The floor was cold and hard. She took baby breaths that sounded jack-hammer loud to her ears, but she knew nobody else could hear.

A whoosh of sound hit her as the doors opened. Not loud, she told herself, not really.

"Everything is on track, except for your loose end." It was a radio voice, smooth and cultured.

"I'm gonna take care of it." A hard voice. Maggie wished she could see their faces, but no way was she going to risk popping her head up for a quick look.

"Soon, I trust." The radio voice again. Maggie shivered, because all of a sudden she recognized it, knew who it belonged to.

"You can count on me—" The hard voice was swallowed up with the sound of the front doors opening and a car passing by outside.

The doors closed, a sonic boom to her heart, then silence. She breathed a sigh of relief, cut it short when she heard someone charging down the stairwell behind her. Horrified she reached behind herself for the gun. It wasn't there. She'd left it in the car and any second someone was going to come bursting out of the stairwell and she'd be the first thing he saw, because although she'd been hidden from the elevators, she was in clear sight of the stairwell.

Nowhere to go. No time.

The door burst open.

He stopped, breathing hard, caught her with a hard glare.

"What are you doing here?" It was Gordon.

"I was worried?" Maggie pushed herself to her feet, brushed herself off.

"You should have stayed in the car."

"You took so long."

"I was waiting outside that PI's office. After a few minutes I figured out I made a mistake."

"A few minutes, more like fifteen." Maggie was whispering, but frantic.

"Not so loud. I heard the elevator, thought I could catch them," Gordon said. Then, "Did you get a look at them?"

"No."

"Damn!" Now Gordon was loud.

"But I know who it was, not the guy in the BMW, but the one he came to see."

"How?" Gordon said.

"Fifth floor." Maggie pointed up at the legend.

"What?" Gordon followed her finger. "The Congressional Office?"

"Yeah," Maggie said, "the Congressional Office, you know, where the Honorable J.L. Nishikawa works when he's in the district."

"Johnny Nishikawa got the medal of honor in Vietnam," Gordon said. " He's honest to a fault, beyond reproach. You've gotta be mistaken, that can't be where the BMW guy went."

"He was talking to someone when he went out. I heard his voice. It was him, I know, I've heard him enough times on television."

"The only thing that proves is the congressman was in his office tonight. The guy in the BMW could still be up there."

"No, the other guy sounded like the man who followed me into the liquor store."

"You sure?"

"I bet the Beemer's gone," Maggie said.

"Let's see." Gordon crossed the lobby, pushed his way through the double doors, looked down the street. The BMW was gone.

"I forgot to tell you something." Maggie passed him, got in his Ford.

He got in after her, slid behind the wheel. "What?"

She told him about Ichiro Yamamoto who used to work for Congressman Nishikawa and who went to the police with a story about conflict diamonds and weapons. She told him about the man Striker, who used to be Nishikawa's administrative assistant and now worked for Nakano Construction, which used Yakuza money. And she told him that Ichiro Yamamoto was in that convenience store when Frankie Fujimori was shot to death.

"That was a lot to leave out," he said when she'd finished.

Chapter Sixteen

Jesus wept, he'd been shot. His head was ringing. Horace couldn't hear. He forced himself out of the fetal position, struggled to sit, back against the wall. He had to move, any second the place was gonna to be crawling with cops. Pain wracked his side. He put a hand inside his jacket, pulled it out. Wet, sticky. Blood.

Using the wall as support, he fought his way to his feet. Standing, he took a few breaths. The breathing hurt, but he didn't taste blood, didn't think he'd been lung shot. He moved along the wall to the kitchen. The room was spinning. The pain was intense. He left a bloody trail across the carpet from the bathroom to the dining room, then across the white kitchen tile.

Bloody prints on the knob as he opened the back door. More prints on the rail. Thank God for the gloves. Blood on the stairs as he stumbled down the steps. Blood on the side of the garage as he scooted around it. Blood on the wall. Blood on the driveway. So much blood.

He climbed up into the van, expecting any second to be bathed in light, covered in guns as hands wrested him to the ground. But it didn't happen. Lights came on. But they were lighting up the front of the house. No one out back. He fumbled the key into the ignition.

He was barely conscious as he drove down Lakewood Boulevard toward the motel. Blood ran down his face, getting in his eyes. He couldn't understand that, he'd been shot in the side. He pulled off the surgical gloves, ran a hand against the wet on his forehead. It came back sticky.

A head wound and it was throwing blood like a squall does rain. He'd been shot twice. How could he have been so dumb? The house felt alive because it was. He'd never even considered the bathroom. And the woman had been there all along, with that gun, waiting. Was she clairvoyant or something?

He passed the turn to the airport, turned into the motel parking lot, parked in front of his room, grateful the place was doing lousy business. In the room he hustled to the bath, stood before the mirror. He bit his lip to keep from passing out. He looked like he'd lost a fight with a Rottweiler or something worse, an alligator. He ran water in the sink, wetted a washcloth and went to work.

He'd heard head wounds bleed worse than they are, and now he knew it was true. It was only a graze, but it took the better part of an hour to clean up and stop the flow of blood. He should have stitches, but hospitals and doctors had to report gunshot wounds to the cops. He'd suffer enough for ten men before he'd allow that. He'd been busted before, barely escaped jail. That's all he wanted of that. The thought of it sent cold blades knifing up his spine.

He still had the wound in his side to worry about. He should get the bomber jacket off and give it a look, but it would have to wait. Besides, it didn't hurt too much now. He left the bathroom, started toward the phone, took two steps, got light-headed, the room started spinning. He turned, grabbed onto the door jamb, held himself up. The nausea passed in a few seconds. He took slow steps to the bed, sat and eased his way to the phone on the nightstand.

He punched nine, then Striker's number.

No answer.

Horace clenched his teeth, stood and went back to the bathroom where he pulled off the jacket. He didn't want to get blood all over the motel room, too. The bloody shirt came after the jacket. He tossed it in the wastebasket. Then he took the still damp washcloth and dabbed at the wound. The bleeding had stopped. Another graze, but it hurt like hell.

His lucky night.

"Not," he grumbled. He'd been shot, no luck there. But it could have been so much worse. Maybe he was lucky after all. Lucky the broad was such a lousy shot.

Convinced he didn't have to go to the hospital, he picked the bomber jacket up from the floor, turned it inside out and scrubbed as much of the blood off the lining as he could with hand soap and the washcloth. Then he hung it over the shower railing. He loved that jacket.

He couldn't have the maid come in tomorrow morning and find blood in the sink, so he washed it up. Then he rinsed out the cloth, wrung it out, dumped it in the trash.

The bathroom clean, he examined his wounds again. Although the bleeding had stopped, they were going to have to be bandaged or it would start up as soon as he strained himself or bumped into something. Besides, he could hardly walk around with that gash in his forehead.

In pain, but able to walk, he went out to the van, that too he was going to have to clean, but it could wait till he took care of himself. He had no first aid kit, but he had a tool box and in it a roll of duct tape. Back in the bathroom, he folded a clean washcloth and duct taped it over the wound on his side. Then using a utility knife from the tool box, he cut a one by two inch piece from one of the motel towels, placed it over the wound on his forehead and taped it into place.

Finished, he studied his handiwork in the mirror above the sink. He looked daring, he thought, like a pirate with that great hunk of grey tape covering his forehead. And unforgettable. That wasn't good. He had more work to do this night, and if seen, he didn't want to be remembered.

Horace left the bathroom, went to the closet where he pulled another pair of slacks from a hanger, another silk shirt. At the bureau he took out a clean pair of Jockey shorts. He slipped off his loafers, stripped the pants and underwear from his body. Thought about a shower, rejected the idea. He didn't want to get the makeshift dressings wet. Then he put on the clean clothes and cleaned the blood out of the van, but he couldn't clean away what he was setting out to do. Horrible as it was, he had no choice.

Twenty minutes later he drove by the Ocean View Towers on Ocean Avenue, a nineteen story luxury apartment complex on the beach. He parked half a block away and took the steps down to the beach. Stars lit the sky, the moon was up, a sliver of a sideways smile. He was on the sand, two stories below Ocean Avenue. He walked along the bike trail toward the Towers.

He missed his bomber jacket. He hated stuff in his pants pockets. Shit in pockets broke up the natural look of his profile, made him look cheap. He pulled the picks out of a hip pocket, grit his teeth and sauntered up to the Tower's beach door. He had it open in seconds.

Inside he walked through an underground parking garage. He was breathing heavily now, his side on fire. Walking was difficult, painful, as if stabs of hot fire were shooting from his side down his right leg with every step. He couldn't walk without a limp. He caught his reflection in a round overhead mirror used to warn residents of cars coming around the ramp from the floor above. He looked like a stroke victim.

He shuffled to the elevator. Lifting his feet caused bolts of pain in his side. He pushed the call button. After a minute that seemed like a month the doors opened. It was empty. He stepped in, pushed the button for the seventeenth floor.

During the ride up he tried to shut out the pain. Eyes closed, he imagined a cool place. A ski lodge in the mountains. A log fire, girls laughing, drinking. By the time the doors opened he was focused, the pain gone, for now. He didn't know the time, didn't have a watch, but he guessed it was around midnight, maybe a little later. He was taking a chance, he knew it. He'd left the Beretta back at the motel in case he got stopped by a cop because his driving wasn't what it should be. A cop saw the tape on his forehead, he might search the van. Busted with a handgun was the last thing he needed.

He walked out of the elevator toward the Wolfe apartment. He stopped at the door, listened for the sound of a television, music, anything. Nothing was what he heard. Odds were they were asleep. Horace always played the odds. Again the picks were out.

Inside the place was dark. He stood still as stone, left the door open a crack. He heard the steady breathing of someone deep in sleep coming from the back of the apartment. Horace slipped off his loafers, walked to the full window that ran the length of the living room, looked out upon the beach, the sky, stars, the moon.

This was the kind of view he could have if it wasn't for Ma. She insisted on staying in Lakewood. And like a good son, Horace couldn't leave her. He saw the lights of a small plane over the ocean. A night flyer. Horace loved flying in the dark. The sense of freedom.

All of a sudden he knew how he was going to do the kid. At first he'd planned on quietly smothering him in his sleep, but now he didn't know if he could keep holding the pillow while the kid struggled.

There was a balcony to the right of the living room. Horace eased open the sliding glass door. It wasn't locked. Stupid Mom. He stepped out into the night, went to the railing, looked down at the beach below.

Time for work.

Back in the apartment, he followed the sound of the sleepy breathing. There was a bedroom at the end of a hall. Mom was curled all scrunched up with the covers. He backed out of her bedroom, found the kid's room across from the bathroom.

Horace stood in the doorway for a second, then took three quick steps into the room and was at the kid's bedside. A blanket went up to the kid's waist. Horace pulled it down. It would be best if he could do this without waking him. A small mercy. Horace scooped his hands under the tiny body, lifted it.

A silent gasp as pain racked his ribs. Horace clenched his teeth as he made his way out to the living room. He moved though the apartment like an apparition, silent and quick. In seconds he was out on the balcony. The kid was still asleep. Horace resisted an urge to kiss his forehead.

The kid opened his eyes. Wide, afraid.

Horace tossed the boy into the night.

He fought puking his guts out as he took the elevator down to the parking garage. Outside, back on the beach, he heard someone screaming. Head down, he jogged along the bike trail to the stairs up to Ocean Boulevard. He pulled away from the curb expecting sirens. He didn't hear them till he was past the Safeway where Virgil had grabbed onto that bitch's shopping cart.

If only he could go back and live that few minutes over, Virge would still be alive.

He turned into the Safeway parking lot, parked and locked the van. He crossed the lot to the country and western bar where he'd hoped to catch the bitch. Inside he ordered a tequila shooter. He passed on the salt and lime, drank it straight down, ordered another. Then he saw the pay phone on the wall at the end of the bar.

"Got quarters?" He dropped a dollar on the bar.

Ken Douglas

"Guy over there's been playing the juke all night," the weightlifter of a bartender said.

"It's for the phone." Horace turned, saw a slim guy with dirty jeans and unkempt hair drop quarters into the jukebox. Springsteen started singing 'Born in the USA.' "A sign." Horace tossed the second drink down.

"What?" the bartender said.

"It's a sign. My brother's favorite song. He's trying to tell me something."

"You want another shooter?"

"Naw. I was gonna call my boss, then get drunk, but now I'm gonna call a girl instead."

"I hear ya." He put four quarters on the bar.

"Wish me luck." Horace scooped up the coins, headed for the phone. Most things Horace forgot right away, but he had a head for phone numbers.

"This better be good," Sadie said instead of hello. "It's the middle of the night and I have to work in the morning."

"Sorry, I wasn't thinking."

"Horace?"

"You know my voice?"

"I don't exactly tell all the men I meet to call. Of course I know your voice."

Horace was flattered. "I'm in kind of a spot, plus I feel about as low as hound dog at the bottom of an outhouse."

"That sounds pretty low."

"I could use some company."

"Where are you?"

"You know that cowboy bar out by the pier?"

"Give me ten minutes." She hung up.

Now his wounds didn't hurt so much. He signaled the bartender, raised a finger to let him know he wanted another drink. He gulped the shooter, then dialed Striker's number. He wanted business out of the way before he saw Sadie. Striker sounded like he was out of breath when he answered. Horace told him about his evening.

"So you okay?" Striker said when Horace was finished with the telling.

"I think so." He ran his hand along the wound in his side. "Feels like the bullet seared along my rib cage, like I was cut with a knife, but it didn't enter. And I got a graze on the forehead, bled like a pig, but I got it under control. I just saw that gun in her hand and started back-peddling. I was lucky. That's one tough bitch."

"And you say she looks like the Kenyon woman?"

"I only got a quick look, but yeah, except for the hair, it's her. Must be twins, only thing I can think of."

"Margo Kenyon didn't have any sisters. Maggie Nesbitt didn't either."

"They sure look alike," Horace said.

"They say everyone's got a double," Striker said. Then, "Regarding the gunshots. You should be in the clear. A black-and-white responded. Neighbors heard shots, but nobody knew from where."

"How do you know this stuff so fast?"

"I was a cop a long time. I got friends."

"I left a lot of my blood up there."

"Any prints?"

"No."

"So, it's not a problem. When the news guy gets home and sees the mess, he'll call the cops, but so what?"

"What about the woman?"

"That is a problem." Striker told Horace about the woman he'd followed into the liquor store and how she had dark hair. Then he told him about the car chase and how he saw the Porsche crash into the sea. "But apparently she didn't die," he added, "because I was outside that duplex. I heard the shots and saw the same woman run out. I followed her and the guy from downstairs out to a warehouse by the airport, then I lost 'em."

"So who's the broad, the news guy's wife or the Kenyon bitch?" Horace said.

"She was Margo Kenyon this morning and Maggie Nesbitt this evening," Striker said.

"Something real hinky is going on."

"Yeah," Striker said.

"What do you want me to do?"

"Stay put. I'll put the Japs on it. They've been dying to help, now we'll find out if they're as good as they say they are."

"No, I started it, I'll finish it."

"When?"

"This time tomorrow she'll be toast. You can count on it." Horace didn't want the Japs involved. If they took care of it, maybe Striker wouldn't need him anymore.

"All right. I'll keep them in reserve. And don't blame yourself about tonight, no way you coulda known she'd be in the bathroom with a gun. It was just bad luck."

"Yeah, bad luck." Horace grimaced. His side was killing him.

"Stay cool," Striker said. "If we pull this off, we're gonna have enough money to go live on a Caribbean island for the rest of our lives, sun, sea and more girls than you'll know what to do with."

"Right."

Striker hung up.

Horace thought about the conversation as he replaced his own receiver. Striker had talked to him like a partner, not like an employee. Why did he do that? Was there a lot more in this for him, or was Striker just setting him up? He sighed. And how come Striker took off following the broad after he'd heard the gunshots? Who the fuck did he think the bitch was shooting at anyway?

Horace shrugged. Maybe Striker didn't hear the shots. Maybe he did and didn't think about the consequences. Whatever, point is he'd never known Striker to lie. If he said there was gonna be a big payoff, there was gonna be a big payoff.

For a second his thoughts were clouded with the boy. That was bad. No kid should have to die. But then he thought about what Striker had said. The sun, sea and more girls than he could count. Sometimes sacrifices had to be made.

"Horace." Sadie climbed up on the barstool next to him.

"Hi." He touched the makeshift bandage on his forehead with a finger, then put the finger to his lips.

"Gotcha." She knew enough not to say anything in front of others. Horace admired that.

"Let's get a booth."

"No, let's go to my place. You look like you could use some serious attention."

"Nobody's ever asked me to their place just like that."

"We'll talk about it after we get there. Come on." She took his hand and led him to the door.

"My van's in the Safeway lot." Horace had trouble walking straight.

"We'll take mine. How much have you had to drink?"

"Three shooters. It's mostly shock." He looked across the street, pointed at his van. "Will they tow it?"

"Not until it's been there a couple days." She opened the passenger door to a baby blue, beat up Toyota.

Horace got in.

Two minutes and two blocks later she parked in front of a single family house on Bennett Avenue. The house was sandwiched between a duplex and an apartment building. The apartments looked new. The Shore was crowded, parking was at a premium.

"How'd they get the zoning?" Horace said as she put on the parking brake.

"Owner's brother knows somebody on the city council." She got out of the car.

"Figures," Horace muttered. He got out too, followed her up the walk.

The house was built in the '30s. The furniture looked like it was from the same period, from the sofa and the wing chairs to the baby blue, flower print carpet. Horace shook his head. The rug was the same color as the car. She turned toward him, smiled. Her eyes, too.

"What happened to you?" She wasn't accusing, just inquisitive.

"I was shot."

She gasped. "Did you call the police?"

"I can't. It was a cop that did it."

She gasped again.

"It's not what you think. I was working for his wife, trying to catch him with a hooker in one of those motels downtown. You know the type, they play dirty movies, have mirrored ceilings and waterbeds. Anyway," Horace continued with the bullshit, "I bribed the desk clerk for the key. I figured to open the door, get a couple of shots with my Nikon, and be out of there before he had a chance to get his pants on. But it didn't work out the way I planned."

"What happened?" She was all ears now.

"He started shooting the second I pushed the door open. Got me twice, the forehead and a grace across my side. If I wouldn't a started back peddling so fast, I'd a been a dead man."

"I used to be a nurse. Let me see."

Horace shed his shirt and submitted himself to her care. She rebandaged and dressed the wounds.

"You are an awful lucky man. You're going to have a scar on your forehead if you don't get stitches, but the wound in your side will heal nicely without them.

"Really?"

"Really," she said.

"I've always been lucky." Horace didn't know what else to say. He'd never been good with women. Besides, they usually didn't like him. This one apparently did.

She gave him a smile. "You wanna mess around?" She was wearing a baby-blue T-shirt, same as the eyes, carpet and car. She pulled it over her head. She wasn't wearing a bra.

"It's never happened for me like this." He felt like the PI he said he was. No, like James Bond, he felt like James Bond. A secret agent man who couldn't take his eyes off her tits. Not big, but not small either. He forced his eyes up to her face. She wasn't as young as he'd thought and she looked a little road weary, thin and a bit hard, like maybe she did speed, but hell he wasn't no angel himself.

"Let's go into the bedroom," she said as she kicked off loosely tied, black high top tennis shoes. "I mean, if you want." She pushed down her jeans. She wasn't wearing panties either.

On the bed she pulled off his shoes and socks. Then his pants. She left the light on and he couldn't take his eyes off her. He lay on his back as she mounted him and watched her pupils dilate as she moaned her pleasure. But his own pleasure was dulled by thoughts of what he was going to do to the Kenyon-Nesbitt woman tomorrow night.

He wished he really was a private investigator, wished he'd never met Striker. But then he thought of the payoff Striker promised as she rocked him to completion.

He moaned himself.

Tomorrow was the last time. He had to do it because he needed the money. Then he'd take Sadie with him somewhere far away, maybe the Caribbean like Striker said. Maybe they'd get a boat, sail the seas. He'd never done that, but how hard could it be?

"What'cha thinking, sweetie?" She was maybe forty-five or so, but every line on her face lit up with her smile.

"You wanna learn how to sail?" he said. Then he fell asleep.

Chapter Seventeen

"Mom!" Jasmine shook Maggie's shoulder. "There's a man sleeping on the sofa."

Maggie opened her eyes. Bright sun streamed in the bedroom window. She squinted at the clock. Eight-fifteen.

"Who is it?" Jasmine asked.

"Yeah, who is it?" Sonya echoed.

"His name's Gordon. He's a friend of mine and he's pretty tired, so please don't wake him."

"We're gonna be late for school," Jasmine said. She'd spent the night with Sonya. Maggie was supposed to pick her up when she got back from the police station, but she didn't get home till after midnight, so she decided to let it wait till morning. She hoped Gay didn't mind.

"Where's your mother?" Maggie said to Sonya.

"She had to go into the beauty shop. They have to get the books ready for the tax man, 'coz he's gonna do an audit. My mom hates taxes," Sonya said.

"Everybody hates taxes, right mom?" Jasmine said.

"Yeah, they do. Look, why don't you guys go out to the kitchen and get yourselves something to eat while I get up."

"We already ate," Jasmine said. "Besides, Sonya has to leave right away or she's gonna miss the school bus, so come on, get up or I'll be late."

"How come I have to drive you when there's a bus?"

"Is this another one of those things you don't remember?" Jasmine said.

"Yeah, it is."

"You don't like me riding the bus."

"And why's that?"

"You were in a bus accident when you were a little girl. A bunch of kids were killed. That's why."

"Ah," Maggie said. "You must have thought I was pretty paranoid."

"What's that mean?" Jasmine said.

"It means you're always afraid of stuff that's not gonna happen," Sonya said. "My mom used to be like that all the time, but she's getting better."

"So, now it's okay? You know, if I take the bus with Sonya?" Jasmine said.

"I think so."

"Cool."

"You're gonna love it," Sonya said to Jasmine as they scampered out of the room.

* * *

Horace rolled out of bed, padded into the bathroom nude, raised the toilet seat and pissed. Finished, he lowered the seat. Ma was always real sticky about that. Light eased in the bathroom window and made the pink shower curtains glow. Pink bathroom rug too. It was something Horace wasn't used to, a feminine place.

He stuck his head out the door. Sadie was still asleep. He wondered would it be okay to use the shower. He raised an arm, sniffed. Yeah, it'd be okay. He pulled the curtain aside, adjusted the water to warm, got in, used her soap under his arms, between his legs.

"I got some new shampoo." Sadie stepped into the shower. "Close your eyes." He did and she poured a healthy amount onto his hair, then massaged his scalp, making lather.

"Feels good," he said. No one had ever done that for him. He'd showered with women after sex in the past, but always before it had been in a motel, and it had been get in the shower, get clean and get out—out of the shower, out of the motel room. Sadie couldn't leave, this was her home and she wasn't showing any signs of wanting him to go.

Finished with his hair, she poured some shampoo onto her hand and started up between his legs. This was a definite first and he was hard in a heartbeat. Then she was on her knees and took him in her mouth. He moaned with the pleasure of it. He ran his hands through her hair, fought against release, but after a few minutes he was unable to control it and he let go.

"Ummm," she gurgled.

Then she was on her feet and into his arms, kissing him. He tasted himself on her lips and it tasted good. He was hard again. She laughed as he pushed into her.

Afterwards, over breakfast of coffee and toast, he asked her if he could borrow her car for the day. "I have to follow someone and they might recognize my van."

"Not the cop that shot you?"

"That's the one," Horace said.

"You're going to be careful," she said.

"After last night, you bet."

They traded keys and Horace took her beat up Toyota to Huntington Beach. He wanted to get the business with the Kenyon-Nesbitt woman over with. He needed the money Striker promised for Ma's medical bills, that was true, but now he had something else to live for, some kind of life to look forward to.

* * *

Maggie pulled off the bedspread, rolled out of bed. She took off the pajamas she'd found in Margo's bureau and headed toward the bathroom, ignoring her image in the full length mirror on the closet door as she passed. She didn't need confirmation to know she looked as worn out as she felt. There might be bags under her eyes, but she didn't have to see them.

After she'd showered and changed into a pair of the Levi's and a sweatshirt that she'd heisted from Nick's apartment, she went out into the living room, where she found Gordon sitting on the sofa, reading the *Los Angeles Times*. He lowered the paper as she came into the room.

"It's a new day," he said. "I've made coffee."

"You look like you're about to give me the third degree." She saw a steaming cup on the coffee table.

She picked it up, smelled the aroma. It was just what she needed.

"I am. You told me most of it last night, but now I want to hear it again. I want you to take it slow, leave nothing out, no matter how insignificant you think it is."

She sat in one of the rattan chairs, sipped at the coffee, then started to talk. She told him everything, from when she ran into Nighthyde in the Safeway, to when she faced down the gangbangers last night in the warehouse complex.

"Now you know everything I do," she said when she'd finished.

"So," he said, "the Chicano cop Alvarez gets a long sought after transfer to London. The next day Norton's mother commits suicide in Catalina and he quits the Frankie Fujimori case." Gordon spoke in a quiet voice. "Two cops taken off the case. It's almost as if somebody wanted it to fall through the cracks."

"Maybe you could look at it that way," Maggie said. "But even with Norton and Alvarez gone, it wouldn't fall thorough the cracks, as you say. Norton was going to give the case to someone who would follow up on it. A Lt. Wolfe."

"Wolfe?" Gordon got up, went to the kitchen.

"What?" Maggie said, following.

"I had a late cup of coffee with him the night before last. He's the cop in charge of solving your murder." He told her about how he was one of the first on the scene when Margo's body was discovered and about his conversation with the detective.

The phone was wall mounted, next to the refrigerator. Gordon picked it up. "Wolfe gave me his home phone number and he said to call anytime." Gordon pushed buttons. "Hello, my name is Gordon Takoda. Can I speak to Lt. Wolfe?" he said into the phone. Then, after a few seconds, "I'm so sorry, I know what it's like to lose someone you love. Please give him my condolences." He hung up.

"That was his mother." Gordon was barely breathing. "Lt. Wolfe and his wife were separated. Marriage problems, that's what she said."

"Go on."

"Last night his two-year-old son somehow climbed out on the balcony at the Oceanview Towers where he was living with his mother. He supposedly climbed the rail and fell seventeen stories to his death. It happened sometime around midnight. The boy's screams on the way down woke the neighbors. They woke the mother. She took her life before the police arrived. Shot herself."

"Oh, my God." She followed him back to the living room, sat in one of the rattan chairs.

"After losing his wife and son, I doubt he'll be doing much police work." Gordon sat in the other. Then, "It's too much coincidence. Someone wants the police off the Fujimori case, somebody with a lot of connections."

"They'll just give it to someone else." Maggie gripped her hands together, squeezed tightly. "That's what Norton said."

"What else did he say?" Gordon was looking at her with an intense look she'd never seen before.

"He said it would be given a low priority. As far as they're concerned, Frankie Fujimori got what was coming to him. Wolfe would've tried to sort it out, but no one else will. He was clear about that."

"It's incredible," Gordon said. "Someone wants a detective taken off a case, so he kills a family member and the cop takes time off. Not once, but twice, if it works with Wolfe."

"We don't know for sure that's what happened." Maggie didn't want to believe what she was hearing. "Besides, they couldn't be sure it would work. And even if Norton or Wolfe took leave, they might come back and pick up where they left off."

"Maybe, but probabloy not," he said. "People get murdered all the time. A homicide detective takes a couple weeks away from his desk and a whole new batch of murders are waiting for him when he gets back."

"But it's so uncertain, why not just kill the cops if you want them off the case?" Maggie said.

"Killing cops is a big no no," Gordon said. "Police get very upset about that. But an old woman commits suicide, who knows why, maybe she was depressed. A kid falls off a balcony, a tragic accident. His mother kills herself, more tragedy. But not crimes, nothing for the police to look into."

"This is crazy talk," Maggie said. "You're making this sound like some kind of conspiracy or something."

"It sounds like one to me," he said.

"Come on, listen to yourself. This kind of stuff doesn't happen!"

"I spent twenty years in the FBI and I'm here to say that it has and it does," Gordon said.

Maggie didn't answer.

"I spent a good part of my life wondering who killed Kennedy," he went on. "I believe in conspiracies."

"I don't. I can't," she whispered.

"Maggie," he said, "you were followed from the store, chased on the beach, followed from the police station by the black BMW, your car was run into the bay, this Nighthyde character came at you with a gun, and the black BMW came after us again last night.

Add all that to the fact Margo was killed and her body dumped behind a bar you'd left only a couple hours before, and that ought to tell you the person after you is a little more connected than some crazy who walked into a convenience store and blew away a little shit like Frankie Fujimori."

He got out of the chair, stood over her. "And you put all that together with the one cop's transfer and the bad things that happened to the families of the other two and you have a serious looking conspiracy."

"Then we should call the FBI," Maggie said. "They'd put a stop to this right away."

"Yes, they would," Gordon said. "If they believed you."

"Why wouldn't they?"

"Who'd go to the FBI, Maggie Nesbitt or Margo Kenyon?" he said.

"Oh."

"Yeah." He sat back down. "You'd have to come clean. And that means you go back to being Maggie Nesbitt and that little girl goes to live with her father and you said you didn't want that. And I wouldn't be surprised if they found some way to implicate you in Margo's murder."

"How could they?"

"Lots of motive," he said. "Margo's money for example."

"And I get to keep the baby," she said.

"What baby?" Gordon said.

Maggie told him. It had been the one part of the story she'd left out.

"I had no idea." He picked up his cup from the coffee table, took a deep drink. "So I guess we have to solve this ourselves if you're going to keep on being Margo."

"I guess."

"The first thing we have to do is find somewhere else for you to live in case this guy Nighthyde comes after you again."

"He's not going to come," Maggie said. "I shot him, remember?"

"Let me call Nick and find out about that." Gordon got out of his chair again.

"No," Maggie said. "I don't want to involve him."

"Okay, I got a friend who's a cop in Long Beach. I'll call him."

She followed him back to the kitchen, back to the phone. She listened while he called the Long Beach Police Department, asked for his friend, then identified himself. He lied, saying he was away last night and when he returned home one of his neighbors had told him there was a shooting. He listened for about a minute, thanked his friend and hung up.

"You did shoot someone," he told Maggie.

"Of course I did."

"But you didn't kill him. The police rolled on a shots fired complaint. When they got to the duplex, the neighbors were up, but nobody knew where the shots had come from. When Nick came home, he saw the blood and called the police. There was no body, so whoever you shot either got up and walked away, or someone carried him."

"I fired off seven rounds at him," Maggie said.

"So, you're not a very good shot."

"I saw blood."

"That doesn't mean he's dead." Gordon set his coffee cup down. "I'm going to see an old friend and find out what I can about Congressman Nishikawa. I'll be back before noon. Till then I want you to stay inside with the door locked. Shoot anyone who tries to break in or pick the lock." He was serious.

"You won't get an argument out of me on that," she said.

"I mean it," he said.

"What kind of friend?"

"One that won't talk in front of you, otherwise I'd bring you along."

"He got up, started for the front door, opened it, turned back toward her. "When I get back, we'll have to find someplace for Jasmine to stay till this is over."

"What about me? I thought you wanted me to move out, too."

"I changed my mind. You're staying here."

"Why? I don't get it."

"We're after a big fish. We need bait."

"I don't think I like the sound of that."

"I hate it," he said. "But we don't have much choice if we want to put an end to this without involving the police." And all of a sudden Maggie knew what Gordon was going to do.

"You're going to kill him, aren't you?"

"Yes I am." Then Gordon closed the door and she was alone.

***

Horace went straight to the motel, got his gun, then drove to the Taco Bell on Fourth Street. Coffee and toast didn't cut it for breakfast. He ordered five tacos and a large coke, then went to the pay phone in the back to call Striker. He dropped a quarter into the phone.

"Did you mean what you said yesterday?" he said when Striker picked up.

"If I said it, I meant it, but what specifically are you talking about?"

"Having more money than I can count." Horace felt his knuckles turning white as he gripped the phone. He relaxed his hand.

"Maybe not more than you can count, but you do the woman before tomorrow at this time and I'll have a briefcase for you with a hundred and fifty large in it. Twenty-five for the woman in Catalina, twenty-five for the kid and a hundred for the Kenyon woman."

"I already did the Kenyon woman."

"She's still walking around."

"She won't be tomorrow." Horace grit his teeth. Striker was paying a lot, but it wasn't right about the bitch in the alley. He'd done the job, he deserved to be paid. Besides, he didn't like thinking Virgil died for nothing.

"That's what I wanted to hear." Striker sounded smug.

"I might wanna take a vacation after."

"I understand," Striker said.

"Anything I should know?"

"They haven't pulled her car out of the bay yet, so the cops don't know it was hers."

"She didn't call 'em?" Horace tightened his grip on the phone again.

"No."

"What's that tell you?" Horace said.

"She knows someone's coming for her and she doesn't want the police involved. She's not afraid."

"She's gonna to be ready. That what you're saying?"

"Maybe," Striker said.

"Shit."

"Exactly."

"That's why you're paying so much?"

"If it was easy, I wouldn't need you."

"Okay, but I want twenty-five extra for the bitch in the alley," Horace said. "Fair's fair."

"Deal, but I want the Kenyon woman dead by tomorrow."

"She'll be dead." Horace hung up and went to get his tacos.

***

Maggie took her coffee out to the kitchen, washed the cups. She went to the refrigerator to get some ice and saw the Winnie the Pooh magnet for the first time. There were three yellow Post It notes under it.

She lifted the magnet and pulled the notes off the door. The top one was a reminder for Margo to pick up the cleaning from the Main Street Cleaners on Monday. Yesterday, Maggie thought. The second was to remind her to take the car in for a five thousand mile check up. Maggie laughed, she wouldn't be doing that. *Mom's new address* was scrawled across the top of the last one, followed by an address on Balboa Island.

She went to the bedroom, picked up Margo's purse, then stopped herself. It was way too dressy for faded Levi's and a sweatshirt. She grabbed the backpack, dumped out the school books, then dumped the contents of the purse into the pack. She reached under the pillow, pulled out the Sigma, put it in the pack, too.

Yes, she'd promised Gordon she'd stay inside with the door locked, but Balboa was a straight shot down Pacific Coast Highway on the bus. She could get there, talk to Margo's mother, and be back way before Gordon.

She jogged up to the guard shack, returned the guard's wave, then saw a bus glide into the bus stop.

"Hey, wait!" She ran to the stop, caught the bus just in time.

*　*　*

Horace was about to make a pass by the Sand and Sea Condos, when he saw the Kenyon-Nesbitt woman with the new hair running to catch a bus.

She sure wasn't acting like she was expecting trouble. Not a bit like a woman who'd had her car run into the bay only last night. How come she didn't call the cops, scream bloody murder? She wasn't making any sense.

He let a car get between him and the bus. No problem following. Horace fingered the Beretta in the shoulder holster under his sport coat. He missed the bomber jacket, but she'd seen him in it last night. Besides, it had a bullet hole in it and he wasn't able to get all the blood off it.

He wished he'd had a chance to change the plates on the Toyota, then he could just drive by when she got off the bus and pop her. But he hadn't, and he sure as hell didn't want anyone writing down Sadie's license number.

He couldn't see the woman in the bus, but he'd see her when she got off. "Then what?" he muttered. He couldn't very well follow her on foot. She'd gotten a good look at him in that stop-and-rob in Long Beach and again in that Safeway.

All of sudden he pictured her in the supermarket, the way she looked at him. She wasn't scared. Upset, annoyed, bent outta shape, all that, but not afraid. He tried to concentrate and keep his eyes on the road at the same time, and then he saw the picture in his mind, sure as if he'd been lying in bed with his eyes closed, sure as if he was back in that supermarket. She wasn't afraid when he'd smacked Virge with that magazine, she was relieved.

"Shit!" He pounded the steering wheel. The woman in the Safeway was the news guy's wife. When she got away, him and Virge went to the Condos in Huntington Beach and grabbed the other one and, not knowing the difference, Horace left the body by the dumpster in back of the fag place.

"Shit, shit, shit!" He pounded the steering wheel with each outburst. Striker had him kill the woman in Catalina and the kid at the Towers so the cops wouldn't follow up on the case with the Kenyon woman and she'd been dead all along.

"What a fuckup," he moaned. That old woman, the kid, dead for nothing. Horace just wanted out, wanted to go away with Sadie. But it wasn't gonna happen, not unless he did the woman on the bus. "Calm," he told himself. His hands were white on the wheel. He relaxed his fingers, one at a time, without taking his eyes off the back of that bus.

Twenty minutes later he was fit to be tied. Driving like an old lady had never been his style, but there was no other way without passing the fucking bus. He wondered how far it went. All the way to San Diego? He hoped not.

It pulled to the stop before Balboa Island and she hopped off. He floored it, passed the bus, hung a right in front of it and took the bridge to Balboa. Where else could she be going?

He found a spot in front of a surf shop, parked and waited. It didn't take long before he spotted her. She looked like a college kid strolling up the street with that backpack slung over her shoulder.

She walked right past the Toyota and went into the surf shop. Horace could see her in the store plain as the steering wheel in front of his eyes. A pimply faced kid behind the counter was talking, pointing. She was asking directions.

Horace hoped she bought something good while she was in there, because if he had his way, it was the last time she was ever gonna do any shopping. He clenched his fists on the wheel, then whipped his head around and pretended he was looking out the back window as she turned toward him and came out of the store.

Chapter Eighteen

Maggie strode out of the surf shop, looked up into a cloudless sky. She blinked against the sun as she made her way along the sidewalk. It had been several years since she'd had been on the island. The unique boutiques were out of her price range then. Now, she supposed, she could buy whatever she wanted. Back then she wanted it all. Now, all she wanted was to be left alone so she could have her baby and raise Jasmine. Material things, she didn't need them, didn't want them.

A chill rippled through her, a strange feeling, like she was being watched. She spun around. The sidewalk was crowded with tourists scurrying from store to store, but she saw nothing out of the ordinary. She was being paranoid, she told herself, imagining ghosts when there were none there, like she did when she was a little girl and wanted her dad to come into her room and chase away the monsters. There were no monsters then, there was nobody following her now. After all, she'd jumped onto the bus at the last possible instant, and it wasn't planned. It would be impossible for someone to have followed her.

She took a deep breath, studied faces as people passed by. Nobody was interested in her. Nobody knew where she was. She was perfectly safe. She took a deep breath, sighed, then started on her way.

***

Horace now thought of her as the Twin. And he felt a little bad about what he was going to do. She hadn't seen him blow away Fujimori in the stop-and-rob. She hadn't seen Striker's car. She wasn't the one who stuck the switchblade in Virge's belly. But she'd got a good look at him in that Safeway and that wasn't good. For that reason alone, she had to go.

He saw her stop in the middle of the sidewalk, turn and inspect faces, as if she knew she was being watched, but she never looked to the parked cars. She was an amateur, but why wouldn't she be?

All of a sudden she spun around, took off at a brisk walk, moving away from where he was parked. Horace watched till she turned a corner, then he nosed the Toyota into the traffic. He made the turn just in time to see her make a left a few blocks up. She wasn't quite jogging, but she was walking real fast, swinging her arms as if she didn't have a care in the world. He pushed the accelerator, made the left and passed her. Cars lined the curb, there was no place to park, so he doubled parked with the engine running next to a yellow pickup. Now all he had to was wait, like a spider for a fly.

A quick check in the rearview as she approached. He pulled Virge's switchblade out of his hip pocket. All he had to do was open the door, jump out, pull her between the pickup and the Corvette parked in front of it and do her. It was broad daylight, but he'd be gone before anybody noticed. He had his hand on the door handle when she stopped and stared up at a big white house. She was studying the address. Then all of a sudden she started up the walkway.

"Damn," he muttered as he pulled away from the yellow pickup. No way could he stay where he was. This wasn't New York. You didn't double park in California, not for more than a few seconds anyway, and not unless you wanted some old biddy calling the cops.

* * *

Maggie stood in front of a large, white house, sandwiched between similar homes. The front yard was ringed with a three foot hedge, not a leaf out of place. The lawn looked painted on. There was a *For Sale by Owner* sign in the middle of it. A house like this on an island where small homes were the norm was more then expensive, Maggie knew. This was a million dollar home, maybe more.

If Margo's mother lived here and it was a new address, why the for sale sign? Had she just moved in and not taken it down yet? That didn't make sense. She put the question out of her mind, went up the walk, took the steps up the porch, pushed the doorbell. Chimes rang inside. "Rich people." She shook her head.

The door opened, a little girl rushed out, bumped into her.

"Whoa," Maggie said. The child was younger than Jasmine, four or five years old. She had Orphan Annie red curls and a wide smile.

"Sorry! Oh, Margo, I didn't recognize you."

"That's okay," Maggie said.

"I gotta go check on the sitters." The girl giggled, then scooted past and ran down the walkway.

"Margo, what did you do to your hair?" The speaker was a striking woman who appeared younger than she was. She was tall, almost six feet, and she looked like a model. Maggie looked at her neck, the backs of her hands—even they looked young, but the eyes gave her away.

"I'm not her," Maggie said.

"My, God!"

"Can I come in?"

The woman stepped aside and made way for her to enter. She had shoulder length blond hair, like Maggie's till she'd cut it and dyed it dark. She was dressed in a silk blouse and skirt, as if she were going out.

Inside the house, Maggie saw a plush white carpet, modern furniture—steel and glass, cold and sterile. The walls were white, there were no paintings or anything on them, no wood grain anywhere. It was as if Margo's mother lived in an antiseptic future where people didn't age.

"It's all new," the woman said. "And it's only temporary."

"You don't have to apologize," Maggie said.

"I wasn't. I was explaining, because you looked shocked."

"Maybe I was, a little. This place looks so cold. Is this the kind of atmosphere Margo grew up in?"

"My name's Debra Murrant," the woman said, ignoring the question.

The furniture was different—Margo had beachy rattan stuff, whereas here the sofa and chairs were made out of soft white leather, the same color as the carpet—but the arrangement was the same. Two chairs opposite a sofa with a coffee table between. It was set up as if conversation were expected. Maggie didn't see a television.

"There's no easy way to say this," Maggie said. "Margo's dead."

"Oh!" Debra's hands went to her face. She staggered, as if she were going to fall.

In an instant Maggie was at her side. "I've got you." She helped her into one of the chairs. "Can I get you anything?"

"Water. Kitchen. That way." She pointed.

Maggie found a glass, filled it with water from the tap. Back in the living room she gave it to Debra Murrant, who wrapped both hands around the glass with laced fingers and held it tight without drinking.

"How?"

"I think it was the man who killed Frankie Fujimori. She saw him, she could identify him."

"I told her to leave it alone, but she wouldn't listen." Debra took a sip of the water, fingers white on the glass. "She was like those people who demonstrate in front of abortion clinics. Those people, especially the so called Born Again ones, need a way to show their faith. They need someone to see and applaud. Frankie Fujimori was Margo's abortion clinic."

"You didn't believe in Margo's faith?"

"Not a bit." Debra lowered the glass, looked at Maggie through tear filled eyes. "We used to fight, then we just stopped talking about it. She stopped trying to save me and I stopped trying to convince her that all those people wanted from her was her money. I guess they're going to get it now."

"What do you mean?"

"She had money. Her will leaves it to that Reverend Goodman and his church."

"What about Jasmine?" Maggie said.

"It's one of the things we used to fight about. She said the church would take care of her. They won't, but that's okay, I will."

"No one's getting her money, least of all Goodman."

"What do you mean?"

"They meant to kill Margo, but they killed me instead."

"I don't understand."

"It's a long story."

Debra wiped the tears away from her eyes. "I have time."

"Before we talk about that, I have some questions."

"Of course," Debra said.

"I need to know how she came to live with you and I wound up with my father?"

Debra's eyes were moist, full of sadness. That and something else, a kind of fire. "Like your father, my husband Gil was in Viet Nam when it happened." She stood up. "I'm gonna make some tea. How do you take yours?"

"Milk," Maggie said. "Not cream."

* * *

Horace drove around the block for the third time. Who the fuck was she talking to? How long was she gonna be? Another time around and people were gonna notice. The old lady neighborhood watch types would be on the phone to the cops.

Up ahead the yellow pickup he'd parked next to earlier started to pull away from the curb.

Opportunity knocked and Horace answered. He was behind the truck, easing into the spot, even as it was vacating it.

He got out of the car, went to the hood, raised it. Not the best cover in the world, but believable for a few minutes anyway. He looked at the battery, the oil covered engine. Sadie didn't take good care of her car. It was something he was going to have to teach her. You never knew when you'd have to depend on your vehicle. If you weren't there for it, it might not be there for you.

"What'cha doin', mister?" It was a kid's voice.

Horace grinned, like he was somebody's uncle or something, pulled his head out from under the hood, turned toward a little girl and said, "Who wants to know?"

"I do." The girl had bright red hair, green eyes and a face full of freckles.

"And who are you?" On one hand it was good the kid was talking to him, that way he didn't have to pretend to be working on the car. But it was bad on the other hand, because he didn't want her around when the Twin came out of that house.

"I'm not supposed to talk to strangers."

"Hey, you started it. My name's Horace, what's yours?" Stupid, he told her his real name. He was getting to be as dumb as Virge.

"Yeah, I guess. My name's Virginia Wheetly. I live over there." She pointed to a two story house next to the one the Twin had gone into.

"Ah, next door to—" he paused, "I forget her name."

"Mrs. Murrant, but she likes me to call her Debra. She just moved in till she sells the house. She's my friend."

"Really," Horace said. That explained the for sale sign.

"Yeah, My mom and dad work so I got a sitter."

"Debra's your sitter?" Horace said.

"No, silly. Carole is, but when her boyfriend comes over I go over to Debra's, because they think I'm in the way."

"How can you be in the way if it's your house?" Horace said, still smiling.

"Exactly. That's why I'm glad Debra moved next door. She doesn't think I'm in the way. Margo likes me, too."

"Did she change her hair?" Horace said.

"Yeah, but I still recognized her. I don't think her mom did at first, but I did."

"You're pretty sharp." Horace turned back under the hood, pretended to fiddle with one of the battery cables. "Fixed." He closed the hood. "See ya."

He couldn't get in the car quick enough. No way could he do anything here. Not now, not after giving the little brat his real name.

* * *

Maggie took a sip of the hot tea, then set her cup on the coffee table. She watched as Debra did the same.

"My daughter," Debra said, "my real daughter, died of SIDS, sudden infant death syndrome. She was a brand new baby, only two days old. I was pregnant when Gil went away. I wrote him about Margo right after she was born, but I couldn't write him when she died. I should have, but I was only eighteen.

"I had a job working for your mother at this place called the Last Chance Motel in San Diego, she was the manager.

"One day she asked me if I'd mind staying in her place and watching her baby girls for a few days while she flew up to L.A. in a small plane with a couple of Marines. They were going to a Grateful Dead concert."

"She was just going to leave two brand new babies with you?" Maggie said.

"We were friends, besides, she was a Deadhead. Maybe you had to be alive at that time to understand."

"I know about Deadheads."

"Yeah, I guess you would. Jerry Garcia's gone now, but his fans are still just as crazy about him, more maybe."

"We're getting sidetracked," Maggie said.

"You're right." Debra took a sip of her tea, then continued. "The next day I'd just put Margo down in her crib, but you had a runny nose and wouldn't stop crying. I was pacing back and forth in the living room, patting your back with every step, when the doorbell rang. It was the police.

"They told me the plane had gone down in the ocean somewhere between the coast and Catalina. They couldn't find the wreckage. They knew your mother was on the plane, because when they contacted the base, they found a friend of the pilot's. They also knew about the babies.

"Margo asleep in the bedroom had the same name as the baby I'd lost. It seemed like fate, so I lied. I said your mother left you behind because you were sick, but that she took Margo with her." Debra paused, took another sip of her tea.

"I always wondered why she took one of us on that plane and not the other," Maggie said. "Sometimes I felt like there was something wrong with me, like she didn't want me. But she didn't take either of us. She left us both."

"She was young."

"So were you."

"Yes I was."

"So, did the police believe you, you know, when you told them she took one of the kids on the plane?"

"Without question. They bundled you up and left. The next day I packed and drove up to Huntington Beach, where I got a job waitressing and rented a small apartment a couple of blocks from the ocean."

Maggie looked into the woman's red rimmed eyes. It was wrong what she'd done, but she understood it.

"There's one more thing I'd like to know."

"Ask me."

"I met the Reverend Goodman and Margo's so called boyfriend, real pieces of work. What made her attracted to men like that?"

"Gil was a salesman who made a fortune in real estate. He wasn't religious, but he watched the televangelists. He'd point to the TV and say to Margo, 'Listen up, little girl, that guy is selling!' Unfortunately Margo listened too well. By the time she figured out he wasn't watching because he believed in the junk they were dishing out, it was too late, she'd been sold on salvation. After he died and left her the money, she was ripe for somebody like Goodman."

Maggie picked up her tea, but put it back on the table without a sip. Silence ruled the room for a full minute, then she said, "He never knew Margo wasn't his real daughter, did he?"

"No. He loved her. He was a wonderful father." She paused, started back up. "But he was only an okay husband. He was vain. He needed the fastest car in town, the biggest house on the block, the prettiest wife on the planet. He could buy a faster car every year and a bigger house every three or four, but he couldn't stop his wife from aging, so he did the next best thing. He found the surgeons, arranged for the surgery. Gil Murrant's wife never looked a day over thirty. And in the end, I suppose even that was too old, because he found himself a twenty-three-year-old honey."

She took another sip of the tea, a pause for effect. "Her name was Gloria, she fancied herself a designer. But she killed him with a heart attack during sex. Now she gets nothing and I get her house."

"Her house?" Maggie said.

"Yeah, can you believe this place?" She swept a hand around, attempted a smile. "I didn't get clear title till last week. I'm gonna show it myself and drop the price ten thousand a week till someone buys it."

"She lived here, the girlfriend?"

"Never got a chance to move in. I'm only living here because escrow closed on my house in Laguna Beach three weeks ago. As soon as I dumped this place, I was going to get a condo where Margo lived, you know, so I could be close. Now, tell me about you and what brought you here."

Maggie started from when Virgil grabbed onto her shopping cart in the Safeway and told it all, right up till she knocked on Debra's front door.

"So, you're going to take over her life?" Debra said. "For Jasmine and for your baby. Fortunately she had enough money so you could do that."

"It's not about the money," Maggie said. "You can have it. We can get along without it. We don't need it."

"Don't be so naive," Debra said. "It came from her father. It's yours."

"What are you saying?"

"In about two hours I'm supposed to meet Gil's parents at LAX. Their flight comes in at noon and leaves at midnight. They were going to spend the day with Margo and me before flying off to a six week European tour. They're in their late seventies and still in good health, but Gil's death almost killed them. I can't tell them Margo's gone. I won't."

"You're going to help me?"

"Years ago I made a mistake and it's haunted me every day of my life. I played God with your lives, yours and Margo's. In my defense, I was young, grieving and through all those years I loved Margo as if she were really mine. There's absolutely nothing I wouldn't have done for her, and now there's absolutely nothing I won't do for her sister."

"I'm gonna need all the help I can get." Maggie couldn't believe how different Debra was from her first impression of her.

"I'll make some excuse why Margo and Jasmine couldn't come out to the airport. I'll have dinner with them, tell them how wonderful Margo's getting on and how great Jasmine's doing in school. I probably won't get back till two or three, but first thing in the morning I'll pack and come by. Lord knows I'd rather stay with you than in this modern art mausoleum. I wanted to do that anyway, but Margo was afraid Jasmine wouldn't get any school work done." She smiled. "We do like to play."

"Really?"

"I'm her other best friend. We're the Three Musketeers, Jazz, Sonya and me."

"I used to be in the Three Musketeers—me, Nick and Gordon." Maggie sighed. "I should be getting back." She wasn't quite sure what she thought about Debra moving in. "The bus can be unpredictable and I want to be there before Gordon notices I was gone."

"You took the bus?" Debra got up. "I'll drive you."

Maggie was hardly aware of the time as Debra negotiated her Mercedes through the traffic on Pacific Coast Highway. In what seemed like only seconds, Debra was signaling a left turn into the Sand and Sea Condos, Maggie's new home.

"My, we're looking sharp today," the guard said as he stepped out of the guard shack.

"Back at 'cha, Danny," Debra said.

"Gonna be staying awhile?"

"I was gonna stay in the new house till it sold, but I just couldn't pass up seeing you every day, so I'll be resting here till it's off my hands."

Danny laughed, deep from the belly. "Debra, you're 'bout the best looking woman I've ever laid eyes on, and now that your mourning time is over, we should give some serious thought 'bout stepping out, me and you."

"What about Darnelle and the kids?" Debra laughed too.

"Ah, them." Danny was still laughing as he raised the bar. He turned. "How 'bout if I get an okay from the wife?"

"In your dreams." She put the car in gear and drove through. Then, to Maggie, "Danny's an old scoundrel, but he wouldn't flirt with me if he didn't know I enjoyed it so much." She reached up to the visor and pushed a button on a garage door opener and waited while the gate slid open.

"You have your own clicker?" Maggie said.

"The condos come with two parking spaces. Margo only had one car, the spot next to it's mine." Debra parked next to where the Porsche should have been. Maggie was secretly thankful the parking space was empty. It meant Gordon wasn't back yet. She wanted a little time before she had to explain why she'd been out running around, when she'd promised she'd stay inside with the door locked.

"You really drove the car into the bay?" Debra said.

"I really did."

"Margo would have freaked."

"Yeah, well don't think I didn't."

"I don't know, it sounds like you handled yourself okay."

"It was more reaction then anything else." Maggie got out of the car.

"Okay, I accept your modesty," Debra said. Then, "We'll put our heads together in the morning, me, you, Gay and your friend Gordon."

"Okay."

Debra backed out of the space. Maggie stood and watched till she was through the moving gate and turning onto PCH. She was a nice person and Maggie thought she was going to like her.

Chapter Nineteen

Gordon paced the living room, doing his best to hold his temper in. He hadn't been in the apartment ten minutes when Maggie told him about the excursion to Debra's and what she'd learned.

"I know I shouldn't've gone out, but when I saw her mother was living so close, I just had to." She leaned forward on the sofa, hands in her lap like a little girl.

"You could've wound up like Margo." Gordon stopped his pacing, cut Maggie with a glare. What could she have been thinking?

"I said I was sorry."

"Okay, you told me about your day, let me tell you what I found out. Your pal Norton was right about Nighthyde. He was arrested for breaking and entering when he was twenty-two. Striker was the arresting officer. He put in a word with the court and Nighthyde got probation."

"We already knew that," Maggie said.

"Here's something you didn't know. I did a check with DMV. Striker drives a black BMW."

"So he was the one who chased me into the bay," Maggie said.

"Looks like it," Gordon said. "And it seems pretty obvious Nighthyde is still working for him."

"Brrrrr." She crossed her arms in front of herself.

"So, I figured I'd talk to Nighthyde. I got his address from DMV and his number from the book. The guy's some kid of hit man and he's listed. Go figure. I called and his mother answered, apparently he lives with her. She said he wasn't home. I told her I worked for the IRS and wanted to schedule an audit and needed to talk to him as soon as possible. She told me he was a process server and worked for the district attorney's office, maybe I could get him there. Not only does he not work for the DA, there's no record of him having ever worked anywhere. I called her back and she told me she'd just got off the phone with him. She said he was on his way to Mexico with a girl named Sadie and he wouldn't be back till the day after tomorrow." Gordon sat in one of the rattan chairs, looked Maggie in the eye. "So, it looks like we have a couple of days to figure out what we're going to do."

"I hate the thought that there's somebody out there who wants to do to me what he did to Margo."

"Maybe we should go to the FBI. I have friends in the Los Angeles field office. We could say you're Margo and your twin sister Maggie was killed and that you think the killer's coming after you. You could identify Nighthyde from the picture you saw in the mug book."

"Nick would find out. He'd want to meet his dead wife's twin. How would I face him? I'm already treading on thin ice as it is. I don't think I could pull that off. And Bruce Kenyon would see right through it and take Jasmine. No, I don't like that idea."

"I thought that's what you'd say, so I guess we'll go with plan B."

"Which is?"

"Tomorrow morning I'll pay a visit to Striker at Nakano. I'll tell him everything we know. I'll tell him it's all written down and in a safe place, and for added emphasis I'll tell him if anything happens to you, I'll personally come by and cut his balls off."

"I like this plan better."

"But to make sure nothing happens to you or Jasmine, I'll also have to tell him you're letting it lie."

"What do you mean?"

"They grabbed Margo here. They dumped her body behind the Whale. They followed you from the police station when you were Margo. They followed us from my house, where Maggie lived. Let's face it, unless they're stupid, they've made the connection between you and Margo, and they know they killed Margo. They know you're Maggie, and they know you're masquerading as your sister."

"I hadn't thought it through that far."

"I'll have to tell Striker if he stays away from you, you'll forget anything you might've learned about him, Nishikawa, Nakano and Nighthyde."

"They get away with Margo's murder?"

"And you get away with Margo's life."

"What about Norton's mother?" She got off the couch, started for the kitchen. Stopped, turned back.

"And ... and, what about Wolfe's little boy and his wife? What about them?"

"What about Jasmine? What about your baby?" He got up too, went to her, took her hands. "What about them?"

"It's so unfair."

"Yeah, well you know how that goes. Besides, we don't know for certain they had anything to do with that. It could just be coincidence."

"Norton said he doesn't believe in coincidence," Maggie said. "I don't either, not anymore."

"If you want to raise Jasmine and your baby here, you have to forget it."

"I hate it."

"I'm sorry, it's the best I can come up with."

"What if he doesn't go for the deal?"

"He will." He looked into her eyes, gave her hands a squeeze. "You'll see. He'll think you're doing it for Margo's money. That's something he can understand. It'll be over, really over."

"I really, really hate it." She let go of his hands, backed away, slumped down on the sofa. "But I guess I don't have any choice." She looked fragile.

"I know it seems lousy, but sometimes you have to go with the flow. I'll see Striker first thing in the morning. Then you can get on with living your new life."

He came over to the couch, sat down next to her and put a hand on her stomach. "I don't feel anything."

"You will soon."

"It's going to change your life, this baby."

"My life's already changed."

"Yeah, I guess it is."

The front door burst open and Jasmine and Sonya poured in. They were home from school. "Girl's night out," they squealed in unison.

"What?"

"We decided since I don't have to go to Tuesday Bible school, we could go to the mall with Gay and Sonya," Jasmine said. "We're gonna have dinner, then the movies after."

"Oh, we decided, did we?" Maggie said as Gay came through the front door.

"Yeah, me and Sonya. So you should hurry."

"But it's a school night."

"That never stopped us from going to Bible study," Jasmine said.

"She has you there," Gordon said.

"I'll get my coat." Jasmine ran into her bedroom with Sonya right behind.

"Do you have a cellphone?" Gordon asked Gay.

She patted her purse. "I take it everywhere."

"Keep an eye on the rearview. If you see a black BMW or anything else that looks suspicious, call 911."

"You're not coming?" Maggie said.

"Girls night out," Gordon said. "Besides, I've got a call to make. You know, to set up that meeting for tomorrow."

"What meeting?" Gay said.

"We're ready," Jasmine said as the girls came out of the bedroom.

"She can tell you all about it when there's no little ears around," Gordon said.

"I hate it when adults do that," Sonya said.

"Tough break." Gordon saw them out. The sun was hanging over Catalina Island, twenty-six miles away. It reminded him of Norton's mother and

DEAD RINGER

Wolfe's wife and son. Nobody should get away with murder.

He got Nakano's number from information, made an appointment with Striker for 10:00 the next day. Then he stretched out on the sofa and closed his eyes, just for a minute. He opened them as the sun was going down. Hungry, he decided to walk up to Johnny Rocket's and get a burger. He liked the '50s art deco decor, the jukeboxes on the tables, the young crowd and the good food.

* * *

Horace sat outside at the picnic tables in front of the Taco Bell on Fourth Street in Long Beach and watched the sunset as the cars went by. On the table in front of him was his usual, five tacos and a large Pepsi, but he couldn't eat. Half a day had passed since he'd talked to Ma on the phone and he was still seething. Someone had turned him into the IRS. It burned him. With every fiber in his being, he wanted to know who'd done it.

Lucky he thought fast. Telling Ma he was going to Mexico with Sadie bought him a few days, but it wasn't enough. Once those IRS guys got their teeth into you, they never let go.

Maybe Striker could help him out. Those Jap business types he worked for must have plenty of high powered accountants on their payroll. Already feeling better, he chomped down on a taco. But that woman better be dead the next time he talked to him. He didn't wanna have to explain why she was still walking around if he was gonna ask him for help with one of those accountants.

He jumped from the table, grabbed the box of tacos, gulped at the Pepsi on his way to the van. He could be at her place in thirty minutes. He ate as he drove, his mind on fire. He saw himself knocking at her door. She opens it. He pushes her inside, sticks her with the knife, then he's outta there.

Then the mind pictures screeched to slow motion. What if the kid was there? Could he do another? What choice did he have? His earlier plan had been to sneak in around midnight, do the woman and get out of the apartment without anyone the wiser. But now, with this tax thing, he didn't have the luxury of waiting. He wanted to call Striker as soon as possible, get the Feds off his back.

In Huntington Beach he parked on PCH, got out of the car, walked around the fenced complex to the bike trail that ran along the beach side of the condos. It was dark now.

A couple of kids, teenagers, a boy and girl, passed him on Rollerblades. He turned and watched as they zoomed along the concrete trail. Young love, he understood that. It's what he had with Sadie. Somebody pumping a mountain bike was coming fast, whizzed by the blading teens. In an instant it was past. Horace spun around, grabbed onto the fence and scrabbled over it, landing like a cat on the other side.

He darted a look around. Nobody had seen. He stood and started for her condo, swinging his arms as he walked, as if he had every right in the world to be where he was.

Her condo was dark. He knocked on the door. No answer. He knocked again, louder. Still no joy. He had the lockpicks out and the door open in seconds.

"Anybody home?" He pulled the Beretta out of the shoulder holster. "Anyone home?"

Again, no answer.

He holstered the gun, pulled the knife out of his hip pocket. He pushed the button, flicked it open, closed it, did it again. There was nothing for it but to wait. Sooner or later she'd come home and that would be it. He closed and flicked the blade open again.

* * *

Elvis was playing on the jukebox as Gordon left his tip on the table. He'd had the burger and fries, finished up with apple pie and vanilla ice cream. Seldom did he eat so much, but tonight he was ravenous. His emotions had run the gamut the last couple of days, from the unbelievable low when he thought he'd discovered Maggie dead behind the Whale, to the exaltation that shocked though him when he discovered her at the other end of his gunsight only last night.

And he'd spent the day as a cop. Something he hadn't done in years, and it wasn't over. Tomorrow he would face down Larry Striker and make everything okay for Maggie. He'd never felt so alive.

Outside he inhaled the night air, looked to the heavens, sighted the Big Dipper, the only constellation he could identify. A slight breeze was blowing as he jogged across PCH at the Main Street light. He waved to the security guard, got a nod and a smile back.

He walked along the fence, the bike trail and the beach on one side, the walkway through the condos on the other. He ran his fingers through the chainlink, like a kid would a picket fence on his way to school just before summer vacation. He felt like a kid, too, and it was a change he liked. Somewhere along the line he'd blinked and gotten old.

Close to Maggie's condo now, something moved in the bushes outside the front door. Gordon stopped, hand still on the fence. Often times he sat on his front porch and watched the cat from next door stalk a bird across the street at the beach. The animal could sit forever without moving a hair. He was that cat now as he took silent breaths, waiting, watching.

It moved again.

It was an animal. At first he thought maybe it was a cat, he had cats on the brain, but as his eyes got used to the dark he saw that it was a possum. He smiled, started for the door. The possum scurried between the hedge bushes and the wall, ducking out of sight.

He keyed the lock, entered laughing at the possum when something smacked into him. Gordon rolled with the punch as the lights came on.

"Fuck! Where is she?" The man was wiry, with squinty eyes and he had a gun pointed at Gordon's belly. There was no doubt it was Horace Nighthyde. He looked like a ferret.

"What are you doing in my apartment? What do you want?" Gordon reached up, massaged his jaw. It was going to be sore in the morning, if he lived to see the morning.

"Don't give me any crap. This isn't your place and we both know it. So tell me what I want and I'll be out of your face."

"Can I get up?" Gordon pushed himself to his feet without waiting for a reply. His own gun was in Maggie's bedroom in a bureau drawer, the others out in the trunk of his car. None of them any help now.

"I said, where is she?" Nighthyde had sweat running down his forehead. His gun hand was shaking.

"Who?"

"Don't play stupid with me. I followed you from that bar in the Shore to that fag place the other night. You went in, I saw."

"That's why you dumped the body there, because you saw us together?"

"So, tell me where she is and you can live to go there again." Nighthyde's dark eyes glowed, the pupils were pin pricks, as if he'd been doing drugs. Was it fear?

"Come on, Horace. How many people are you going to kill because you fucked up and shot Frankie Fujimori by mistake?" Gordon edged to the right.

"Don't move."

"I'm just going over to the sofa. You popped me a good one, I'm a little dizzy."

"What do you mean, mistake?" Nighthyde motioned toward the sofa with the gun, signaling it was okay for Gordon to go over and sit.

"Your pal Striker screwed up." Gordon eased over to the sofa, sat down with a sigh. He continued to rub his jaw as if he were in pain. "Fujimori was a child molester and a killer of little girls, but not the man you were supposed to kill."

"What do you know about it?"

"I know another Japanese man, a guy named Ichiro Yamamoto was in that store. I know he used to work for Congressman Nishikawa and that he was selling out Nishikawa to the cops on a diamonds for weapons scam. I know Striker used to work for Nishikawa and that the company he works for now operates with Yakuza money. I know Nishikawa's thick with the Yakuza and I know he hates the idea of some little punk sending him to jail." The last two were a guess, but he thought the odds were pretty good they were as true as everything else he'd said.

"Striker woulda told me if I got the wrong one."

"No he wouldn't, you fucked up and the next day Yamamoto decided to clam up. He told the cops he made the whole thing up, therefore Striker didn't have any reason to have him hit anymore. So even though you got the wrong guy, Striker couldn't tell you because he needed you to get rid of the witness." Gordon was really guessing now, but it all made sense. It couldn't have happened any other way.

* * *

"Aw fuck." All of a sudden Horace felt drained. The guy on the couch was too scared to lie. Horace wanted to puke. He'd killed that old lady and the fucking kid for a mistake. For a God dammed mistake.

"You don't look so good, Horace."

"Shut the fuck up. Fucking faggot, think you know it all."

"Gordon," the fag said.

"What?" Horace tightened his hand on the gun as he watched the fag holding onto his jaw. He grinned, he still had a mean right cross.

"Gordon, that's my name."

"I oughta do you and get it over with." Damn faggot had balls.

"Do me, as you put it, and Mr. Striker and yourself will wind up holding your breath in that iron room. How long can you hold your breath, Horace?"

"The fuck you talking about?"

"The gas chamber, Horace. For you for sure. A cop's mother, another's kid. The kid's the capper, you'll get the chamber, no doubt."

"So, if I'm going down, what's one more body?"

"Tomorrow I'm gonna meet with Striker. I have a deal that ends it. You walk away, we walk away. As far as the cops are concerned, the world's better off without Frankie Fujimori. And as of now, they believe Wolfe's kid climbed over that balcony and fell, his wife ate her gun, and Norton's mother took her own life. Maggie's twin will just have to go down as unsolved."

"Twin?"

"Don't act so surprised, you've already figured it out. And yes, you got Margo Kenyon. That was another mistake, dumping her body behind the bar. We never would've been involved if you hadn't done that, never would've figured it all out. And before you think you can shut me up by pulling that trigger, you'd better wonder whether or not I wrote it all down and left it in an envelope with someone to go public with if anything happens to me or Maggie."

"Don't make sense, nothing in it for you." Horace tightened his grip on the gun.

"Margo Kenyon inherited over a million dollars from her father when he died. We get to keep it, me and Maggie."

Horace was stunned. They get to keep a million bucks if they keep quiet, but if something happens to either one of them, someone opens an envelope somewhere and tells the world about how fucking stupid he'd been, hitting cops' kin. Yeah, Striker would leave 'em alone, at least until he found out who had that envelope.

He saw the payoff for the Twin sinking down a rat hole. No way could he do her now. Striker might even try to renege on the old broad and the kid. It wasn't fair. Minutes ago he was looking at a fortune, now this clown and the woman were getting it.

"So you and Striker got it all worked out?" Horace moved in closer, stood above Gordon, pointed the gun at his head.

Gordon looked past him, said, "Jasmine, you're not supposed to be up. Get back to bed."

The kid was here? Horace sneaked a quick glace over his shoulder.

And pain blasted through his hand.

Horace spun his eyes back toward the fag. The fucker was in flight, coming toward him like a killer bird. He tried to bring the Beretta to bear, but it was gone. Bastard had kicked the gun from his hand.

Then the faggot was on him. Hands circled his neck, claws dug in, cut off his air. Pain thundered from his groin, bastard had kneed him in the balls. No air, can't breathe. He was falling backward, fucker on top of him.

Air, need air.

Horace jabbed a fist into the faggot's belly, but he didn't let go. He hit him again and still he held on, thumbs digging into his windpipe. Again, again, again, but each blow was a pale imitation of the one before it. Horace had no power behind his fists. He was a two year old trying to stop a train.

His head pounded into the carpet as he thudded to the floor with the faggot still on top of him, hands still on his neck, still squeezing. Horace was getting dizzy. He was going to die here. Fucking faggot was killing him. He could feel his eyes popping out as he stared into the faggot's cold glare. There was no mercy in those eyes, the faggot was going to kill him. No doubt.

Horace struggled a hand into a back pocket, fingers snaked inside, closed around Virgil's knife. He was going to pass out, but first his thumb hit the button, flicked the knife open.

No strength for a good thrust, but he gave it his best effort, a swipe at the fucker's chest.

The faggot screamed, jumped back.

Horace sucked air, wheezing like a sick dog, he couldn't get enough.

All of a sudden the faggot was on the other side of the room, his yellow Hawaiian shirt covered in blood.

DEAD RINGER

Horace rolled over, pushed himself to his knees. His balls felt like they were going to explode, but he had to get up before the faggot came at him again. Fuck, the guy was strong. Horace climbed to his feet as the faggot ripped out a shivering scream. Not pain, one of those karate screams.

The bastard was coming at him again, rage in his eyes. No knife was gonna stop something like that. Horace dropped it, picked up a lamp. The base was a thick glass bowl stuffed full of sand and sea shells. Heavy as cement. He ripped the cord from the wall and smashed it into the charging faggot's head. Fucker was so blind angry he never saw it coming.

The faggot went down like he'd been shot and Horace dashed to the door. No telling who heard that scream. In an instant he was outside. For a second he thought about going back for the gun and knife, but a light went on down the way and it made up his mind. He ran.

* * *

Gordon came to with the mother of migraines. Everything was black. Something cold was pressed against his forehead. He tried to get up.

"No, lay still." It was Maggie's voice.

"I'm okay." He opened his eyes. Concern was written all over her face. She looked like an angel. He was on the floor, head in her lap. Gay was looking over her shoulder.

"No, you're not."

"Where's the girls?"

"Still at the movies. It was a double Disney thing, we left after the first one. And it's a good thing we did, you were bleeding all over everything."

"I'll call 911," Gay said.

"No," Gordon said.

"We have to get you to a doctor. You've lost a lot of blood and that cut on your chest is going to need stitches."

"Don't feel it," Gordon said. But he was beginning to.

"It'd be quicker if we took him to the hospital," Gay said.

"No, call Jonas. He'll know what to do."

"Gordon!" Maggie said.

"No doctor, no police. Call Jonas. Tell him what happened, he'll fix it."

"I don't think so, Gordon," Maggie said.

"It's the only way. I'll be all right."

"I'll take over so you can make that call." Gay sat down and Maggie shifted Gordon into her lap. He fought to stay conscious as Maggie went out to the kitchen and the phone. In a few seconds he heard her talking to Jonas. Heard her explaining how she was still alive and why she'd called. Then he closed his eyes.

Chapter Twenty

"I THOUGHT YOU WERE GONNA take the kids to your house." Maggie pushed her hair out of her eyes. She was in Jonas' kitchen in his apartment above the Whale. She leaned on the counter by the sink. She was tired.

"I decided it was a bad idea. It didn't seem safe, not after what happened tonight." Gay whispered so the girls in the other room wouldn't hear. She'd gone to pick them up right after they'd delivered Gordon to Jonas'. She'd only been back a few seconds when Maggie whisked her into the kitchen. "How's your friend?"

"He's going to be all right. The doctor's with him now. It doesn't look like a concussion."

"What about the knife wound?"

"Fifteen stitches, he's going to have a scar."

"So what's the deal, are these guys some kind of crooks or something?"

"No." Maggie laughed. "Gordon used to be in the FBI. Jonas, well I don't know, but I know he's got a lot of friends and that he doesn't like cops."

"That's obvious," Gay said.

"Yeah, I can see how it looks like something out of a bad movie," Maggie said. Jonas had a doctor waiting for them when they showed up with Gordon. A young guy she'd seen working the pinball machines downstairs in the Whale. He didn't make any noises about getting Gordon to a hospital or calling the police.

"They just put him to bed and started working on him like it's something that happens every day," Gay said.

"They're close." Maggie turned, looked out the window over the sink.

"Checking to see if anyone's outside?"

"That's the dumpster where he left her, right down there. God, I've been so stupid. I feel like this whole thing is my fault."

"Nonsense. None of it is,"

"Especially tonight, I should've stayed home."

"Then that would be you cut up, or worse, Jasmine. And you guys might not have been so lucky."

"She's right," Jonas said, coming into the kitchen. "Gordon's all drugged up and mumbling, but he's a tough old bird, it'll take more than a scratch across his chest and a bash to the head to do him in. Doc says he's going to be right as rain, but he's stuck in bed for a week or so."

"Thank God." Maggie favored Jonas with a weak smile. "What are the girls doing?"

"Television in the den, music videos," Jonas said. "They think my place is cool, but they're distressed that I don't have any Sugar Frosted Flakes and they're upset about not having their schoolbooks. What's the fifth grade coming to, school's supposed to be fun at that age, isn't it?"

"I'll go and get the books after I get back from the liquor store with the cereal." Maggie started for the back door. It opened on a landing, the steps went down to the alley behind the Whale.

"Where do you think you're going?" Gay said.

"The liquor store's only a couple blocks away."

"You're not going alone," Gay said. "And especially not down there."

"I'll be okay, I've got my trusty Sigma." She turned, raised her sweatshirt so Gay could see the gun tucked between her Levi's and the small of her back.

"Where did that come from?" Gay said. "Do you know how to use it?"

"I stole it." Maggie wondered if Nick had noticed it gone yet. "And yes I know how to use it." She went to the back door, opened it.

"I'm still going," Gay said.

"Just be careful," Jonas said. "Gordon will have my neck if anything happens to you two on my watch."

"Nothing's going to happen," Gay said.

"You can help make sure." Jonas left the room, returned after a few seconds. "Take this." He was holding out Nighthyde's gun. "It's easy to use, just point and pull the trigger."

"I know how they work." Gay took the gun, pulled her blouse out from her jeans and stuffed it between them and her back, like Maggie. "God I feel like we're Bonnie and Clyde."

"Thelma and Louise," Maggie said.

"Whatever."

At the liquor store on the corner Maggie said. "You go in and get the milk and cereal, I've got something I need to find out from information." Maggie started toward a phone booth in front of the store.

"What?"

"Horace Nighthyde's address."

"You're kidding."

"It's my only chance. I have to convince him it's all over. Gordon was right about that. It's the only way."

"Yeah, and look what happened to him."

"He said Nighthyde was listening to him when he took a chance and knocked the gun out of his hand." She picked up the phone, dialed information and got the phone number. At first the operator didn't want to give out the address, but when Maggie pleaded, saying she just needed it to address a birthday card to her stepfather's brother, the operator gave in.

"God you're good, you sounded just like a little girl."

"It's easier to bend the rules for children." Then, "He lives in Lakewood, on Daneland."

"You never were going to get the schoolbooks, were you?"

"No."

"What if this Nighthyde character doesn't listen to you?"

"He's not gonna shoot me on his front porch."

"I'm going with you?"

"I know."

"Let's go get the cereal."

Inside the store Maggie picked up the Frosted Flakes, a half gallon of milk and a bottle of Sutter

Home Cabernet. "To celebrate with when this is all over."

"Big spender," Gay said as they were at the check out.

"Yeah, I guess I'm not used to all the money yet." Maggie bagged her purchases. "In fact, I hope I never get used to it."

"You'll do fine," Gay said.

"You think?"

"Look out." Gay pushed Maggie aside as a young Asian man burst through the doorway. He was wearing fringed jeans, not Levi's, and a black leather motorcycle jacket with the sleeves cut off. Tattoos peppered his arms. It would have been a head on collision, but thanks to Gay's fast reaction he only brushed against Maggie. "He didn't even apologize."

"Yakuza copycat," Maggie said. "Japanese type Mafia."

Back at the apartment Gay said. "We'll have to stop and get gas, Gordon's Ford is almost out."

"Take mine." Jonas fished a set of keys out of his pocket, handed them to Maggie.

"I hate these high tech Volkswagens," Gay said as she got in the passenger side of Jonas' car.

"Bright red, new and improved." Maggie took off the hand brake, started it.

"It's twice the size of a regular Beetle. It's like a pregnant Bug." Gay pulled on the shoulder harness.

"At least it's not an automatic," Maggie said.

As they took the on ramp to the 605 Freeway, Gay said, "Yesterday you seemed so lost, but not now. You've changed."

"I don't feel any different."

"You are."

Fifteen minutes later they turned off the freeway. Another couple of minutes and Gay said, "Daneland, that's it, that's the street."

Maggie turned, drove slowly, found the address, parked in front. "Lights are off. No car in the driveway. Doesn't look like anyone's home."

"Car could be in the garage," Gay said. The neighborhood was middle class tract homes built after the Korean War. Sidewalks in front, driveways led to garages in the back. People either parked their cars in the drive or through the gate and in the garage. There was only one other car parked on the street on the whole block. The red Volkswagen stood out like a tomato in a bag of onions.

"Could be, but I don't think so." Maggie restarted the car, drove down to the corner, turned and parked next to a park at the end of the block.

"Now what?"

"He broke into my house. I'm gonna break into his." Maggie got out of the car.

"What?" Gay got out too, joined Maggie on the sidewalk.

"I'm tired of this guy stalking me. This time I'll be the one waiting with the gun."

"Like when you hid in that bathroom?"

"That was different, I was scared, surprised."

"And you're not afraid now?"

"I'm terrified."

"That's reassuring," Gay said.

On foot in front of the house Maggie saw a neatly manicured lawn with a picture perfect flower bed, roses ran along the front of the house. She wondered if Nighthyde kept the lawn looking that way or if he had a gardener.

She passed the lawn, hooked a left up the driveway. She took quiet breaths as if the neighbors could hear. The gate had a string through a hole above the latch. Maggie pulled it, the latch clicked and the gate opened with a screech that shivered up her spine. Surely someone had heard. But no lights came on.

Gay followed her through and Maggie steeled herself as she screeched the gate closed. Inside she found they were protected from the neighbors' eyes by a five foot brick fence that surrounded the backyard. The yard, like the front, looked professionally managed.

"I still think this is a stupid idea." Gay was so close behind Maggie that she felt her breath on the back of her neck.

"Let's check the back door." Maggie stepped up the back porch, tried the knob. "Locked."

"Maybe we should go."

Maggie backed away from the house, studied it. "The bathroom window's open a crack." She went to it. "Give me a boost."

"Right." Gay laced her fingers together. Maggie stepped into them.

Maggie slipped her thumbs under the window, slid it up. "Piece of cake."

"This is stupid."

"Oh stop."

"Stopping."

"Can you boost me a little higher?"

"Boosting." Gay pulled Maggie up enough so she could squirm through the window, like a gopher squeezing into a hole, she thought.

Then she was in and falling. She hit the floor on her backside as an animal roar filled the bathroom.

Bear was her first thought.

Then it was on her.

"Gay!" she screamed

The thing wrapped itself around her and squeezed. Maggie smelled its breath, foul as if raw meat were decaying in its mouth. It wheezed as it squeezed, choking her, suffocating her. It had her arms pinned to her sides. She was helpless.

She kicked against it and it answered by gripping harder. Maggie was caught in its killing embrace and there was nothing she could do about it. Blood rushed to her head as she thrashed like a netted fish trying to get away, trying to breathe.

From somewhere in the distance she heard the sound of breaking glass. She heard her name shouted, then light replaced the dark as Gay screamed, "Let her go!" And Maggie saw into the dead eyes of the old woman who had her in her grasp, saw Gay's hands grab the old crone's hair. "I said let her go! Let go or I'll rip your head off!"

But the old hag flexed her great arms and crushed Maggie into her bulging breasts. The monster woman wailed as Gay jerked her backwards by the hair. Maggie kneed the woman in the groin, kneed her again, felt the woman's grip slacken. Somehow Gay had gotten an arm around the old hag's throat and now the two woman were riding a bronc from hell as the hag bucked and thrashed about the bathroom, banging herself, Maggie and Gay into the cabinets below the sink, the bathtub and the toilet.

Then all of a sudden she let go her grip. Maggie rolled away and Gay jumped back as flabby arms flapped against the floor like a great seal's flippers. She was on her back now, head banging the tiles.

"What's going on?" Maggie said, out of breath.

Vomit spewed from the hag's mouth.

"Grand mal seizure!" Gay went to her knees. "Help me turn her onto her side so she doesn't drown in her vomit."

Maggie grabbed onto her shoulder, Gay her buttocks, and they heaved, but the old woman flung an arm around and caught Gay full in the face, sending her flying across the bathroom.

In an instant Gay was back. "Come on, she could die."

"Okay, push," Maggie said and she did. "It's working, she's going over."

But as quickly as they'd rolled her onto her side, the hag flipped herself back again, flinging Maggie and Gay aside.

"Get her!" A man's voice rang through the bathroom.

Maggie turned, barely able to register that the man was shouting in Japanese, before something slammed into her chest and knocked her wind away. She gagged, sucked air, tried to get up when the man slapped her face with an open palm, knocking her back to the floor.

There was another Asian on Gay. Maggie struggled to stay conscious, saw a tattooed arm slam Gay to the floor, spin her onto her stomach even as the man on her spun her onto her own stomach. Head turned to the side she saw grotesque tattooed hands frisk Gay, find the gun as she felt her own attacker pull the Sigma out from behind her.

Who were these men, why were they shouting in Japanese?

Hands pulled her to her feet, were dragging her out of the bathroom. She tried a feeble kick, got hit on the side of the head for a reward. She gave up, let the man drag her down a hallway, though the living room and on into the kitchen. He pulled a chair from a breakfast table and flopped her into it as the other man dropped Gay into its mate.

They were silent now. Maggie saw one had a roll of duct tape. They were quick and efficient as they taped her hands behind the chair. Then they went to work on Gay. The men taped their feet to the legs of the chairs. They were trussed up like rodeo calves.

Able to breathe now, Maggie took in her captors. They were Japanese. They wore black leather motorcycle jackets with the sleeves cut off. Their arms were covered with tattoos. They were young and one of them was the man who had brushed against her in that liquor store when she was buying the Frosted Flakes.

He was short, with a scar under his left eye, as if he'd been the loser in a knife fight. His hair was cropped close and he danced around on the balls of his feet. The other one was slightly taller, with long hair pulled into a ponytail. He was thin but muscular, and he had twice the tattoos as Scarface. His black eyes were glued to Maggie. Maybe he was going to kill her, but it was obvious what he wanted to do first.

Yakuza thugs.

Why?

"What's going on here!" The voice tore through the kitchen like a gunshot. Maggie turned her head toward it, saw Horace Nighthyde. His face was going red. He didn't look stable.

"Mr. Nighthyde," one of the Japanese said in heavily accented English, "these women entered your house though a back window. We surprised them as they were struggling with your mother."

"What?"

"She's on the bathroom floor. We were just about to move her to the sofa," Ponytail said.

Horace Nighthyde ran out of the room.

DEAD RINGER

The Japanese started whispering among themselves in their own language, unaware that Maggie understood every word.

"We should kill them all and go," Scarface said.

"No, Mr. Striker was very specific. First we find out how much they know and who they've told," Ponytail said. "You will take Nighthyde to the others while I question the women."

"I know what you want." Scarface laughed.

"Find out everything, then do them all. The children, too. Nobody in that house gets out alive. When you're finished make it look like Nighthyde put a gun to his own head and killed himself."

The children! The words pierced Maggie's heart. She struggled against the tape, tried to get out of the chair. Ponytail slapped her across the face and she sank back, again fighting to stay conscious.

"It's almost like she understands." Scarface laughed, louder than before.

Ponytail laughed too.

"She's okay," Horace said as he came back into the kitchen. "She usually sleeps after one of her spells. She won't wake up for awhile." In his right hand he held his own gun, the one Gay had come into the house with, in his left he had Maggie's Sigma. Apparently the Japanese had left them in the bathroom. Now Horace Nighthyde had them.

" You two get her to the couch." Horace waved at the Japanese with the Sigma. The guns gave him control of the situation and clearly he wasn't ready to give it up.

The Japanese obeyed and shortly they brought the blind woman out of the bathroom. From where she was Maggie was able to see through the kitchen door and into the living room. The Japanese each had one of the old woman's arms around their shoulders, she was slack between them. The seizure was past, but she seemed dazed. They led her to the sofa, laid her on her back.

"You can't keep us here like this!" Gay called out.

"Tape their mouths," Horace Nighthyde said.

"You can't!" Gay said.

"We can." Ponytail picked up the duct tape, wrapped some around Gay's head, shutting her up. He leered at Maggie as he did it, then he came to her. Maggie fought a scream as the man wound the tape around her mouth and the back of her neck.

They were all in the kitchen now, Horace Nighthyde with the ferret face and the two Japanese.

Nighthyde came over to the women. "So you come after me with this?" He stuffed his gun in front of Maggie's face. "My piece! Mine!" He held up his left hand. "Is this the one you shot me with?" He touched Maggie's cheeks with both guns. "I ought to blow your face away right now."

Maggie's eyes went wide.

"Yeah, that's right." He moved the guns to her forehead. "Two bullets, one for each of you, Maggie Nesbitt or Margo Kenyon, whoever you are."

Maggie felt her heart thump. He was going to do it.

"Mr. Nighthyde, wait!" Ponytail said.

"And who the fuck are you guys?" Horace spun around. Now he had a gun trained on each of them.

Maggie let out a quiet sigh.

"We were following Mrs. Kenyon, in case you needed some help disposing of her," Ponytail said.

"Striker ask you to do that?" Horace Nighthyde said.

"We are only to assist. You are in charge," Ponytail said.

"Just so we know," Horace said. Maggie thought he sounded like a puffed up peacock. Ponytail was buttering him up and he was falling for it. However he didn't lower the guns.

"But we have more problems now. The woman has told others. We must find out how much."

"You mean her faggot friend?"

"Yes, and now there may even be another who knows. There seems to be no end to it. If we don't act right away, Mr. Striker might be hearing about himself on the local news. That, my friend, would make him very unhappy."

"You're not my friend." Horace Nighthyde held the guns steady, but at least they were pointed at the Japanese men and not at Maggie and Gay.

"It was a figure of speech. We followed these two while they took the man you injured in Huntington Beach to a place in Belmont Shore. Curiously enough, it's above the bar where you left the nude body of her twin sister. Now we have to go there and find out how much they know and deal with it."

"Right." Now Horace Nighthyde looked confused.

"My companion will go with you while I stay and watch over them." Ponytail pointed a stiff finger toward Maggie.

Scarface started toward the door as if he expected Horace Nighthyde to follow.

"I didn't see a car when I came in." Now Horace sounded wary.

"We left it at the end of the block, behind theirs, across from the park."

"Anything in it?" Horace hadn't moved toward the door, didn't look as if he wanted to go with Scarface.

"Our weapons," Ponytail said. "We didn't want to walk the street after dark with them, just in case we ran into a curious policeman, but they're locked in the truck."

"You should bring the car here, park it in the driveway," Horace said to Ponytail. He seemed more irritated than angry now. "You can come with us and drive it back."

"What about them?" Again Ponytail pointed at Maggie.

"You did them up fine. They won't be going anywhere. Besides, you can be back in less than five." Now Horace started for the door. "Are you guys coming or what?"

The two Japanese followed him out. Scarface first, without a look back, then Ponytail. He turned, looked into Maggie's eyes and winked.

Chapter Twenty-One

"Ma is up. Tell me where you are." The blind woman's voice slurred through the kitchen. She sounded demented. Maggie remembered her strength, had no desire to mess with her again. "I know you're here." The woman was at the kitchen door. She was big, with ketchup red hair, curly and long, uncontrolled, a wild mane, swirling as Ma jerked her massive head back and forth. No ferret face on this woman. If anything, she was a grizzly.

"That's right, they taped your mouth. But not to worry, I can find you."

The old woman cackled as she went to a drawer by the sink. She opened it, pulled out a giant knife, serrated, sharp, gleaming in the kitchen light. Still laughing that witch's laugh, she moved toward Maggie.

Maggie took in air through her nose, held her breath. She pushed with her bound feet against the floor. The chair screeched as she backed away from the crazy looking woman. She was sure Ma was about to finish what Horace Nighthyde and his Yakuza thugs had started.

But Ma stopped her laugh. "You don't have to be afraid." She held up the knife she clutched in her right hand. "It's for the tape." She had her left hand in front of herself, fingers moving like stubby worms. She found Maggie's head, fingered through her hair, found the tape. She jerked it off.

"Ouch!" Maggie said.

"Better to do it quick," Ma said. "The way doctors do. Otherwise the hurt lingers."

"That's all right, I'm just glad it's off."

"Hold up your hands."

"I can't, they taped them behind my back."

"Okay." Ma felt along Maggie's shoulder, down her arms, found the tape and sliced through it. "Take it now." She held out the knife. "You can do the rest."

Maggie took it, cut off the tape that bound her feet to the chair. She winced as the blood rushed to them. Her wrists hurt too. She dropped the knife on the floor, massaged her ankles.

"Hmmmm." It was Gay, humming through the tape to get Maggie's attention.

"Oh, sorry." Maggie picked up the knife again, cut Gay loose. But she let Gay pull off the tape wrapped around her neck and mouth.

"Christ," Gay said, once she had it off. "That really sucked."

"Yeah," Maggie said.

"You have to hurry, one of them's gonna be coming back," Ma said.

"Are you okay?" Gay said.

"I'm old, I'm blind, I'm an epileptic with cancer. No, I'm not okay. What are you, stupid?"

"Why did you do this?" Maggie said. "You know, cut us free after we broke into your house?"

"He thought I was out like a dumb light bulb, my boy Horace. He was wrong. Used to be when one of them fits was over, I'd be out for two-three hours after." Her words were slow, labored. "But I learned I recover quicker if I just go with it when I feel one coming on." Her breathing seemed to be getting better as she spoke. "I feel like an old whore left to die in the snow." She laughed at her joke. "But I ain't no whore. I know when right's right, and wrong's wrong." She was serious now. "I heard what he said, my boy. All this time I thought he was working for the district attorney, doing good, and he was doing the Devil's work."

Outside they heard a car pull up in the driveway.

"It's not one I recognize," Ma said. "So it must be that man coming back. You should go out the back way. Shimmy over the fence. He won't know which way you went, the neighbors on either side or the ones behind."

"We're not gonna leave you to him." Maggie remembered the man's leer. "We'll surprise him when he comes in the front door."

"No!" Ma said. "I can handle it. You go. Now!"

Maggie heard a car door opening. "But—"

"No buts, get on outta here." Ma stamped her foot. Her jaw was firm.

"She's right," Gay said. "We can't leave you here."

"No one's gonna hurt me. My boy will see to that. But I wouldn't give a tinker's damn for your chances if you don't get out of here right now!"

Maggie heard footsteps coming up the porch and all of a sudden she remembered what Ponytail had said about the children. They were gonna kill them all. Gordon, Jonas, Jasmine and Sonya.

"We're going!" Maggie grabbed Gay's arm and started toward the back door.

"What?" Gay said.

The front door started to open.

"Now!" Maggie jerked on Gay's arm, propelled her toward the back door.

"I'll hold him off." Ma started toward the living room.

Maggie heard a crash behind her as she followed Gay through the service porch. They were moving fast, fueled by fear. Gay got the door open, then they were in the yard, running toward the back fence.

They were at it when a gunshot tore through the night. They stopped, turned back toward the house.

"Ma," Maggie said.

"Shit," Gay said.

"He killed her," Maggie said.

"We can't do anything." Gay gasped out the words as she sucked air. "We gotta go."

"He's coming!"

Ponytail was in the service porch now, backlit by the kitchen light behind and framed by the doorway. He had a pistol in his hand and he was pointing it at them. He was going to shoot.

"Come on!" Gay was halfway over the fence when a gunshot rang out. Rocky fragments blasted into Maggie's arm as she scurried over the wall. He'd shot into the fence, missing her by inches.

"Dog!" Maggie screamed as a back porch light came on. A dark German Shepherd was charging toward them. Maggie dropped to a crouch, blocked her neck with her left arm as the animal leapt. Teeth sank in, pain blasted up her shoulder, down her side, stinging her to the bone.

"Release!" Gay reared back, kicked the dog in the head. It let go of Maggie's arm, but not because it obeyed the command.

"Next house!" Gay charged toward another brick fence, was over it as someone came out onto the back porch.

"Get back inside!" Maggie shimmied over the fence as the man on the porch slammed his door shut, leaving his whimpering dog to greet the man with a gun coming over his back fence.

Another shot. The dog screamed, almost human like. Then it was silent.

"Come on, come on!" Gay charged through the next backyard, Maggie right behind. Another fence. Gay was in the air and over it.

Maggie's arm screamed. She was a runner but her lungs felt like they were going to explode. Her heart thudded. Sweat ran through her hair, down her neck, but the thought of the girls and what those men might to do them was like a shot of speed. She leapt at the fence, pulled herself to the top, rolled over the side.

Sirens sounded in the distance. Ponytail hadn't been too discreet, shooting his gun of like that. People were up. Cops were on the way.

"No time to catch your breath. He'll be coming." And as if to add truth to Gay's words, they heard someone rooting around in the yard they'd just come out of. "Checking the bushes," she whispered. "To see if we're hiding."

Without further talk they jogged across the yard, attacked another fence. They slipped over it and two collie dogs went wild, barking up a storm.

"Shit." Maggie ran across the yard toward still another fence, this time ahead of Gay. The barking dogs loped alongside, alerting any around that there were intruders here, but they made no attempt to attack or hinder.

Maggie was over the fence first this time. She hit the ground running toward still another fence. Their pursuer would have heard the dogs and he'd be on their trail.

Gay caught up to Maggie, grabbed her shoulder, pointed left. Maggie nodded. The yards were back to back, fences between them as they were between every house on the block. Right now they were jumping the fences and running through the yards on the street behind the Nighthyde house. But each yard gave them two choices, run ahead to the next fence, or hop over the back fence and go through the yards on Nighthyde's street.

Maggie and Gay went over the fence and landed in a thicket of bushes. Maggie poked her head through the hedge-like growth. It ringed the yard, almost as high as the five foot fence. Several fruit trees, a cactus and two palm trees grew in the yard. Whoever lived there had the greenest of thumbs. Mr. Greenthumb was probably retired, probably spent hours in his yard, shaded by his trees.

Maggie stood, started through the bushes. Gay grabbed her shoulder, softly squeezed. Maggie stopped.

"What?"

"I have to catch my wind." Gay pulled Maggie down to her knees. It was pitch dark, but their eyes were inches apart. Maggie tasted Gay's breath.

"Okay." Maggie took Gay's hand, led her crawling along the fence, between it and the hedge bushes. They went fast, squirming along like Brer Rabbit in his briar patch, stiff branches scraped their arms as they struggled to get away from the spot where they expected Ponytail to come over the fence.

The collies they'd encountered in the backyard diagonal to Greenthumb's went berserk. One was howling. Ponytail was getting close. They heard him grunt as he went over the fence. Now he was in the yard behind. Either he'd keep going, in which case Maggie and Gay could exit through Greenthumb's gate and be out on Nighthyde's street, but then they'd still have to get to the car, or he'd come over the back fence. For reasons she couldn't explain, Maggie thought he'd come over the fence.

And he did, thudding and cursing as he crashed into the bushes. He bullied his way through them, an elephant in a nursery, was halfway through the yard, stopped in the center, under one of the palm trees. It was as if he knew the women were close. He moved to the tree, seeking cover. In his right hand he held a pistol. It looked like a revolver. Didn't they hold six shots, like in the old cowboy movies? He'd fired three, so he had three left, at least.

The back porch light came on. Mr. Greenthumb, alerted by the collies who were still barking to beat the band. Ponytail dashed from the palm to the base of a plum tree, stepped behind its trunk.

Greenthumb came out onto the back porch. An old man, Maggie saw him clearly through the bushes. He appeared confused. He put a hand to his forehead as if he were shielding his eyes from the sun. The gesture wouldn't help him see into the dark, it was just a reflex, Maggie thought. For a second he seemed to be staring right at her, then his gaze turned to the palm trees, then to the plum that hid Ponytail.

And it started to rain. Not a passing cloud, but a quick shower. Greenthumb stood, feet at parade rest and looked up into the night sky. Water fell around him, but he didn't seem to mind. He turned back toward the door, but the collies started barking even louder. Greenthumb ran a hand through his hair, turned away from the door, took a step down from the porch. The dogs had helped him make up his mind. He was going to check out his garden despite the rain.

Now the sirens vied with the dogs for attention. They weren't off in the distance any more. They were close and getting closer, loud. The collies continued their wailing, but apparently Greenthumb decided it was the sirens and not intruders that had set them off, because he turned, climbed the porch and went back into the house. He eased the door closed after himself. The light went out.

The bushes were keeping Maggie and Gay dry, but wouldn't for much longer. One siren screamed louder. A police cruiser had turned the corner on Nighthyde's street, was fast approaching Greenthumb's. Maggie reached out, squeezed Gay's elbow, then started along the fence toward the garage as the cruiser roared by out front. The siren covered their noise.

The bushes stopped at an area behind the garage. There was about a three foot space between it and the fence that ran behind it. Maggie peered into the dark, a long tunnel like affair. Greenthumb had extended the garage roof so that it covered the area.

Maggie slipped out from the hedge bushes, moved behind the garage. Gay followed. It was dark as a cave, but it was dry, whereas Ponytail wouldn't be. Maybe the rain would drive him away. Maggie hoped so. It started to fall harder now, beating a metallic tattoo on the overhang above. Tin, Maggie guessed. It sounded like African drums, war drums.

She put a hand out, felt the back of the garage. It was dark, she was blind as Ma now. The thought of Ma gave her pause. That bastard out there killed the old woman, was trying to kill her and Gay. All of a sudden Maggie knew he wouldn't leave. He was like a bird dog and he had their scent. The others were going after the children. He was coming after her and Gay. Maggie clenched her fist. She'd been running so much lately. No more.

She put a hand on the wall, moved along it, back into the dark tunnel. She was looking for something, anything she could use against the man in the yard. She found it. A wooden handled thing leaning up against the garage. Like a broom. She felt down the handle. Not a broom. A rake. The kind with curved metal spikes to gather up dead grass and leaves. She picked it up. It was heavy.

She scraped it against the garage wall.

"What are you doing?" Gay whispered, urgent, fear in her voice.

"Get back!" Maggie said. "I need room to swing this."

"What?"

"Hurry, you'll be in the way."

Gay moved back into the tunnel. Maggie backed up a little too. Her heart thumped in her chest, matching the tattoo of the rain.

Then, suddenly as it started, the rain stopped, but it wasn't quiet. The collies were both howling now. And they were close, only a few feet away. The dogs hadn't attacked them before, but they might now. Maggie and Gay were at the back corner of

Greenthumb's yard, the collies at the back corner of theirs. The only thing between the dogs and them was the fence. Maggie wondered if they could jump it.

She moved back to where Gay was, put her mouth to her friend's ear. "Get down, in case he shoots into the dark."

"He wouldn't."

"He might," Maggie said.

Gay crouched down on her hands in knees.

Maggie moved against the back of the garage, willed herself to be invisible, hoping Ponytail would be as blind, staring into the tunnel behind the garage, as she'd been. She raised the rake above her head. She had to choke up about halfway on the handle or the rake would hit the tin roof.

But he didn't come. Maybe the dogs drowned out the sound of the rake scraping against the garage. She scratched it against the wall again.

And then he was there, at the entrance to the tunnel, looking in. He stood, legs together, relaxed, arms at his side, gun still in his right hand. In her mind, Maggie knew he couldn't see through the dark, but the way he seemed to be looking right at her chilled her more than the cold night or wet rain ever could have done.

"Come on," she mouthed. For an instant she thought she'd said it aloud, but it was only her lips moving in the dark. "Come on in, just a little."

He took a tentative step forward, then stopped, as if waiting for his eyes to get used to the dark. Could they do that? Maggie wondered. Maybe they could. After all, she could see him. But that was because what little light there was from the night was behind him.

"Come on," she mouthed again.

And as if he heard, he took another step forward, arms still at his side, gun still pointed toward the dirt. But he stopped again, turned his head to the side, cocking it like a frightened deer listening for the wolf.

Maggie held her breath, tightened her grip on the rake. "Come on, get closer. Just a couple more steps." Sweat trickled her face, caught on her lip. She licked it away.

And Ponytail took another cautious step into the dark. He stopped again, brought the gun up, pointed it ahead of himself, moved it back and forth. If Maggie wasn't afraid to breathe, she'd have sighed. He couldn't see. But he knew they were back there. Felt it. He was a hunter.

But he wasn't a very good one, Maggie thought, because he pointed the gun toward the back of the tunnel. If he fired, the round would go well over Gay's head and it wouldn't even be close to Maggie.

"Come on," she silently said. "One more step."

And he took it. Gun hand in front of himself, finger on the trigger.

Maggie brought the rake down with everything she had, hitting him square on the head. He slumped to the ground without a sound. The gun went flying, and for a second Maggie thought it might go off, but it didn't.

"Shit," Gay said as the smell of human excrement filled the enclosed space.

"Exactly," Maggie whispered. Ponytail's bowels had cut loose. The body jerked for a few seconds, then stopped. Maggie crouched, felt for a carotid, sought a pulse, found nothing. "He's dead."

"We gotta go," Gay said.

"Just a second." Maggie ran her hands around the ground, found Ponytail's gun. It was a revolver. She shoved it between pants and back as she got up. "Okay, let's get the F out of here."

She stepped over the body.

Another siren ripped up the night.

"The streets must be crawling with cops," Gay said.

"We'll go over the fences till we get to the end of the block where we left Jonas' car. There can't be that many more."

"Okay." Gay gave Maggie's arm a squeeze. "Don't worry about him. You did good here. Better than I could've. Now, let's move."

Maggie sprinted across the yard, Gay on her heels, the collies howling in the background. When she reached the fence, she climbed over, then she was up and running to still another, then another, then another.

Chapter Twenty-Two

"Miserable is how I feel." Horace closed the door after himself, stepped into Sadie's small apartment. "Rain's coming down like it was the Everglades."

"You gonna leave the car in front? I like it in back, it's not such a good neighborhood." Sadie toked on a joint, held it out to Horace.

"I don't do that stuff." Horace waved it away. He wanted to take off his wet jacket, stay awhile, but he still had work to do.

"Might make you feel better."

"I gotta go back out. I just wanted to check, make sure you were all right."

"I'm okay, babe. Why wouldn't I be?" She took another hit. It bothered Horace. He didn't hold with drugs. He'd have to talk to her about that, but not now. Not tonight.

"I didn't want you worrying about the car, so I brought it back. I can use the van for the rest of what I gotta do."

"You sure you have ta go?" She draped arms over his shoulders, pulled him in for a languid kiss.

"I got someone in the car. He's the impatient type, Japanese. I'll take care of business and get back quick as I can."

"You do that." She reached between his legs, grabbed his crotch and squeezed. Pleasure rippled through him. "Sure you don't want a toke?"

"What the hell." He took the joint, sucked in deep. It had been years, but he still knew how. He took a second toke as she lowered herself to her knees and pulled down his zipper and a third as she took him into her mouth. He held the joint in one hand, with the other on her head for balance. He sucked in deep, held his breath and let go, shaking on quivering legs as she swallowed.

"That's a reminder, so you come back quick." She wiped her mouth with the back of her hand. The look in her eyes told of a thousand more delights.

"I'll be as quick as I can." He zipped up, glad he'd insisted on taking his car and not the Jap's. And doubly glad he'd made the asshole wait outside while he came inside to swap keys. The fucker didn't want to come by Sadie's. He wanted to go straight to the Shore and get the faggot, but Horace had put his foot down. He'd wanted his van. It was souped up and built for speed. Besides, you had to show that kind who was boss or you never got any respect.

"I parked your van 'round back. You can drive mine around and park behind it." Sadie was still on her knees, hadn't bothered to get up.

"Thanks, Sadie," Horace said, then he was out the door.

* * *

Maggie came over the fence after Gay to the sound of automatic gunfire that drowned out the yapping dogs four yards back. Whoever lived in this house—the corner house and the last yard the women had to cross—was playing some kind of war movie through a mega sound system with the volume cranked up loud.

Gay put her mouth to Maggie's ear. "Only one more fence."

"Okay, let's get out of here." Maggie sprinted across the yard, attacked the side fence, pulled herself over it as if she'd been doing it all her life.

A wet wind blew her hair as she hit the grass. It was going to rain again. She sighed when she saw Jonas' red Volkswagen parked across the street where they'd left it.

Gay came over, squatted on the ground next to her, huffing like she was out of breath.

"You okay?" Maggie was breathing hard herself, but the adrenaline sparking through her made her high. Even her arm didn't hurt any more.

"Yeah." The rain came down, sheeting cold. "We're safe now."

"No we're not. Nighthyde and that Scarface character are on their way to Jonas'. They're gonna kill the girls, Jonas and Gordon, too. Then Scarface is gonna shoot Nighthyde in the head and make it look like suicide."

"How do you know this?" Gay sounded stunned.

"It's what they were talking about when they didn't think I understood them." Maggie shivered.

"You speak Japanese?"

"Yeah." Maggie wiped water from her eyes.

"Let's go!" Gay got up and started for the car, went to the passenger side.

Maggie fished the key out of her pocket, had it in the driver's door when a Sheriff's cruiser came around the corner, tires hissing. It stopped as Maggie was getting in the car. A window came down.

"What are you ladies doing out in the rain?" The deputy was young, maybe twenty-two or three.

"Going for pizza," Maggie said.

"In this?" The deputy pointed to the sky.

"Kids don't care about the rain," Maggie said. "Not when they can send the moms out for the pepperoni and Pepsi."

"Where are these kids?" the cop said.

"There." Maggie pointed to the corner house, the one they'd just walked away from. "You can go annoy my husband if you want," she said. "My kids would love that, but we're getting wet so we're outta here." Maggie started to get in the car.

"You know about the trouble up the street?"

"Mister," Maggie said, "the only reason I'm talking to you is because I thought the neighbors called because the kids got the TV up in the stratosphere. If you have other business, I'd appreciate it if you'd go about it and let us be on our way."

"Kinda late for kids to be eating pizza," the deputy said.

"And they're gonna get it a lot later if you don't stop hassling us."

The cop looked to the house. Saw the flickering light from the television. He couldn't help but hear the sounds of movie gunfire. It sounded like a war was going on over there. "Okay, sorry to have bothered you." He rolled up his window and the Sheriff's car drove away, turning left onto Daneland, Nighthyde's street.

"That was close," Gay said.

"Yeah." Maggie pulled away from the curb.

"Uh oh," Gay said. The Sheriff's car turned its lights on, pulled into a driveway, backed out again. "Guy with that German Shepherd must have seen us, told the cops about the two woman in his backyard."

"Could they have got it over their radio that quick?"

"Only takes a second once they know," Gay said.

Maggie jerked the wheel to the right and the VW climbed up the curb.

"What are you doing?"

"No way can this thing out run that cop car." Maggie felt the bump as the rear tires thumped over.

"So we should pull over and tell them what's going on."

"Like they're gonna believe us." Maggie shifted into second, pushed the accelerator to the floor. The rear wheels spun on the park's wet grass, the car slipped to the left, Maggie, in her element now, turned into the slide as the wheels found traction and the little red car scooted forward as the police cruiser turned on its siren.

"I can't see anything," Gay said.

"We're driving blind." Maggie hadn't turned on the lights and the rain was sheeting down now.

"But he's not!" Gay was looking out the back window. "He jumped the curb. He's gonna be on us in a second."

"I see him in the rearview." Maggie turned on the lights, hit the brights. Ahead she saw manicured grass. She shifted up into third. She didn't know how far the grassy savannah went, she couldn't see beyond it.

"Oh shit!" Gay screamed. "He's gonna run right over us."

The siren was deafening as the Sheriff's cruiser climbed up onto their tail. Red and blue lights flashing on the cruiser, coupled with its bright lights, lit up the inside of the VW. Blinding white coming out of her mirror fought with the eerie glow from the Christmas tree on top of the cruiser. Red, blue, blinding white. Red, blue, blinding white. Like no Christmas Maggie ever knew. A Christmas from Hell maybe.

All of a sudden the VW shook and went into a long slide to the right.

"Bastard rammed us," Maggie said. This time instead of turning into the slide, she turned away from it, felt the Gs as the VW's rear end whipped around.

The kid cop in the cruiser slammed on his brakes as the VW spun through a one-eighty.

"Holy shit," Gay screamed as Maggie popped it down into first, stomped on the gas and let out a whoop herself as the little car's tires dug in again.

Caught by surprise, the deputies could only watch as the VW sped by them, engine screaming against the abuse Maggie was inflicting upon it. But their surprise was short lived. In seconds the cruiser was wheeling around, digging up the grass as its powerful engine roared, cutting off the whine of the VW's.

"Look out!" Gay yelled.

"See it." Maggie jerked the wheel just in time to avoid hitting a baseball backstop.

"You went the wrong way, turn, turn, turn!"

Maggie pulled the wheel back, but not in time, and the Volkswagen scraped along the bleachers. The sound sent shivers screeching up Maggie's spine as she struggled with the wheel. Finally she got control again. She pulled the wheel to the right, away from the stands. The VW shot toward the pitcher's mound, past it and continued on toward second base.

"They're coming!" Gay said.

The deputies had swung a wide right to avoid the backstop and were now coming at the women from right field. Maggie pulled on the wheel, jerked the car toward left and shifted up into second.

"Look ahead," Gay wailed.

Maggie did, and saw a long hillock, six or seven feet high. It was covered with pine trees, the kind her parents had had every Christmas as far back as she could remember. Only these were much bigger. The hillock and trees ran the length of the baseball field, separating it from the residential neighborhood across the street.

"Hang on." Maggie clutched, grabbed the shift lever, pulled it down into first, put her foot to the floor and aimed the car to a small space between two of the trees.

"You're crazy!"

Again the car was flooded with light. The cruiser was coming up fast, gonna ram them again. Did. The VW went right, Maggie pulled it back, engine screaming. For a second she was off course, didn't think she was going to make it, but she did, threading the car between the trees as if she did it all the time.

Pine branches screeched against the sides of the car and once again sound shivered through her, but Maggie screamed, "Yesssss," as the car passed out of the trees and they were careening down the hillock.

A loud crash thundered behind them.

"They didn't make it!" Gay yelled out as the little car shot over the curb. The wheels squeaked as they hit the street. "You did it!"

Maggie shifted up into second and took the first left. They sped down a residential street and came to a four lane road.

"I know where we are," Gay said. "That's Woodruff. Turn right, then left at the light, it'll take you to the freeway."

* * *

Horace glanced over at the Japanese out of the corner of his eye as the wipers click clacked water off the windshield. He was staring ahead as if he could see through the rain, stiff and still as Buddha. It was unnerving the way he could hold himself like that. Fucker didn't even blink. Couldn't be good for his eyes. All of a sudden Horace couldn't stop himself from blinking. His eyelids fluttered out of control and for a second he thought he was having one of Ma's seizures.

Someone told him once they were hereditary, but he didn't believe it. He couldn't afford to.

He turned onto Ocean. A couple minutes and he'd be at the fag bar. If life could be the way he wanted it, Horace would walk away right now. But when did you ever get what you wanted? The woman had seen him, her black friend, too. Got a real good look even though they were all tied up.

He shook his head, stopped for a light, listened to the rain pounding on the roof. How the hell had those bitches tracked him to the Lakewood house? And what was Ma thinking about all this? One thing for certain, he was gonna have to make it up to her somehow. Not just for the deal about Virge not coming back, that was gonna be bad enough, but Ma was never gonna let him hear the end of tonight.

The light changed and he took his foot off the brake.

"The women gotta go," Horace said. "That's a fact."

The Japanese grunted, kept his eyes forward.

"Maybe even that faggot. I can see that."

The Japanese nodded. Horace caught it out of the corner of his eye.

"But I'm here to tell you, we're not hurting them little girls." It was bad enough he had to throw that kid off that balcony. Little fucker's scream was gonna be with him for the rest of his life. He wasn't about to add any more kids to the list.

"Whatever you say," the Japanese said.

"Just so we got that understood." They were approaching the fork where Ocean branched off into Second Street. Horace kept to the right, stayed on Ocean.

***

Maggie kept her foot on the floor and threw the VW into third as she took the off ramp onto Studebaker Road. She'd had the little car up to ninety on the freeway, despite the rain. And through blind luck, the grace of God or both, she didn't get stopped. She flew off the ramp at seventy-five, tires squealing. In seconds she careened the car around the corner and was speeding into the Shore.

"Faster," Gay said.

"It's on the floor," Maggie said. They raced down Second Street. Maggie slid the car through the first left past the bridge onto Bayshore Drive, downshifting through the middle of the turn.

The car rocked up on the two right wheels, sliding like a bar of soap on a wet floor.

"We're gonna go over!" Gay screamed.

"No we're not!" Maggie cranked the wheel into the direction of the slide, got control, but not enough to keep the car on the street. They jumped the curb and now the VW's tires were churning sand as they shot along the beach.

"Look out!" Gay yelled.

"Holy shit!" Maggie pulled the wheel and barely avoided a couple making love on the beach. The couple rolled away, white arms and legs caught in the headlights. Maggie felt the fear in their wide eyes sure as if she'd been right there with them.

"It's after midnight," Gay said. "And it's pouring cats and dogs."

"Maybe they're drunk, horny and got no place to go." Maggie aimed the car back toward the road, downshifted to second. The lovers looked like kids, barely old enough to get into a bar. A long time ago, in her other life, she and Nick had made love in the rain. A beach in the Bahamas on their honeymoon. But it wasn't nearly so cold.

"Hang on! Maggie braced herself as the VW went over the curb. It was a miracle the tires still held air. They thudded onto the street and once again were in a slide, but Maggie got control of it in time to make the turn onto Ocean. She downshifted through the corner with her foot on the floor.

"Now you've got the hang of this!" Gay said.

"Yeah!" Maggie had gone around the corner without so much as a chirp from the tires.

"There's a parking spot right across the street," Gay said.

"Yeah." Maggie slipped into the space, parking next to the beach sand, opposite the Whale.

* * *

Horace slowed the van for a couple of women crossing the road. He shook his head. They didn't belong out so late alone. Anything could happen.

"It's them!" The Jap said.

"What?" Horace looked through the wet windshield and the clacking wipers. It was the two women. The Twin and the black one they'd left tied up at Ma's. They were in the middle of the street, crossing right in front of him as if he didn't exist, as if he was nothing. "How?"

"Get them!" Now the Jap was excited.

Horace jammed his foot to the floor. The back tires squealed on the wet pavement. The Jap screamed, an animal wail that filled the van, like he was a karate guy charging an army, Horace thought.

The women looked up and Horace hit them with his brights. Almost on top of them now. They jumped away, one going forward, the other jumping back as he plowed down on them. Horace screamed himself as he sped past, then he was braking, looking for a spot to turn around.

* * *

"Are you okay?" Maggie called across the street. Gay had jumped back, was in front of Jonas' battered VW.

"Yeah."

The van's tires screeched as its driver stomped on the brakes. No doubt in her mind as to who it was. It was the same black van Horace and Virgil had that night they'd chased her on this same beach. He was going to be coming back and fast.

"Get down, play dead!" Maggie screamed.

"What?"

"Just do it!" Maggie ran across the street as Gay dropped to the pavement. "Get closer to the car. Stick your legs under it."

"What for?"

"So he doesn't run over you when he comes back."

"Swell."

"I'm gonna take off across the beach, lead them away from the apartment. When they come after me, you go up there and get the kids away. Hide."

"Where?"

"Climb a fence, hide in someone's backyard. You should be good at that now."

"This is a stupid plan."

"No time to argue." Maggie dropped to her knees by Gay. She bent over her, as if examining her, pulled out the gun as the van spun around at the corner where the bay joined the ocean, tires sliding and squealing through a hundred and eighty degree turn.

"Shit, he can drive," Gay said.

"Okay, here he comes." Maggie got up. "I'm outta here. Good luck." She took off at a dead run toward the pier.

* * *

"There she goes." The Japanese was hopping in his seat now, pointing toward the Twin who was running over the sand.

"Deja-fucking-vu!" Horace cranked the wheel left and the van jumped the curb as if it wasn't there. She got away from him before on this beach. She wasn't gonna do it again.

"What are you doing?"

"Gonna run her down." The brights nailed her sure as a laser sight. Horace pulled the van down into low, insides tingling as it kicked in, but the wheels dug into the wet sand, shooting it out from the wheel wells.

"What?" The Japanese screamed.

"Stuck!" Horace pulled the trans into reverse and the tires spun in the other direction.

"She's getting away." The Japanese was yelling into Horace's ear like he was deaf or something.

"Cool your jets!" Horace put it back into first, tried to ease out of the rut the tires had dug into, but couldn't.

"I can't see her." The Japanese fuck was out of Horace's face now. He opened the door, jumped out.

Horace jammed it into reverse, floored it. The engine screamed, the tires kicked wet sand six feet into the air, but he'd only dug himself in deeper.

"Fuck!" Horace pulled it into park, pulled his door open, pulled out his gun and charged off into the rain. Anger raged through him. His head throbbed. Rain pelted him, a cold shower killing his sight. Straining, he barely saw the Japanese bastard blundering ahead. Horace could only assume he had the Twin in sight. He had no choice. He charged after him.

* * *

Rain soaked through Maggie's clothes as she ran. The Olympic pool was between her and the street. A murky monolith cutting off the real world. She was running in a dark, alien place, where murder was the order of the day and death is king.

She'd put on a burst of speed when the screaming truck jumped the curb, sprinting away from it. But all of a sudden she realized it had stopped. Had they given up? She stopped too, turned into the rain. She was drenched now, cold. Her lungs demanded air and she sucked it in, bent over, hands on her knees, like a baseball player in the infield waiting for a line drive, the only difference, she held a gun in her left hand instead of a mitt in the right.

Then she saw him, short and squat, hulking out of the night. Scarface, a dark apparition, blurred by the sheeting rain. Ponytail's revolver wasn't like her Sigma automatic. It seemed too small, almost a toy. She snugged it up under curled fingers while the palm of her hand rested on a bent knee. She brought it up, fired at Scarface.

She missed.

Either it wasn't as accurate as her Sigma or there was a trick to the revolver she didn't know.

But the gunshot didn't even slow him down. He kept coming and now she saw someone behind him. Nighthyde, had to be. They seemed to be moving in slow motion as thoughts raced through her head. Fire again or wait and get a better shot? If the gun held six, she only had two left.

Every fiber in her being said run. She took off toward the pier, running for all she was worth. It was close. Was it going to be her salvation or her tomb? She didn't want to die. She had so much to live for, her unborn child, Jasmine. From deep inside she pulled out that extra bit of energy, that piece of heart she needed to increase her speed. She pumped her arms the way Olympic runners do to get their legs to match the killing rhythm.

The pier loomed larger out of the pounding rain with every breath, with every step. Almost there. Something grabbed her around the waist, killed her wind. She dropped to the wet sand, breathless, felt the gun ripped from her hand.

Somehow one of them had gotten in front of her.

It was all over now.

But it wasn't.

She heard a gunshot, gasped when she saw Scarface stop, as if a giant hammer had smashed into his chest. Arms flailed, windmilling around his dying body, fighting for balance, fighting to stay on his feet.

But in a heartbeat the battle was lost and Scarface flopped face forward onto the sand.

"He didn't hurt you, did he?" Darley Smalls dropped to his knees. Rain washed through his beard. For an instant she was worried about the baby, but she was fast getting her breath back. It was gonna be okay.

"She's gonna be fine." Now Theo Baptiste was on his knees. She saw the gun in his hand. He'd shot Scarface. There was nothing wrong with the gun. It had been her. She'd been scared, too scared to shoot straight.

"There's another one." Maggie grabbed the gun from Theo's hand. Turned as Horace Nighthyde came charging forward. He hadn't seen them, low as they were. Maggie took aim, steadied herself, and shot him between the eyes.

Chapter Twenty-Three

MAGGIE FLIPPED THE BURGERS on the grill, added some barbeque sauce. Jasmine had told her many times that she had always liked her meat well done, but Maggie persisted in eating it medium-rare. She laughed every time Jasmine said it. She took hers off the grill.

"You might as well eat it raw," Gordon said.

"Not you too." Maggie laughed.

"Me too." Gordon was stretched out in a lounge chair, eyes shielded from the sun with a new pair of reflective sunglasses. Jasmine and Sonya said they made him look like an old highway patrolman and they constantly teased him about not having a motorcycle. The kids loved him, probably because at heart he was a kid himself. It was as if he'd been a part of their lives forever instead of just six months.

"Such a nice day," Gay said from the lounge chair next to Gordon.

The sun was hanging low, an orange ball over the ocean. Jasmine and Sonya were laughing and dancing in and out of the surf, but their parents had them in sight from where they relaxed in front of Maggie's Condo.

"Oh shit!" Maggie staggered back from the grill.
"What?"
"It's time!"
"Now?" Gordon went white.

"Get the girls," Gay told him as she jumped from her chair. She was at Maggie's side in an instant. "Just take it easy. We'll get your bag, then we're off to the hospital."

"Yeah, the bag," Gordon said.
"Get the girls!" Gay said.
"Yeah, yeah." Gordon took off for the beach gate.

Maggie barely remembered the ride to the hospital. The labor pains were like a mule kicking her in the gut. She thought she was going to die. At the hospital a young man and woman in white helped her from the back seat of Gordon's clunky looking Ford into a wheelchair. In no time she was in the delivery room looking up at Gordon's masked face.

"I'm glad you're here." She squeezed his hand, then yelled as a monster pain ripped through her.

"Push," Gordon said.
"I am."
"Again."
"I am!"
"Harder."
"I am, God dammit!"

"I see the head," someone said.
"Push. One more time. A big one."
"I'm pushing!"
"It's a girl!"
"A girl." Maggie sighed, then drifted off.

She woke in a cool hospital room. Gordon's smiling eyes were the last thing she'd seen in the in the delivery room and they were the first thing she saw when she woke up. He was always there for her.

"Where's the girls?"

"Down the hall with Grandma Debra looking at the baby." Gay was next to Gordon, wearing the biggest smile Maggie had ever seen.

"I'm cold."

"I'll get a blanket." Gordon pulled one off the bed next to hers, draped it over her. "Do you have a name yet?"

"Yeah, I do," Maggie said. It seemed they'd talked about nothing else for the last month. A million ideas, a million rejections. Maggie wanted something original, but not something corny. She wanted the baby to have a name that stood for something. A name she could live up to.

"Well?" Gordon said.

"Darley Theo Kenyon."

"After the men under the pier," Gordon said. "I like it."

"Yeah, after them." She sighed, closed her eyes for a few seconds and cast her mind back to that night.

"Are you all right?" Theo had asked her after she'd shot Horace Nighthyde.

"Yeah." But she thought she was going to be sick. Maybe she'd never really be all right again.

"You get up now and go back to your life." Rain cascaded through Darley's dark hair, sluiced around his black face. "Me and Theo will take care of things here."

"What?"

"He means we'll take care of the bodies," Theo said. "No need for you to be concerned. So let me help you up." He rose, took her arm, helped her to her feet.

"We'll walk you to your car." Darley took her other arm.

Halfway they ran into Gay coming toward them out of the rain.

"She's with me," Maggie mumbled.

"She can see that you're safe from here." Darley let go of her arm.

"Can you stand by yourself? You okay?" Theo was still holding on to her.

"Yeah. I'll be alright."

"Then we'll leave you now." Theo let go and the two men backed away into the rain. And the bodies of Horace Nighthyde and Scarface the Yakuza thug turned up the next morning in a parking lot across from the police station.

Also that morning, Gordon called Larry Striker and made the deal. If Striker left them alone, forgot they existed, then they'd forget about him, Nighthyde, Congressman Nishikawa and what had happened to Norton's mother and Wolfe's wife and son.

Striker agreed and more than lived up to his end of the bargain. Somehow he'd assisted the Long Beach Police Department and the Lakewood Sheriff's in connecting the bodies in the parking lot with the ones in Lakewood. With his help the police concluded that Horace Nighthyde had walked in on two Yakuza thugs right after they'd murdered his mother, and chased them as they ran out the back door and went over the fence where one of them killed the neighbor's dog. Nighthyde caught one and killed him. Then he tracked the other one to the parking lot, killed him, then put the gun to his own head.

How Darley and Theo got the bodies all the way downtown, Maggie never knew. But she owed them a debt, thanks at least. She'd gone back to the pier several times after dark, but they were never there. They'd disappeared, leaving her with nothing but the memory of the rough men who lived a rough life. Two great bears she'd never forget.

"Mrs. Kenyon."

Maggie opened her eyes, looked up.

"Detective Norton," she said. "Believe it or not, I was just thinking about you." Norton was wearing khaki Docker's and a pink Hawaiian shirt with hula girls on it. He looked as if he were on vacation. But the expression on the albino's face said he wasn't. He looked serious, dead serious. No wonder the girls called him the Ghost.

"And lately I've been thinking about you."

"Me too." The man with Norton was wearing a Dodgers sweatshirt and faded Levi's. His head was shaved. He looked serious, too.

"Detective Wolfe," Maggie said. "Gordon's told me about you."

"Yeah. But Mr. Takoda is Maggie Nesbitt's friend. He's not supposed to know you."

Maggie looked beyond Wolfe to Gordon, who was standing next to Gay, behind the two policemen. His expression was blank. She'd always been able to read him. Not now. The open book of his face was closed to her. She was afraid.

"Just say what you have to say and get it over with." She balled her hands into fists to keep them from shaking.

"The Lakewood Sheriff's had a homicide a few months back," Detective Wolfe said. "A blind woman, Helen Nighthyde. Gunshot in her own house."

"I don't see what that has to do with me." Maggie struggled to stay calm. How could they come here now, on this, her happiest of days?

"Because of the quick way it was closed the Sheriff's didn't follow up on the prints they took in the Nighthyde house, but we did, Abel and me. Yours were all over the place, Mrs. Sullivan's, too."

"Of course, that wasn't possible," Norton said. "You're dead." He smiled. "You can relax. We're not here to cause you any trouble. We just wanted to see the baby."

"I don't understand."

"If you'd ignored the little girl you inherited and started throwing the money around like rice at a wedding, well, we'd have stepped in," Norton said. "You'd be in jail now and Jasmine would be with her father. But you didn't, you've become what every child needs, a parent who gives a shit."

"So, I've been on probation?" Maggie was angry now.

"But not anymore," Wolfe said. "It's over. The prints and any other evidence taken from the Nighthyde house that might have pointed a finger at you or Mrs. Sullivan have been destroyed."

"Why'd you do this?"

"We've both lost loved ones recently," Norton said. "I guess it made us compassionate. Plus you have a strong advocate in Gordon Takoda. He can be very persuasive."

"So you knew about this?" Maggie said to Gordon.

"Don't be mad," Gordon said.

"I'm not."

"Now we're your advocates, too," Wolfe said. "Gordon has enlisted us as godparents for you, Jasmine and your baby?"

"How?" The short lived anger had melted away.

"It's best you don't know. Just know this, we're in his debt and through him yours. If you're ever in trouble, call us and we'll come."

"Gordon?" She met his eyes.

"I have to leave with them for a bit," Gordon said. "But I'll be back."

* * *

In the hospital parking lot, Gordon said, "We'll take my car."

"You got the stuff?" Wolfe said.

"It's in the trunk."

"That kind of dangerous, driving around with it like that?" Norton said.

"No more than what we're about to do."

"Guess you're right about that." Norton went to the shotgun door. Wolfe got in back.

As Gordon made the right onto Pacific Coast Highway, Norton said. "Sorry it had to be today, the baby and all."

"Don't be. I said I'd be ready. Besides, you didn't have to let me come along. I appreciate it."

"If you hadn't told us, we never would've known," Wolfe said.

They rode in silence, like paratroopers flying above a combat zone, waiting for the drop. Gordon glanced over at the albino, sneaked a look at Wolfe in the rearview. If he added both men's ages, they probably couldn't match him in years, but they were old in a way he'd never be.

Gordon had fought in Vietnam, spent twenty years with the FBI, lost loved ones to war, cancer, heart attacks, old age and AIDS. He'd killed when he'd had to and even when he didn't have to. He'd experienced more life than most. Seen more than most. Lost more than most. But a child's smile still delighted him, and not a day went by that something didn't surprise him. These two policemen riding with him, Gordon didn't think anything surprised them. For them, life had lost its wonder, and that was too bad.

It was 6:15 when they pulled up in front of the steel and glass building where Congressman Nishikawa had his district office. The setting sun, catching all the pollutants in the Southern California air, gave the sky a hue of oranges, pinks and purples.

"Nothing prettier than an L.A. sunset," Gordon said when he shut off the engine.

"Yeah." Norton got out of the car and went to the trunk.

Gordon and Wolfe met him there. Gordon opened it. He took out a Glock, handed it to Norton, gave another to Wolfe, kept a third for himself.

"These are new," Wolfe said.

"Virgins," Gordon said.

"We could have used throw downs," Norton said. "Saved you a bunch."

"For some things you just don't count the cost." Gordon closed the trunk.

"You're right about that," Wolfe said.

Gordon walked to the entrance of the glass office building, the bald detective on his left, the long haired albino on his right. He opened the door with a key.

"Where'd you get it?" Norton said.

"Followed the watchman to a bar and waited for him to get drunk. Then I picked his pocket, made an impression and put it back. He never missed it."

"You learn that in the FBI?" Wolfe said.

"I picked it up somewhere, maybe there." Gordon pushed the call button for the elevator. The congressman's office was on the fifth floor, but Gordon didn't feel like walking up the five flights. Now he just wanted to get it over with.

Gordon was first off the elevator.

"You got a key for his office, too?" Wolfe said. "Or are we gonna knock?"

"It's a pass key, opens 'em all." Gordon put it in the lock, turned it. Gun first, he entered the plush office. Light and dark furniture, teak and oak, from one of those places that sold furniture from Denmark or Sweden, not American looking at all.

Wolfe whistled. "Classy fuck."

"Who's there?" The shouted question came from a room behind the Danish modern reception desk.

"Company." Gordon went through the door to the inner office, Glock still in front of himself. Norton and Wolfe were right there with him.

"Get out." Congressman Nishikawa was wearing a white suit, with a cream colored tie. Three shots rang out as one, turning the suit crimson red.

"What the fuck?" Striker said as the three men trained their weapons on him.

"I wish I could say I'm sorry about this," Gordon said. "But I'm not."

"We had a deal." Striker was also in a suit, dark and expensive. He looked like a million bucks, like he owned the world. "You gave your word."

"I lied."

The Bootleg Press Catalog

Ragged Man by Jack Priest
Bootleg 001 — ISBN: 0974524603
Unknown to Rick Gordon, he brought an ancient aboriginal horror home from the Australian desert. Now his friends are dying and Rick is getting the blame.

Desperation Moon by Ken Douglas
Bootleg 002 — ISBN: 0974524611
Sara Hackett must save two little girls from dangerous kidnappers, but she doesn't have the money to pay the ransom.

Scorpion by Jack Stewart
Bootleg 003 — ISBN: 097452462x
DEA agent Bill Broxton must protect the Prime Minister of Trinidad from an assassin, but he doesn't know the killer is his fiancée.

Dead Ringer by Ken Douglas
Bootleg 004 — ISBN: 0974524638
Maggie Nesbitt steps out of her dull life and into her dead twin's, and now the man that killed her sister is after Maggie.

Gecko by Jack Priest
Bootleg 005 — ISBN: 0974524646
Jim Monday must rescue his wife from an evil worse than death before the Gecko horror of Maori legend kills them both.

Running Scared by Ken Douglas
Bootleg 006 — ISBN: 0974524654
Joey Sapphire's husband blackmailed and now is out to kill the president's daughter and only Joey can save the young woman.

Night Witch by Jack Priest
Bootleg 007—ISBN: 0974524662
   A vampire like creature followed Carolina's father back from the Caribbean and now it is terrorizing her. She and her friend Arty are only children, but they must fight this creature themselves or die.

Hurricane by Jack Stewart
Bootleg 008—ISBN: 0974524670
   Julie Tanaka flees Trinidad on her sailboat after the death of her husband, but the boat has a drug lord's money aboard and DEA agent Bill Broxton must get to her first or she is dead.

Tangerine Dream by Ken Douglas and Jack Stewart
Bootleg 009—ISBN: 0974524689
   Seagoing writer and gourmet chef Captain Katie Osborne said of this book, "Incest, death, tragedy, betrayal and teenage homosexual love, I don't know how, but somehow it all works. I was up all night reading."

Diamond Sky by Ken Douglas and Jack Stewart
Bootleg 012—ISBN: 0974524697
The Russian Mafia is after Beth Shannon. Their diamonds have been stolen and they think she knows where they are. She does, only she doesn't know it.

Bootleg Books are Better than T.V.

The bootleg Press Story

We at Bootleg Press are a small group of writers who were brought together by pen and sea. We have all been members of either the St. Martin or Trinidad Cruising Writer's Groups in the Caribbean.

We share our thoughts, plot ideas, villains and heroes. That's why you'll see some borrowed characters, both minor and major, cross from one author's book to another's.

Also, you'll see a few similar scenes that seem to jump from one author's pages to another's. That's because both authors have collaborated on the scene and—both liking how it worked out—both decided to use it.

At what point does an author's idea truly become his own? That's a good question, but rest assured in the rare occasions where you may discover similar scenes in Bootleg Press Books, that it is not stealing. Writing is a solitary art, but sometimes it is possible to share the load.

Book writing is hard, but book selling is harder. We think our books are as good as any you'll find out there, but breaking into the New York publishing market is tough, especially if you live far away from the Big Apple.

So, we've all either sold or put our boats on the hard, pooled our money and started our own company. We bought cars and loaded our trunks with books. We call on small independent bookstores ourselves, as we are our own distributors. But the few of us cannot possibly reach the whole world, however we are trying, so if you don't see our books in your local bookstore yet, remember you can always order them from the big guys online.

Thank you from everyone at Bootleg Books for reading and please remember, Bootleg Books are better than T.V.

Ken Douglas & Vesta Irene
Wangarai, New Zealand

Printed in the United States
24214LVS00005B/28